MUNDANE MORNINGS AND ENCHANTED EVENINGS

STEPHANIE K CLEMENS

THE ENCHANTED WOODS COTTAGECORE COLLECTION

Mundane Mornings & Enchanted Evenings

Stephanie K Clemens

Adventures with Ink

To everyone that believes in magic.

Castle Ruins
Bram
Sweet Shoppe
Everett Estate
Duskmoor Estate
Wylde Cottage

WICK
LIBRARY
GILDED KETTLE
ROAD TO QUILLMERE
BRAMBLES & BUTTER
BOOK STORE
APOTHECARY
COVINGTON ESTATE

Chapter 1

Bramblewick, England 1912

Tatianna Wylde's fingers trailed in the water as her rowboat cut through the lake, ripples cascaded off the side of the boat and drifted behind her. Wind caressed her cheeks. The cool breeze was a stark contrast to the heat of the sun. Days like these were her favorite, the perfect balance of weather, begging her to linger outside. She untied her hat, freeing her dark curls from the straw cage and tilted her head back, letting the sun warm her cheeks. A content sigh escaped as she lay down in the rowboat.

"Tati, Mother is insisting you come inside. She says you'll freckle if you stay out there any longer," Leondria called out.

Tati's sigh lacked the contentment of earlier. She didn't understand her mother's concern with freckles, since she already had a smattering of them across her nose.

"Coming," she responded. Tatianna pointed her finger at the water, drew a U-shaped figure, and flicked her fingers twice. The boat turned around and moved across the water, heading straight for the dock in front of the Wylde's estate, her family home.

Her mother hated when she used her magic without a spell to control it. But she wasn't good with spells; magic though, that came naturally.

The boat stopped next to the dock. With the grace of a newborn colt, she leapt out of the boat, skidding to a halt mere moments before falling into the lake. She felt bands of air tighten around her waist like ropes, preventing her descent into the water.

"When are you ever going to learn?" Effie Wylde's patronizing tone was something Tatianna was all too familiar with.

Her mother was always annoyed with her, and everything she did. Her dark curls were too wild, her cheeks too rosy, her freckles too prominent. She never wore shoes. And dirt was always under her fingernails. Tati heard the litany of her mother's complaints in her head, all in her mother's unique, exasperated voice.

"Thank you, Mama." Tati regained her balance and turned away from the water. "I already went for a swim today."

"Tatianna!"

She giggled as she skipped down the dock to their cottage, leaving her exasperated mother standing by the abandoned rowboat.

Tati stood in front of her family's quaint-looking cottage. Its window boxes, filled with every color of flower imaginable, contrasted with the white stucco of the small structure. She stared up at the straw roof before opening the blue door that led inside. When she crossed the threshold, the familiar sense of wonder came over her as she looked at the sprawling château she called home. No one would expect to walk into a two-story home based on the cottage's modest exterior.

"There you are, Tati! I've been looking for you everywhere. Where've you been?" Celestine practically bounced on the balls of her feet before seizing Tati's hands with the determination of someone about to spill a very juicy secret.

Tati opened her mouth to speak, but it was a useless endeavor as her sister continued to prattle on and on and . . . She shrugged. After all, Celestine was dramatic, it was an integral part of her character.

"Never mind, there's no time for explanations—I have *news!*" Celestine said, incapable of containing herself; her magic coursing off her in waves.

Before Tati could say a word—in question or protest—Celestine yanked her through the foyer and down the hall at a pace that suggested they were being chased by goblins. They skidded to a stop outside the morning room, where Celestine impatiently shooed her inside.

"Sit," Celestine commanded, though she didn't exactly give Tati much choice. The next thing she knew, her sister was tugging her onto the sofa as she plopped down beside her, so close their knees collided.

Tati rolled her eyes as she rubbed her knee, certain there would be a bruise in the morning.

"Two new gentlemen just moved to town," Celestine began, her eyes sparkling with mischief. "One of them bought the Covington Estate!" She leaned in conspiratorially, vibrating like an over-caffeinated hummingbird.

Even though Celestine wasn't actively using magic, Tati could *feel* it radiating off her, completely untamed. It was a miracle the room hadn't spontaneously combusted from it. Thank goodness Celestine used spells to keep her magic in check. Without them, she was a walking disaster. Honestly, Tati sometimes wondered how they all survived growing up with her.

Each of her sisters' magic perfectly matched their personalities: Celestine was chaos in human form, Leondria was annoyingly precise in *everything*, and Rhiannon stuck to books like her life depended on them, casting only the most thoroughly researched spells. And then there was Tati—different from them all. She couldn't cast spells from books to save her life, but she could wield magic with a thought and flick of her wrist, and she could sense the magic around her like a spider feeling vibrations on its web.

Celestine clapped her hands, her face practically glowing. "Isn't it *exciting?*"

Tati blinked, realizing she'd missed the last part of her sister's news. "Sorry, what was that? Something about . . . gentlemen?"

Celestine groaned dramatically and threw herself back into the mound of pillows behind her, clutching her heart like she'd been wounded. "I said they're planning a ball! In the meadow at the Covington Estate! Just imagine it—dancing under the willow trees, surrounded by wildflowers and lightning bugs. It's going to be *magical*." She paused, her eyes wide with delight. "And"—Celestine paused again to make sure Tatianna was still listening—"they hired fairies to plan the whole thing!"

Tati opened her mouth to reply, but her attention shifted to the doorway. She could feel the hum of magic just before her other two sisters made their grand entrance, undoubtedly drawn by Celestine's excitement.

"My darlings, what is all this *commotion*?" Leondria asked, gliding into the room like a ballerina taking the stage. Her white lace-trimmed skirts swirled around her as she perched primly on the edge of a chair, her movements precisely perfect in every way.

Rhiannon followed with far less theatrical flair, her boots making the faintest sounds against the floor. Her simple blue cotton dress brushed softly along the Turkish rug as she slipped into her usual seat by the bookshelf, her expression already one of barely veiled exasperation.

Tati sighed dramatically, fiddling with the covered buttons running down her blouse. "If you must know, Celestine is chattering about our new neighbors—two gentlemen—and she's completely *twitterpated*."

Rhiannon's head whipped around like a hawk spotting a mouse. "You know Mama doesn't approve of gossip, especially about men." Her tone had that unmistakable edge of eldest-sister righteousness despite only being thirteen months older than Celestine and with two sisters that were actually older than her.

Celestine shrugged, entirely unbothered. "Then don't listen. I'm not forcing you to. It's not like I'm standing here with my wand to your head." She leaned back and crossed her arms, radiating her particular brand of sass.

"Do you even know if they're witches?" Leondria asked, adjusting a strand of perfectly coiffed hair. "Mama won't let us meet them if they aren't. You know how she feels about non-magical men."

Celestine's wide blue eyes expanded dramatically, giving her the look of an affronted owl. She blinked twice before she spoke. "They hired fairies to plan their ball. Of course they're magical. The fairies would never work with the non-magical. Honestly, have you met a fairy? They'd sooner turn them into frogs or something worse for the insult of just asking." She leaned forward, clearly not finished putting her sisters in their place. "Besides, Mama's obsession with only finding magical husbands is so . . . *outre.*"

For once, Tati found herself nodding in agreement with her sister. "I can't believe I'm going to say this, but we should go to this ball. Even if Mama doesn't approve. Dancing among trees and fireflies? It sounds . . . fun."

Celestine smirked. "Nice of you to agree, Tati, but I wasn't *done.*" She lowered her voice conspiratorially, forcing all three of her sisters to lean in. "I heard one of them is related to Lady Cordelia Blackthorn."

Leondria gasped softly, her posture somehow becoming even more straight "*The* Lady Cordelia Blackthorn? Old established magic?"

"The very same." Celestine's grin widened as she delivered her final flourish. "She's about as established as it gets. Mama will see the value in that connection, even if one of them can't brew a potion to save his life."

Tati snorted. "If Mama sees value, it'll be because she's already writing the wedding announcement for the newspaper."

"Which is why"—Celestine paused, a gleam in her eye—"we should get in on the fun before Mama gets any ideas."

Chapter 2

Archer Thornfield had endured many injustices in his life. The latest was standing in the center of the library of his new home—Lysander Goldvale, his closest friend, paced excitedly while rattling off a list of unnecessary embellishments for the ridiculous event he was hell-bent on hosting.

"A ball, Archer! A proper ball to announce our arrival. It's a necessity," Lysander declared, "especially since I've already sent out the invites."

Lysander's magic rippled off him in his enthusiasm. When he threw his arms wide in excitement, Archer half expected the walls to tremble and books to fall off the shelves. Thankfully, Lysander's magic required words to direct it, whereas Archer's magic could only amplify spells that were actually cast.

Archer remained unimpressed, perturbed that it was too late to prevent the ball from happening. He stood by the large window overlooking the sprawling estate and let his gaze linger on the tree line beyond the meticulously cultivated gardens. It was quiet here in the countryside, far from the noises and intrigues of the city. He rather hoped it would stay that way.

"We don't need a ball," Archer said flatly, clasping his hands behind his back as he turned towards his friend. He knew he was fighting a battle he would not win. But he couldn't stop himself from trying.

"But we do," Lysander argued. "If we wish to establish ourselves, we must make an impression. The *right* impression."

"Your wealth and magical bloodlines already do that," Archer pointed out. "If anything, a grand affair will only attract unwanted attention."

Lysander waved a hand. "Is there really such a thing as unwanted attention? The town will talk regardless." He turned to Lilith, his sister, who sat poised on a settee, idly flipping through a book of fashion plates. "What say you, dear sister?"

Lilith didn't even glance up. "I say, I would much rather be anywhere else than listening to the two of you argue over something that has already been decided."

Archer crossed his arms. "Nothing has been decided."

Lilith looked at him, her ice-blue eyes sparkling beneath her perfectly arched golden-blonde eyebrows, lips curving into a knowing smile. "Hasn't it?"

He exhaled sharply, resisting the urge to pinch the bridge of his nose. He thought planning the event was his own personal hell, but actually attending a ball with all the noise and pointless conversations about the weather? Just thinking about going made his palms sweat.

"*I* think it's a marvelous idea," Aisling said, entering the room with the same light step she always carried, as if she were floating instead of walking. His sister moved with an ease and silence that made it difficult for anyone to catch her listening outside the door. Which was shocking, because she was always listening in at a door.

Lysander grinned. "See? Even Aisling approves." He walked over until he stood behind her and squeezed her shoulder.

"She always approves of things that cause me distress," Archer muttered.

"I take offense to that," Aisling said breezily. "It's not my fault you dislike *fun*." She perched on the arm of the chair nearest to him, her dark hair catching the light, highlighting an undertone of red, as she regarded him with an expression that was far too amused for his liking.

Archer did not appreciate them ganging up on him. However, he knew when to throw in the towel. He turned back to Lysander. "Do what you like. But try to keep it modest."

Lysander beamed like the golden god that he was.

Lilith laughed, as usual finding amusement in his current predicament.

And Aisling? Aisling just looked far too pleased with herself. And that should have been his first warning he was in over his head.

The Wylde household was in chaos.

Her older sister, Leondria, would never allow any of them to say that, of course. She would say something like, "Even in chaos, there is *order*," but Tatianna knew better. The preparation for the ball had turned their dressing chamber into a tornado of gowns, lace, and stray sparks of magic.

Tatianna sat before a mirror, running her fingers along the silver embroidery of her gown. Thoughts only needed to float through her mind for the fabric to shift and shimmer in response—her gown was not woven of the typical silk or any other natural fibers as one would expect, but of dew drops and moonlight. Needless to say, the fairies had outdone themselves, creating gowns of beauty that complemented each one of them perfectly.

She could feel her sisters' magic humming around her, as distinct as the voices in the room.

Leondria's magic was sharp and exacting, a precise force that clipped through the air like the measured strokes of a master calligrapher.

Rhiannon's was structured, steady, bound to the pages of the books she so adored—magic that needed to be spoken, conjured, controlled.

Celestine's? Celestine's magic was barely restrained chaos, coiling like an unruly storm held back by the binding spells painted on the inside of her wrists.

And then there was Tatianna's. She had never been able to explain it properly. But she could feel all the magic around her at all times. She could sense who had magic, what type of magic it was, if someone was casting a spell, and if they were using magic for benevolent or nefarious purposes. She didn't know of anyone else that sensed magic the same way she did. When she tried to explain it, everyone looked at her as if she had grown horns.

Then there was her problem with spells. Anything from books felt foreign to her, unnatural. The words on the pages refused to behave, making it impossible for her to decipher and regurgitate them. She could never quite make them work. But with a flick of her fingers and a thought, she could shape magic into reality.

Sometimes reality liked to play tricks on her, but recently, magical things had been going smoothly.

"Hold still," Leondria ordered. Her golden gown glimmered in the candlelight as she finished pinning Rhiannon's deep brown curls into place. "Honestly, is going tonight really such a hardship?"

Rhiannon wrinkled her nose. "I'd rather stay home and read than attend the ball."

Celestine laughed. Her dark gown glowing like the Milky Way. "If you keep scowling like that, you'll frighten away potential suitors, dearest Rhi."

"Good," Rhiannon muttered. "Perhaps they'll leave me alone to read in peace."

Leondria sighed. "You're impossible."

"And yet, you still try to fix me," Rhiannon replied sweetly.

Tatianna laughed, picking at the curls the fairies had pinned into her dark hair. "She can't help herself, Rhi. Leondria was born with the incessant need to make everything and everyone perfect around her, including us. After all, she is the oldest."

The look Leondria cast her way would have scared a lesser soul, but Tatianna was used to it. She waited for a retort. Instead, her sister turned her gaze to Celestine, who had been quietly whispering something under her breath, the designs on her wrist now glowing.

"Celestine," Leondria said, suspicion creeping into her tone. "What are you doing?"

Celestine went silent. She blinked her eyes wide, giving her the appearance of an owl. "Nothing."

A strand of Leondria's perfectly arranged blonde hair slipped out of its pins and floated upward, curling into a loose spiral.

Leondria inhaled sharply. "Celestine."

"It was an accident," Celestine said, not apologizing for her shenanigans.

Tatianna could hear her sister grinding her teeth. To ease the tension, she imagined her sister's hair back in place and flicked her fingers. Leondria watched her hair move back into place and smoothed her hands over her curls, making sure each one was in the exact spot she wanted it to be.

Tatianna laughed. "You really can't help yourself, can you?" She looked at Celestine, who was still standing there pretending to be innocent.

"She's a menace," Leondria said. "One day, those containment spells of hers won't be enough to keep her magic from tearing apart reality."

"You do realize I'm sitting right here?" Celestine interrupted her older sister's diatribe.

"Celestine, don't forget your bracelets, you're going to need an extra boost to contain your magic tonight. We wouldn't want you to set the place on fire because you got overly excited about a profiterole."

"That sounds rather dramatic"—Celestine giggled—"even for you."

Leondria ignored her, turning her gaze back to Tatianna. "And you? Is your gown finished this time, or will it shift into something inappropriate halfway through the night again?"

Tatianna laughed at the memory of the time she tried making her own gown, with magic of course. When halfway through the ball, an errant thought about swimming in the lake flitted through her head due to the evening's oppressive heat, and her ballgown shifted to a swimming outfit. Society was scandalized. Her mother was not pleased and refused to believe it hadn't happened on purpose.

"Will you ever be able to let that go." She held out a hand, watching as the silvery fabric of her gown rippled and reshaped itself, catching the dim light like water under the stars. "I suppose we'll see what happens tonight. But if something does happen, it won't be my fault, *this* dress was made by the fairies."

Leondria sighed. "You're all impossible."

"And yet," Celestine said, wrapping her arms around Leondria from behind, resting her head on her golden sister's shoulder so they both looked into the mirror, "you still try to fix us."

Rhiannon smirked. "Maybe she just enjoys constantly failing."

Leondria muttered something under her breath, laughing despite herself; a small smile tugged at the corner of her lips eventually turning into a full grin.

Tatianna stood, brushing her hands along the shimmering folds of her gown. "Shall we?"

Her sisters stood beside her. They turned to the door, their magic humming in harmony—a symphony of precision, structure, chaos, and feeling.

No matter what happened tonight, the Wylde sisters were going to have a good time.

By the time Archer realized just how much control he had lost, it was too late.

Lysander had not only arranged for the ball to be anything but modest—he had hired the fairies to organize the event.

"Fairies? Really, Lysander?" Archer repeated slowly, struggling to keep his temper in check as he and Lysander stood on the outskirts of the lavishly decorated meadow while the aforementioned fairies flitted around the field and finished decorating the refreshment table and any other necessary last minute touches. The border of willow trees filled with fireflies set the tone for an evening of enchantment. "Tell me you're joking."

Lysander, to his credit, had the decency to look sheepish. "They throw the best events."

"They require anyone who employs them to have magic."

"Yes, well . . ." Lysander trailed off, rubbing the back of his neck. "That's not entirely a problem."

Archer's jaw clenched.

It was a problem. Society believed the Thornfields were without magic. The only reason society welcomed them at all was their relation to Lady Cordelia Blackthorn, a well-known powerful witch. Archer didn't know where the belief that he was magicless had started, but it was an assumption Archer had never corrected, one he had every intention of maintaining because it allowed him to go through society unnoticed.

Now? Now there would be questions. Anyone who knew the fairies would know they would not have worked with him if he was magicless. He would be expected to participate in society and to prove that he belonged among the magically gifted elite—people he had always shown disdain for, Lysander and Lilith being the only exceptions.

Archer stared at the fairies diligently going about their work, hands clasped behind his back. "This is a disaster."

"Only if you let it be. After all, this is Lysander's ball, not yours," Aisling said behind him.

He turned towards her. "He put my name on the invitation."

She adjusted the shimmering green sleeve of her gown, her eyes dancing with mischief. "Everyone will make assumptions, correct or not, that you had nothing to do with the planning or execution of this ball. Allowing them to believe that the fairies didn't care one way or another about you. It's not like the fairies are going to gossip about you to others. They are the very best and quite discreet."

"This is all too much. I don't want just anyone to discover what I've kept secret." He ran his hand through his hair.

Aisling shrugged. "Think of it this way, dear brother: if they already assume you're powerless, they will expect very little of you. A little misdirection, and no one will know the difference."

"You make it sound so simple."

"It is simple," Lilith chimed in, appearing at Lysander's side. "Unless, of course, you're truly incapable of managing it."

Archer narrowed his eyes at her.

She smirked.

They didn't understand. His magic was not like most. He had the ability to amplify any spell, which, on its own, seemed fairly harmless. But if someone was powerful enough, they could use his magic whether or not he wanted them to, making him a commodity to many in society, or it would if they knew he had any power. He was lucky everyone believed the lies about his lineage: that the magic was gone.

This ball was going to call that into question for anyone intelligent enough to make the connection.

He sighed, glancing at the dance floor the fairies had just conjured. The music had already started. On the other side of the border of trees, laughter and conversation spilled over the canopy of leaves like the tide that would soon drag him under.

He had been right from the start.

This was a mistake.

And yet, there was no stopping it now.

Chapter 3

"It is considered both improper and irresistible for a young lady to introduce herself without formal summons at a magical gathering; however, should she do so with wit, grace, and impeccable posture, society may be persuaded to forgive her... eventually." Miss Maplethorpe's Modest Manual of Magical Manners by Mistress Augusta Maplethorpe

The wind whispered through the willow trees that framed the meadow, their branches swaying as if they too were enjoying the distant melody of the string quartet. Fireflies drifted lazily through the air, making the sky look as though the stars had decided to drop in for a dance along with all the guests.

Tatianna walked ahead of her sisters, drinking in every enchanting detail until the beauty intoxicated her. This was, without question, the most magical ball she had ever attended. The fairies had outdone themselves—everything shimmered, from the air itself to the very ground beneath her feet, it was clear the entire night had been dusted with fairy magic.

Unable to resist, she twirled as she stepped into the meadow. The skirts of her gown—woven from dewdrops and moonlight (or so the fairies had insisted)—flared around her, swirling around her ankles when she finally stopped. Laughter bubbled from her lips, light and airy, like a sprite skipping across piano keys.

Behind her, Leondria let out a knowing chuckle. "Your hair has already come loose, Tati. Honestly, I think it's *allergic* to hairpins."

Tatianna sighed with exaggeration, running her fingers through the unruly curls that had been artfully arranged just moments before. "Oh well," she said, shaking her head, freeing her hair and letting it tumble down in wild waves to her lower back. "It feels *so* much better this way."

Leondria rolled her eyes. "Yes, well, the fairies didn't spend an *hour* styling it just so you could shake it out like a mischievous woodland nymph."

Tatianna grinned. "They *should* have known better."

Tatianna looped her arm through Leondria's and tugged her towards the refreshment table, her steps light, as if she were skipping rather than walking.

"Tati! Leondria! Wait for us!"

Celestine's voice rang through the meadow as she came bounding towards them, Rhiannon in tow like an unwilling dance partner being dragged into a reel.

If the fairies had intended to outdo themselves with the dresses, they had succeeded spectacularly. Celestine shimmered in a gown the deep purple of midnight woven with the very essence of stardust. Rhiannon's gown refused to settle on a single color, shifting between magenta and green like the northern lights with every movement. And then there was Leondria—practically glowing, draped in golden sunlight from her golden-blonde hair to the very tips of her perfectly polished shoes.

"You look radiant, Leondria," Tatianna teased. "Like the queen of summer court."

Leondria lifted her chin. "I am a queen, Queen of the Wyldes."

Tatianna snorted in the most unladylike manner. "I think Mama would very much disagree with that claim. I don't think she's ready to relinquish the title. She might not ever give up her crown."

Leondria huffed dramatically. "You're right, our mother may never pass on the title."

Celestine threw her hands out and spun. "At least Mama wouldn't argue with my appearance as an entire constellation. Now move, I see cinnamon cakes."

Laughing, Tatianna let her sisters surge ahead, weaving their way deeper into the shimmering wonderland the fairies had conjured. She, however, did not let her mother catch up—none of them, especially Tatianna, were quite ready for her to make her presence known by lecturing them into oblivion. Effie Wylde had a way of dampening a good time.

She watched as her sisters made a beeline for the cakes before allowing her own gaze to wander over the crowd for the first time. It was an interesting mix of the familiar and the unknown.

Her best friend, Evangeline Duskmoor, was in the middle of a lively reel, dancing with a rather handsome soldier—spinning so fast that Tatianna wasn't entirely sure if it was the magic in the air or the sheer force of Evangeline's enthusiasm keeping them upright.

And then there were the newcomers, or so she assumed, based on her lack of recognition.

Two gentlemen, potentially their hosts, stood deep in conversation on the far side of the refreshment table. They were opposites in every possible way.

One shone like a sunny afternoon—his hair, his skin, even his smile seemed designed to bring warmth and light to a room. He practically radiated charm and affability.

The other? He was nightfall. Dark skin, darker hair, and an expression that suggested he had never encountered anything remotely amusing in his entire life. Not once had he cracked a smile, despite the sheer merriment swirling around him. It was almost impressive.

Tatianna arched a brow. *Well, well, well,* she thought. *This evening was going to be more fun than I originally thought.*

Tatianna tilted her head, her green eyes homed in, studying the two gentlemen from across the magic-lit meadow. She had always been good at reading people, sensing the way magic pulsed around them. It was almost like reading their aura.

The golden-haired one? *Charming. Effortlessly sociable. The sort of man who probably left bouquets on doorsteps because he wanted everyone to feel adored, and whose laughter was infectious, creating joy for all those around to hear it.* She couldn't help but give him the nickname Mr. Sunshine.

The other? *A looming thundercloud wrapped in an impeccably tailored three-piece suit.*

Dark-haired, brooding, and standing with the stiff posture of someone who was dragged here against his will, he was wholly unmoved by the surrounding revelry. His hands clasped behind his back, his expression a dark cloud of disdain, and when his companion spoke with obvious delight, he merely responded with a slow measured nod.

Fascinating.

"You're staring," Leondria murmured, sidling up beside Tatianna, her gloved fingers curled around the stem of a delicate glass of enchanted champagne—tiny golden sparks fizzled from the bubbles before vanishing into the air.

"I'm *observing*," Tatianna corrected, twirling the drink she had somehow acquired without realizing it.

Celestine materialized, a cinnamon-sugar pastry in one hand and a knowing gleam in her eye. "Ohhh, are we discussing the new gentlemen? What does everyone think?" She took an unladylike bite, then mumbled around it, "I'd be happy to claim the golden-haired one as my dance partner."

Tatianna rolled her eyes. "You cannot simply claim a person, Celestine."

Celestine swallowed dramatically. "Watch me."

Rhiannon, who had been quietly perusing a floating book she had brought from home, sighed. "Mama is going to loathe this."

Tatianna smiled, a mischievous gleam in her eye. "Even more reason to enjoy it."

The air shimmered with laughter, music, the faint scent of honeysuckle, and starlit magic. Couples waltzed beneath the willow trees, their branches glowing faintly with luminescent dust, while fireflies danced like tiny constellations among the revelers. Overhead, enchanted lanterns floated lazily, casting a golden glow over the festivities.

It was the kind of night where anything felt possible.

Which meant it was time for Tatianna to do something reckless.

She lifted her chin, squared her shoulders, and, with the confidence of a woman who knew what she wanted, at least for tonight, she strode towards the two gentlemen.

Leondria made a strangled noise behind her. "Tatianna—!"

She might have stopped, but she could feel Leondria following her.

Celestine clapped her hands in delight. "Oh, this will be marvelous."

Rhiannon sighed. "If she embarrasses us, I'm pretending I don't know her."

Tatianna barely heard them. She had a mission now, and that mission was to determine whether Mr. Stormcloud and Mr. Sunshine were worth all this fuss.

As she approached, Mr. Sunshine noticed her first. His eyes lit up, and his lips curved into an effortless smile that had likely charmed everyone he had ever met.

Mr. Stormcloud merely turned his head, fixing her with an unreadable gaze. The air around him carried a subtle hum of restrained magic—controlled, leashed, contained.

Tatianna curtsied gracefully. "Good evening, gentlemen. I don't believe we've been introduced."

Mr. Sunshine's smile widened. "The pleasure is ours, I'm sure."

Mr. Stormcloud? He merely observed her in silence, as though deciding whether she was worth his time.

Tatianna smiled sweetly. *Oh, this is going to be entertaining,* she thought as she analyzed the challenge in front of her.

Mr. Sunshine took her hand in his. "I'm Lysander Goldvale, one of your hosts for this evening."

Tatianna held Lysander Goldvale's gaze as he grinned, his golden hair catching the lantern light as it danced overhead. He clearly found delight in all things. His enthusiasm was tangible. "Tatianna Wylde, a pleasure to meet you."

"I hope you're having an enchanted evening," he said, bowing with a flourish. "I do believe the fairies have outdone themselves. Though, I suspect the true magic of the night comes from the company."

Tatianna almost rolled her eyes at the obvious flattery from someone who flirted with ease. But she played along. "A generous sentiment, Mr. Goldvale."

Lysander turned towards his companion expectantly, waiting for him to join in the conversation, but Mr. Stormcloud remained rigid beside him. The dark-haired man regarded Tatianna with a cool, assessing gaze, his features impassive.

The contrast between them was highlighted by this interaction. Tatianna's eyes took in Lysander's relaxed stance, his smile warm and inviting. Her eyes moved to Mr. Stormcloud, who looked as though someone had physically dragged him here, and he was plotting their demise.

It only increased Tatianna's interest in the man who wouldn't smile.

Lysander, unperturbed by his friend's lack of social graces, took it upon himself to fill the silence. "Allow me to introduce my dear friend, Mr. Archer Thornfield. It took some time, but I convinced him to leave the estate and enjoy the festivities."

Archer inclined his head but did not bow, nor did he make any attempt at pleasantries.

Tatianna raised a brow. "A man who prefers not to speak, such a rarity."

Lysander's gaze shifted to something over her shoulder and his smile widened to the point it was almost blinding. Tatianna glanced back to see Leondria standing behind her.

"Hello, I'm Lysander Goldvale." He extended his hand as he bowed. "Would you care to dance?"

Leondria nodded, her cheeks turning a lovely shade of pink before she turned and walked to the dance floor with Lysander. Together they looked like sun deities.

Tatianna's eyes followed her sister, feeling a tad wistful. She would love to be dancing right now. She looked back at Archer; it was clear he was not going to ask her to dance. *What a shame.*

"It appears you have been abandoned, left alone with my company. Should we talk about the weather or stand awkwardly next to each other, not speaking?" She glanced over, eyebrow arched, a mischievous gleam in her eye.

"I prefer to observe. Too many people speak to fill the silence, or worse, only to hear their own voice," Archer interjected, his voice smooth but firm. "The night is already full of enough noise."

Tatianna's lips twitched. He was a challenge. She found it incomprehensible that anyone couldn't find something to enjoy in a night like this. But somehow, Mr. Stormcloud, Archer Thornfield, found laughter and music off-putting. His distaste didn't seem realistic. Even with her reading of his character, his disdain felt like an act.

"Then let us hope you can find somewhere with less sound," she countered, tilting her head in mock seriousness. "Otherwise, you might find yourself dreadfully bored."

For a brief moment, the corners of his mouth flicked upward. It was as if he found her amusing.

Before he could respond, a young woman approached. She was striking, with waves of dark hair and intelligent hazel-brown eyes that took in the little party with the confidence of someone well-versed in society's expectations, but not overly concerned with them, at least not anymore. Her gown, clearly designed by the fairies, looked like it was made from forest and frost.

The young woman stepped to Archer's side, placing a hand lightly on his arm. "Forgive my brother," she said, her voice lilting with humor. "He has yet to master the art of small talk."

Tatianna's eyes widened. "You're his sister?"

The young woman smiled. "Aisling Thornfield."

Tatianna warmed to her immediately. There was something about Aisling; she reminded Tatianna of herself—it felt like she could see straight through a person, see exactly who they were and decide not to hold it against them. Or maybe Aisling could read people, just like Tatianna could.

Celestine stepped to Tatianna's side, clearly having abandoned all pretense of subtlety. "Well, this is a surprise," she said with a teasing grin. "Mr. Thornfield, you never mentioned you had a sister." Her manner flirtatious, even if her words were nonsensical since she'd never interacted with him before.

Archer stiffened at her attention. Aisling, however, was undeterred. "That's because my brother is dreadfully quiet, at least at first." She looped her arm through his. "But I assure you, he is much better company once you get past his frosty exterior."

Tatianna glanced at Archer, whose expression had become unreadable once more. He was quite an enigma.

Aisling turned to Tatianna. "And what of you? Are you enjoying the evening?"

Tatianna smiled. "Immensely. It's been a delight meeting you." She cast a sidelong glance at Archer. "And I do hope your brother is as well."

Archer, standing rigid as ever, met her gaze, his dark eyes closed like the cover of the novel she had yet to read. "That remains to be seen."

Tatianna grinned. "Then let us hope, Mr. Thornfield, that you are amused by something before the night is over."

Chapter 4

"While a waltz may stir the heart and enchant the senses, one must never forget: a single dance may spark whispers, but a moment alone in the shadows can set reputations ablaze." The Charmed School: A Guide of Magical Etiquette for the Modern Witch by Elspeth Rosemoor

Archer looked at the young woman with her dark auburn hair cascading down her back, sparkling moss green eyes, and mischievous smile standing beside him, chatting with his sister—Tatianna Wylde, one of the daughters of Effie Wylde, a powerful witch on her own, with four daughters that were said to have even more magic than their mother.

He took a step and held out his hand. "Would you care to dance?" He felt his eyes widen because those were not the words he expected to come out of his mouth. Now that the question was hanging in the air, he hoped she would agree.

"Brother, are you feeling unwell?" Aisling asked. "I don't think you've ever asked someone to dance without being pressured first."

Archer turned his attention back to Tatianna, ignoring his sister's teasing. He watched as her lips curved into a knowing smile. "I'm flattered, Mr. Thornfield. I would be delighted." She slipped her hand into his.

He looked down at their hands, her long elegant fingers wrapped around his palm. His skin tingled where they touched, even through the gloves they both wore.

The orchestra struck up a waltz, the elegant notes filling the enchanted meadow with a rhythm that demanded twirling. Archer led Tatianna onto the dance floor, his posture stiff, his grip steady, but distant. As they moved to the music together, the silence between them grew, stretching between the beats of the music like an unspoken spell. Archer wanted to break the silence, but he was unsure of what to say.

Tatianna tilted her head, amusement flickering in her eyes as they turned with precision while travelling around the outside of the dance floor. "You realize that it is customary to converse while dancing, Mr. Thornfield?"

Archer cleared his throat, focusing on the rhythm of the waltz rather than her penetrating stare that felt like she could see everything there was to know about him. "I imagine you find no shortage of willing conversational partners, Miss Wylde."

She laughed, the sound light and teasing. "Ah, but none quite so enigmatic as you. Should I be flattered or concerned that you have yet to say much more than a sentence to me?"

He exhaled sharply, his lips pressed into a thin line. The waltz required them to move closer, and for the briefest moment, he caught the scent of citrus and something more elusive—magic, perhaps, humming just beneath the surface of her skin. It unsettled him more than he cared to admit. Every muscle in his body tensed as other dancers moved closer to them, causing their legs to brush together as he took each step of the dance.

Tatianna sighed dramatically. "You know, Mr. Thornfield, this dance would be far less awkward if you stopped looking as though you were solving mathematical equations to determine where each step should land."

Archer let out the breath he was holding, the corner of his mouth twitching despite himself. "I prefer precision."

Tatianna grinned. "That is an admirable quality in the correct setting. Dancing should be felt, not calculated."

He led her around the floor, moving between couples twirling around them. Snippets of conversation floated through the air. 'Isn't it a shame Mr. Goldvale has someone like him clinging to his coattails.' . . . "His name was on the invitation, but it's obvious Mr. Goldvale is the true host.'. . . 'Do you think her mother knows she's dancing with him?' . . . With every couple they passed another tidbit of gossip came their way. He wanted to comment on everything they'd heard, but the words to do so escaped him.

He spun Tatianna as the last notes of the song faded into the wind.

"Well, that was—interesting." Her eyes conveyed so much more than her words. "Come, let's escape the crowd. I know a place where even you might forget about precision for a moment."

Before he could protest, her hand clasped his, and she pulled him towards the edge of the meadow where the trees stood like sentries, weaving between the clusters of guests as she did so. He thought about stopping her, not wanting to give tonight's guests anything more to talk about, instead he let her lead him away. The music softened behind them as they stepped beneath the swaying canopy of willow trees. Fireflies flickered in the twilight, and a wooden swing, adorned with vines and tiny glowing orbs, hung from one of the branches.

Archer wondered how she knew the swing was in this spot.

Tatianna grinned and gestured to the swing. "Sit. I promise it won't betray your sense of balance."

Archer hesitated, then, with a sigh, lowered himself onto the swing, creaking softly under his weight. Tatianna took hold of the ropes and gave him a gentle push, her laughter as light as the breeze.

"See? Not everything has to be calculated," she said, watching him carefully.

Archer, to his own surprise, smiled fully. "Perhaps not."

Out of the corner of his eye, he saw Tatianna flick her fingers subtly, and the swing kept moving on its own, as if enchanted by the wind. He arched a brow, realizing what she had done without the use of a single word. Before he could comment, she darted in front of the swing, her moss green eyes sparkling with mischief, and leapt onto it.

The moment her feet left the ground, he knew she had miscalculated her landing. The swing moved forward completely underneath her. Her skirts tangled around her feet as her backside flew over the wooden seat. Archer acted on instinct and reached out, catching her just before she fell. His arms secured her to his side, sitting her on the swing, their bodies touching from shoulder to thigh.

For a heartbeat, they were frozen in place. Her wide eyes stared into his, their faces inches apart. Then Tatianna let out a breathless laugh. "Perhaps I should have considered precision this time."

Archer couldn't hide the slight curve of his lips. "Perhaps."

He didn't understand why he felt so drawn to her; she was impulsive, unpredictable, everything he found unsettling and yet—he couldn't stop his eyes from wandering to her lips and watching as her tongue darted out, wetting her lower lip right before she scraped her teeth across it.

He leaned in. The only thought in his mind was how much he needed to know what her full lips felt like pressed against his in this moment.

"Tatianna Wylde, where have you disappeared to?" Her mother's sharp tone destroyed the moment, shattering the spell she and Archer were under.

Tatianna's head snapped forward, and she groaned under her breath. "I have to go," she muttered, looking at his lips one last time before she stood. "Please, stay here for a few moments after I'm gone."

With one last smile, albeit a weak one, she turned swiftly, smoothing her gown as she stepped away from the seclusion of the willow tree, willing her racing pulse to slow. What had possessed her to let things go so far? To let him look at her like

. . . to enjoy it, then to lean into the moment as if it meant something? How could it, when she had just met him?

Her actions were just going to cause people to talk about her, and the last thing she needed was to become the center of town gossip.

"Mama," she hissed as she approached her mother, "must you call my name so loudly? It's embarrassing—and entirely unnecessary."

Effie Wylde's expression was cool, like it was whenever her mother looked at her, her gaze assessing. "Embarrassing? You're speaking to me of embarrassment when I find you alone, in the shadows, with *him*?"

Tatianna fought the urge to roll her eyes. "It was harmless, Mama. I was merely getting to know our new neighbor. All the different sounds were bothering him. I just wanted him to feel comfortable at the ball he helped arrange. Why must you turn everything into a scandal?"

"Harmless?" Effie scoffed. "You were alone with him."

Tatianna let out an exasperated breath. "He is pleasant enough company, I suppose, but you needn't worry, Mama. I'm unlikely to form an instantaneous attachment."

She clasped her hands behind her back. While her statement should have been true, she wasn't sure of its actual veracity.

Her mother's lips pressed into a thin line. "I should think not."

Tatianna didn't react—she had expected this response from her mother. But for some reason, her skin prickled, as if someone were watching. She shook the feeling away.

"A tangential relationship to Lady Cordelia Blackthorn does not give him true standing in society," Effie continued. "Not to mention his family's magic is practically non-existent. In fact, I have heard he doesn't even have magic. You would do well to remember that."

Tatianna didn't disagree. She didn't argue, even though she knew it wasn't true. What would be the point? There was no changing her mother's mind when she was like this. Tatianna sighed. "Let's go back to the dance then."

She linked her arm through her mother's and allowed herself to be led away, back into the swirling lights and music of the meadow. But she couldn't shake the feeling of something left unfinished.

"Have you not heard all the talk tonight? Just think, if any one of those ladies saw you run off for a private tête-à-tête with Mr. Thornfield you would be the first story in tomorrow's society pages." Effie continued her lecture without missing a beat. "Your reputation would be in shambles, with very little we could do to get it back."

"Yes, Mama." She bowed her head, hoping her mother would interpret the gesture as acquiescence.

She did not turn to see if Archer was still there, watching her walk away.

She didn't have to.

She could feel it—the weight of his disappointment after hearing her words, the silent wounding of his pride.

And yet, she kept walking, disappointed with herself for not standing up to her mother.

Chapter 5

Archer remained in the willow tree's sanctuary. He took a deep breath and Tatianna's scent teased his senses, causing his fingers to curl into fists as the faint sound of her footsteps faded away, overcome by the musical quartet. He concentrated on controlling his breathing, blocking out her lingering scent. He schooled his face until it was impassive—ensuring he would remain composed to those around him.

But inside? He was in turmoil, fury and pain twisted together in a dance he had learned to ignore long ago, but tonight he could not ignore it.

It wasn't the dismissal from Mrs. Wylde. He was accustomed to society overlooking him because they believed that magic defined a person's value. Throughout his entire life he had endured polite disinterest, thinly veiled condescension, and the quiet certainty that he was not worth the time of the magical elite.

But this? This cut differently.

It had felt like *she* was different as they sat together. Her recent actions proved him wrong, and yet, despite the anger, something deep inside of him continued to insist she was not like the rest of society.

Tatianna Wylde, with the mischievous glint in her eyes that should have prepared him for her amusing wit had left him befuddled as they sat together. It didn't help that even her magic was different, that against all odds it bent the natural world to her will as if the very essence of the earth longed to make her smile, just so it could be in her radiant presence—which is why he had allowed himself to believe, for a moment, that she *saw* him.

Not as a Thornfield, only accepted because of his money.

Not because he was the nephew of Lady Cordelia.

Not as the man with too little magic to be worth society's time.

Not as a polite obligation or an inconvenience to be endured.

But he had been mistaken. He had let his guard down for just a moment, and it had not turned out well.

Pleasant enough. Unlikely to form an attachment.

A muscle in his jaw twitched as he heard her words over and over again in his head.

Archer had never let the whispers of high society determine his self-worth. Despite the fact that for as long as he could re-member, there had always been gossip circling around his family and their lack of magic, he had remained proud. But there was something deeply humiliating in hearing his worth—his very presence—so easily dismissed by Effie Wylde. She had dismissed him in a manner he was meant to hear and feel.

And worse still? Tatianna had not even tried to dissuade her mother. Even though everything about her had felt different, she had proven herself to be just like the rest of them.

His hands flexed at his sides, his pulse a steady drum beneath his skin. He was not a fool; he knew better than to let the words of one conversation unmoor him. He knew his place in their world—or rather, the place they expected him to occupy without complaint.

But damned if he would make it easy for them.

If Tatianna Wylde thought he was a man easily forgotten, a man to be brushed aside without consequence, then she would find herself sorely mistaken.

He took a step towards the edge of the willow tree, straightening his shoulders. A breeze ruffled the tree's branches that still blocked him from the festivities, the cool night air did little to temper the slow burn in his chest as he prepared himself to return to the ball, to return to a gathering of people who believed his name was worth so little.

It wouldn't be the first time, nor would it be the last.

Let them underestimate him.

Let *her* underestimate him.

He had no intention of staying in the corner like a well-mannered afterthought, noticed only when they deigned to acknowledge him before once again turning away and ignoring his very existence.

Tatianna Wylde would remember him. She would discover that he was so much more than *pleasant* enough.

One way or another, she was going to discover he was so much more than her mother gave him credit for.

Archer forced his expression into something composed as he stepped out from beneath the willow's shadow. The hum of conversation and distant laughter from the meadow ahead assaulted his ears. The sound almost changed his mind, and he turned toward the estate. He did not allow himself to run as much as he wanted to. The cacophony of the party continued, trying to welcome him back into the fold of the ball, although he found the noise less than welcoming. He walked around the outskirts of the dance floor, the floating lanterns' golden light cast across the festive meadow or how gowns swirled like petals in the breeze was lost on him. The thin layer of charm he had worn earlier in the evening had dissolved, replaced by a quiet, simmering irritation.

A familiar figure materialized at his side before he spotted his friends.

"Lilith," he greeted, his voice controlled, though he did not slow his pace.

"Archer, don't tell me you're going to hide yourself away already?" she returned smoothly, falling into step beside him.

Her words stopped him mid-step. "I was . . ." His eyes darted about, searching for a reason he was storming away from the ball. "I believe we need more champagne. I was on my way to find some when you found me."

Lilith laughed. "Is that all? I swore I saw you disappear under a willow tree not that long ago. I was beginning to think a nymph with wild hair had spirited you away."

He gave her a sidelong glance. "I stepped away for some air."

Lilith Goldvale's mouth curved into a knowing smirk. "Air? Is that what they're calling it these days?"

Archer exhaled through his nose. He had known her too long to be baited so easily, but she was nothing if not persistent.

"How interesting," she mused, tilting her head, golden curls glinting in the lantern light. "I could have sworn I saw you wander into the trees with a certain Wylde sister. The one with the enchanting eyes."

He shot her a flat look. "I do not wander—"

"Oh, don't insult me with a weak denial, Thornfield," she interrupted, waving a gloved hand. "I've eyes, and I've ears. And I must say, I'm a bit surprised you would set your eyes on a Wylde sister. Their mother is an insufferable snob. But if you are truly set on catching the interest of a Wylde, you might do better with one who can cast a proper spell."

Archer's fingers twitched at his sides. He had spent years ignoring the murmurs about his magic—or lack thereof—but tonight, after overhearing Effie Wylde voice what all of society felt but refused to say, the words, coming from the sister of his closest friend, struck a particularly raw nerve.

"I have no interest in any of the Wylde sisters, especially not Tatianna Wylde," he said coolly. "She is insufferable, far too convinced of her own importance. If anything, I pity the man unfortunate enough to fall prey to her charms."

Lilith arched a delicate brow, clearly amused by his vehemence. "Oh, my. Such a passionate speech—I almost wonder if your vehement claim of dislike is a way to hide that your feelings are quite the opposite."

"I assure you, it is not."

A tray of champagne floated by, carried by a fairy, who remained unseen. Archer grabbed a glass before the tray floated away.

Lilith gave an exaggerated sigh, pressing a hand to her chest. "A shame. A romantic interest between the two of you would have entertained the gossips for months."

Archer merely shook his head, unwilling to allow the discussion to continue. He had had quite enough of the Wyldes for one evening.

What he did not see—what he could not know— was that a figure stood just beyond the lantern's glow.

Tatianna Wylde had returned to the edge of the meadow after watching her mother walk away with Lysander. Effie Wylde, persistent as always, had convinced their host to leave the ball to give her a tour of the house. Tatianna shook her head, amazed at what her mother could accomplish and thankful because it gave her time to seek out Mr. Thornfield, Archer. She was drawn back to the dance by a desperate need to clarify the conversation between her and her mother, to apologize, only to hear Archer's words cut through the night like a blade.

She is insufferable. Convinced of her own importance. Pity the man who falls prey to her charms.

A flicker of something sharp curled in her chest—anger, embarrassment, and something she refused to acknowledge.

Fine.

If that was how he saw her, then he would find she was more than capable of proving him right.

Tatianna stood there silently seething as Lilith's tinkling laughter disappeared into the crowd of dancers, whose swirling dresses and patterned steps brought the music to life. For a moment, Tatianna imagined that Lilith disappeared into the tune as she walked away from Archer, instead of just joining the rest of the party. Tatianna moved forward at a sedate pace until she stood next to Archer, not close enough to touch, but near enough that she hoped he could feel her presence and cause him to question whether or not she had heard the terrible things he said about her. She stopped by his side and saw the tension radiate off him. It was apparent from the way his hands were clasped to the sharp lines of his clenched jaw—a stark contrast to the person she had sat next to under the private canopy of the willow tree. She turned until he was almost out of sight, hovering at the edge of her vision and plotted how she could become the person he believed her to be. What could she do in this moment that he would find insufferable? She didn't like this cold version of the man beside her, especially compared to her memory of him from just moments before. The man she sat under the willow tree with no longer seemed real, someone her imagination had created, and not the truth of the man who had sat beside her.

As her eyes focused on the dancers in front of her, her friend Evangeline came into focus. She was dancing with another gentleman Tatianna had yet to meet. The way he moved was graceful and . . . predatory. It was the only other word that came to mind as she watched him move across the floor. He was quite handsome, with the light glistening off his hair, and the manner in which he smiled at her friend. It was apparent that he was the type of man who made the person he was with feel like they were his whole world. She watched as the music ended, and he whispered something in Evangeline's ear. Tatianna was about to call her friend over, hoping for an introduction to this mysterious gentleman when she felt the air change around her. The ball was still alive with music and candlelight, but something in the magic shifted. She felt the difference—like a breeze curling the wrong way, like the moment before a storm cracks open the sky, like something terribly wrong was about to happen.

She rubbed her arms as a chill settled into her bones. A sudden, silent thought bloomed in her mind: *Protection.* Not a scream, not even a word—just instinct. An image of home, safe from any disaster the world might throw at her blossomed in her mind as she forced her arms down by her side. The moment the muscles in her arms relaxed and before the thoughts of a safe haven flitted out of her head, there was a flick of her fingers at her side, not much more than a twitch. In fact, it was so infinitesimal she didn't realize she'd cast anything at all.

The air around her shimmered faintly, a ripple, a soft crackle, like heat rising off stone. The wards she hadn't meant to form swept outward in a slow pulse—and brushed against Archer, enveloping him in a safe cocoon.

He jerked, his movement just enough to draw her attention. His hand hovered near his chest, brow furrowing like he'd felt something, but couldn't name it.

Tatianna tilted her head. "Is something wrong?" She hadn't wanted to talk to him, not after his cruel words, but her question came out of her mouth before she could stop it.

He studied her, dark eyes sharp and calculating. "What did you do?"

She blinked. "Nothing." The word left her without a thought. "Why?"

"There was . . . a feeling, like a spell being cast," he said slowly, as if reluctant to admit it. "A flare of magic."

"I didn't cast anything," she replied, and she meant it. To cast a spell, she had to have the intent to do so, at least she always had in the past.

He stared at her, his eyes boring into her, searching for the truth. "You didn't say a spell? No focus? No book? No wand? No flick of the wrist?"

Tatianna's eyebrows shot up at his last statement. How had he noticed that's how her magic worked in the short amount of time they had spent together? Very few people knew her magic worked in ways that others could not understand. In fact, her family and her best friend were the only people in the world that knew, until now.

Not that it mattered. She shook her head, attempting to remove any self-doubt from her next statement. "I don't know what you felt," she said at last. "But it wasn't me."

Archer stepped back, a slight retreat, as if he was retreating to what he believed was a safe distance from her. "How can you be sure? I witnessed how carefree you are with your spells."

She bristled, her spine straightening. "Are you sure carefree is the word you intended to use?"

His jaw worked, silent, until he finally gave a curt nod. "You're correct, I misspoke. I should have said how careless you are with your magic"

Tatianna opened her mouth expecting a witty comeback to be at the ready, instead there was nothing. Her mouth snapped shut as she crossed her arms and turned away from the insufferable Mr. Thornfield.

The silence that followed wasn't easy. It was tight and formal, full of anger and emotions neither of them quite understood yet nor were willing to acknowledge. The music behind them continued as they stood there, incapable of enjoying what was right in front of them.

Unseen, the shimmer of protection engulfed them, while some other magic rippled across the meadow—neither of them felt the spell as it coursed around the magic Tatianna had unknowingly cast.

Chapter 6

"Emotions, like spells, are often complex. It is not uncommon to experience two seemingly contradictory feelings. Happiness for what the future holds, and fear of, as yet, unforetold change. It is often best to focus on the first and examine the second in private, for change is inevitable even if unwanted." The Book of Etiquette for Acceptable Societal Decorum and the Proper Use of Magic by Honoria Penhaven, Third Duchess of Cheltenham

The meadow glowed behind them, its enchanted lanterns drifting like lazy stars through the night air as the Wylde sisters' carriage creaked down the moonlit road. The last strains of music faded into the distance, muffled now by trees, but lingering like a half-remembered dream.

Inside the carriage, gowns rustled, heads leaned against velvet cushions, while glitter from fairy magic clung to their sleeves and hair as if the night itself refused to let them go.

Celestine sighed, dramatically throwing her arm over her eyes. "I can't feel my feet. I danced with every man under a hundred and even some over a hundred. One of them might've been a ghost. Not entirely sure."

"You say that like it's a complaint, instead of your goal for the night," Rhiannon murmured, her chin resting atop her latest book, which had somehow made it back into her hands. "I doubt you stopped for air."

"I stopped for cake," Celestine said with a satisfied grin.

"Only to steal mine," Leondria said dryly.

"Yours wasn't the only cake I ate tonight. It was all so delicious." Celestine licked her lips just thinking about it.

Their mother, Effie Wylde, sat straight-backed despite the hour, her dark eyes thoughtful as she looked out the carriage window at the fading lights of the Goldvale estate.

"Well," she said at last, "I must admit that Lysander Goldvale certainly knows how to host. Gracious, well-mannered, and effortlessly charming. A suitable companion for any woman of sense and station."

Leondria arched a brow. "He did seem fond of sense. And flattery."

Effie nodded approvingly. "Flattery is not a flaw when it's well-spoken and well-intended. Unlike that Mr. Thornfield." Her voice dripped with disdain. "All scowl and silence. I imagine his conversational skills are stored in a locked cabinet, never to be opened. Although I'm not surprised, such a disgrace to his family."

Tatianna, watching the soft glow of the meadow disappear behind the trees, crossed her arms. "He was not affable, that is for certain. Although far from unpleasant at first, he was incapable of maintaining a polite charade"

Effie sniffed, clearly surprised to hear Tatianna agree with her. "For once, you and I are in agreement. It is unfortunate that Mr. Goldvale considers the man such a close confidant."

The carriage jostled as it turned onto the familiar path toward the Wylde family estate. Lights twinkled in the cottage windows, while the scent of night jasmine drifted through the open slit in the carriage windowpanes.

Once inside the house, the sisters ran upstairs eager to gossip about the ball and its attendees. However, by the time slippers were abandoned and hairpins fell like stars across the floor, yawns overtook even Celestine's endless commentary.

From down the hall they heard their mother's voice—a mix of amusement and mild disappointment—before retiring with a sigh and a muttered, "Girls raised by pixies, I swear it."

"I'm going to sleep for a year," Rhiannon mumbled, heading to her bedroom.

"Wake me if Lysander proposes," Celestine called over her shoulder to Leondria, already halfway to her room.

Tatianna lingered in Leondria's room, a gentle fire crackling as they sat on the tufted settee in their chemises, gowns puddled in the middle of the floor, cheeks still pink from laughter and dancing.

For a while they said nothing, just sat there, Tatianna's head resting on Leondria's shoulder. The quiet between them was filled with the pleasant exhaustion only a perfect night could leave behind.

Then Leondria broke the silence. "You like him."

Tatianna tilted her head, pretending not to understand. "Mr. Sunshine? He's delightful, but a bit too eager for my taste."

"No, not Lysander." Leondria gave her a look. "Mr. Storm-cloud."

"At first, perhaps. He was intriguing." Tatianna smiled faintly, remembering their moment on the swing.

"He glared at the cake table like it had personally offended him."

"That's what made it so fun," Tatianna said with a spark of mischief. "He's so buttoned-up. I wanted to see if I could make him unbutton something. Figuratively, of course."

Leondria laughed, shaking her head. "Mama will lose her mind if you pursue him."

Tatianna leaned her head against the back of the settee, staring up at the carved ceiling. "She's already halfway there," she sighed. "I hate to admit it, but she might be right about him. The things I overheard. He called me insufferable. Not to mention this, 'I pity the man unfortunate enough to fall prey to her charms.' That's what he said, about me, can you believe it?"

Leondria shook her head. "Gentlemen are baffling, I don't know how they can say such hurtful things and still gaze at a person like they are the stars and moon combined."

"They are an enigma." She shrugged. "But you must tell me more about Mr. Goldvale. Such an apt name for someone who looks like a golden god."

"What's there to say? We danced. We talked. He actually listened to me, even when I was discussing the importance of bees, and when the conversation turned to astronomy."

"Bees and astronomy. I think he may be a keeper."

They sat in silence for a few heartbeats more, the fire's crackle the only sound.

Then Leondria reached over and took her sister's hand. "It was a good night."

Tatianna squeezed her fingers gently. "It was."

And outside, as the sisters drifted toward sleep, the last of the fairy lights from the meadow flickered and vanished into the trees—leaving only memories behind.

Late morning light filtered into the breakfast room through lead-glass windows and shined directly into Tatianna's eyes. She raised her hand to close the curtains with magic.

"Tatianna Wylde, you know how I feel about the frivolous use of magic. If you want the curtains closed, walk over there and make the required adjustments." Effie Wylde raised her teacup to her lips as she looked on expectantly.

She lowered her hand with a sigh and placed her palms on the table, about to stand when the door to the morning room burst open. Leondria waltzed through, dancing to a tune she alone could hear, causing her morning gown to flutter around her feet as she moved in tiny circles. Even at breakfast, she dressed as though the Queen might drop in unannounced—the golden frock reminiscent of her ball gown from the night before, her hair coiled into an elegant chignon, and her neckline adorned with a sunburst brooch that shimmered with charm-bound sparkle.

"Well," she announced, sweeping to the table and plucking a grape from a bowl without so much as a glance. "I hope you've all had your tea this morning because the estate is buzzing."

Effie didn't look up from her tea. "If the estate is buzzing, I'd wager it's because you've stirred the hive."

"Please, mother. I only give the bees direction and it always helps make fantastic honey." Leondria flopped gracefully onto a chair and waved for a servant—non-magical, of course—to pour her breakfast tea.

Tatianna, still blinking against the effervescent glow of her older sister, muttered, "Wouldn't dream of closing the curtains with magic, but by all means, summon a servant with a flick of your wrist."

Effie's eyes were sharp as daggers as she glanced over the rim of her cup, a clear warning that Tatianna had crossed a line, at least from her mother's perspective.

"The rules are about restraint. There's no need to flaunt our abilities," Effie said.

Tatianna couldn't help but roll her eyes. Her mother decided every individual's value based on their magical ability, but using said ability was somehow gauche. It made little sense.

"I'm not sure Tati knows the meaning of restraint," Rhiannon murmured as she entered, a leather-bound tome pressed to her chest. She took her usual seat, pushing her spectacles up the bridge of her nose with one hand as her long, ink-stained fingers of her other hand flipped the book open to a dog-eared page before she'd taken the time to even look around the room.

Leondria scoffed. "You're one to talk. You've probably found a spell in that book to charm your toast into buttering itself."

"It's a breakfast spell," Rhiannon replied, without looking up. "And I didn't find it. I actually wrote it and perfected it last week."

"Show off," Celestine declared, breezing into the room last, humming a waltz to herself. Her curls were wild from sleep and piled on top of her head in disarray. She plopped onto the chair beside Tatianna and reached for a croissant—and accidentally knocked over the croissant basket. Celestine whispered an incantation and the entire basket now hovered over the edge of the table, instead of crashing to the floor.

"Celestine," Effie said with the long-suffering tone of someone who had issued this warning many, many times. "Control."

"Oh no," Celestine said brightly, grabbing a floating croissant. "It's the magic again. Must be something in the air. Even with my bracelets on it feels off."

Tatianna gave her sister a sidelong glance. "Maybe you're allergic to rules."

"No," Celestine said with a wink, "just Mama's voice."

The room rippled with laughter—except for Effie, who sighed into her teacup and muttered something about decorum and doom.

Tatianna smiled. For a moment her heart was light as she watched her sisters playfully tease each other and their mother, but the feeling was fleeting. She couldn't shake the lingering sensation from the night before—the effervescent dancers in the meadow, the sudden unwelcoming shift of the air, and, if she had known about it, the spell that had cast itself without her intending to do so.

Not to mention Archer Thornfield.

She hadn't dreamed his reaction. He had felt something, too. Whatever happened last night, it wasn't isolated to her—or to the Wylde sisters.

She sipped her tea, then set it on the saucer with only the briefest of a rattle. Lost in memories of last night, her fingers circled the rim of her cup. Something had happened last night. The question was—what was it and who was it going to affect?

Celestine tore off a piece of her croissant and popped it into her mouth. "So," she said, through a flurry of flaky crumbs, "how was your enchanted evening, Leondria?"

Drawn back to the present by Celestine's impertinent teasing, Tatianna raised a brow and glanced toward her eldest sister, who had suddenly found great interest in stirring honey into her tea.

Effie set her cup down with a quiet clink. "Yes, do tell. I hardly saw you at the ball after the opening dance. You vanished like a well-behaved spell. Granted, I did have my hands full with Tatianna."

"Mama!" Tatianna gasped. "I did nothing untoward last night."

Leondria gave them all a look—cool, practiced, and just this side of smug. It was her, *I'm the eldest* look. "I was occupied. Mr. Goldvale was quite unexpected last night, especially for a man. He was, dare I say, intelligent and affable."

Celestine snorted. "That's rich coming from the woman who has said more than once that men were better off seen than heard."

"I still stand by that but . . . Lysander Goldvale is hardly 'men,' plural," Leondria said smoothly, dabbing at the corner of her mouth with a linen napkin. "And he's not like the rest of them. He's . . . competent."

"That's a low standard," Rhiannon muttered, without looking up from her spell book.

"But he cleared it," Celestine said, grinning. "The real question, though, is did he manage to clear any other barriers?"

"Celestine!" their mother snapped.

"What? I meant emotionally," Celestine said with faux innocence. "Was there a deep and moving heart-to-heart under the stars? Perhaps a shared longing for a new grimoire?"

Leondria rolled her eyes. "We walked. We talked. He asked about Mama. About our estate. About—" she hesitated for half a second, then went on, "the burdens of responsibility."

Tatianna tilted her head. "Did it feel like a conversation or an interview?"

Leondria didn't answer at first. Her fingers curled around the stem of her glass, and for a moment, she looked almost uncertain. "It's a rare thing, to feel truly seen. With Lysander, I wasn't performing or pretending. I could simply be myself—no pretense, no cleverness, just . . . me. And he looked as though he liked what he saw."

That silenced the table.

Even Celestine didn't joke. Rhiannon turned a page more slowly than normal. Their mother, surprisingly, said nothing at all.

Tatianna felt something tighten in her chest and as she looked around the room at her sisters, she could tell they could feel it as well. The Wylde sisters. So often treated as curiosities based on the vast arrays of magic they had, or worse, threats. Society liked to pretend that they were their darlings, but the whispers behind the sisters' backs were never quiet enough to go unheard. Because of this, Leondria wasn't one to open easily, and for her to admit something felt real... That meant something important.

Still, Tatianna asked, "Do you trust him?"

Leondria looked at her. Her eyes were clear and steady. "No. Not yet. But I think I could. And that's not something I ever thought I would say."

Celestine made a soft, surprised sound and leaned back in her chair, visibly impressed and a little jealous. "Well. Since you're falling for him, should we prepare the wedding runes now, or wait until he leaves love notes spelled in rose petals around the cottage?"

"He'd better not," their mother muttered, almost to herself. "That's how you get bees in the draperies."

"Wouldn't that be Leondria's dream?" Celestine grinned. "A swarm of bees and a man who listens and sees."

Tatianna laughed despite herself, though, if her sisters had looked close enough, the tension behind her smile didn't ease. The thought of Leondria entangled with someone who was friends with Archer, friends with someone so cold and calculating as the man that almost kissed her and then called her insufferable, made her want to cringe. His words still stung in the morning light, as did his accusations that she had something to do with the strange shift last night.

Did her sister have to fall for someone who was friends with Archer Thornfield? The man had looked at her like she was a catastrophe waiting to happen.

And if she *was* a catastrophe . . . She pushed that thought away. She loved how her magic worked and refused to believe there was anything wrong with it.

However . . .

Last night something happened and deep down she knew whatever it was, it was just the beginning.

Archer Thornfield sat at the long, sun-drenched table in the east wing's breakfast salon, slowly rotating his cup of black coffee in his hand as if the movement might cause something more than the swirling of dark liquid in a porcelain cup to happen. The whimsical thought of being able to turn back time with a piece of his morning ritual crossed his mind, but it flittered away, leaving behind the reality-based thoughts he was comfortable with.

He raised the cup to his lips, then set it down with a grimace. The deep, rich liquid didn't satisfy as usual. Instead, the morning beverage tasted of bitterness and memory.

He hadn't slept well, tossing and turning until the sheets wrapped around his body. Flashes from the ball taking over his thoughts, cycling through moments. Under the willow tree, Effie Wylde's dismissal, whatever it was that caused the air to shift during the ball. Her response to it.

Tatianna Wylde. It was her eyes that haunted him throughout the night.

He'd told himself—repeatedly—that the Wylde women were a curiosity, not a complication. Her magic was unpredictable and dangerous. He needed to avoid her and the rest of her family. Yet, the moment the magic in the meadow turned, it had been her he looked to. Not his sister. Not his friend. *Her.*

Tatianna Wylde. It was her sparkling laughter he heard as the wind blew by his window all night long.

He couldn't explain it. Not without sounding foolish. Or worse—enchanted. Is that all it took, one evening for him to become enchanted? No, he wouldn't fall prey to something so frivolous.

"She's not even trying," he muttered under his breath to an empty room.

And that was the damnable thing. Tatianna Wylde had scarcely looked at him at the ball. At least not after her mother had taken her away, or so he believed. Her words as she walked away had been crisp, her manner restrained. She hadn't cast any sultry spells, not even before her mother had come along, when she'd been playful, but observant. At the end of the night, she'd stood near him, a combination of moonlight and thorns—her smile reminiscent of her curious demeanor, but then she was surrounded by a prickly exterior that kept him at arm's distance, utterly unaware of the way the world bent toward her.

And then... the magic had changed. Just for a moment.

He felt it. He *knew* it. It wasn't panic or an attack. It was protection. Soft, subtle, like a shield of silk draped across his skin. It had closed around him, and when he turned—there she was. Glancing away like she hadn't done a thing.

But something in the air had tasted like her.

"Lost in thought already? Or just bored with your own company?"

Lilith's voice floated in from the doorway, sweetly mocking.

Archer sighed as he continued to swirl the coffee in his cup, never taking his eyes off the storm brewing in his hand. "I was hoping for a moment of quiet," he said, glancing over at his friend's sister with a measured gaze. They had been friends for long enough that he hoped she would leave him be this morning.

"Clearly," she said, ignoring his wishes as she settled into the seat opposite him with the effortless grace of a woman who knew exactly how much trouble she was capable of. "But quiet never lasts long in a house that has recently hosted the Wylde sisters."

He continued to stare at his cup, suddenly wishing he had asked for the morning paper. Something, anything, that could provide a physical barrier to Lilith's prying.

She plucked a blackberry from a silver dish and popped it into her mouth. She closed her eyes for a moment, savoring the taste. "So. Which one's caught your eye? Not Leondria. Too obvious. I can't see you being intrigued with the bookish one. And not the youngest—her magic's liable to turn your boots into butterflies. That leaves . . ." Her gaze sharpened, amused. "Tatianna."

Archer set his cup down with more force than necessary, abandoning his quest for introspection. "I'm not *interested.*"

Lilith grinned. "I wasn't asking."

He met her eyes, cold and flat. "She's unpredictable. I don't think she knows what she's capable of, which makes her dangerous."

"Mm. Sounds like the two of you have something in common." She picked up another berry, rolling it between her fingers before popping it into her mouth.

"What are you implying?" Archer's jaw clenched. He knew exactly what she was implying, but needed her to say the words.

Lilith sighed as she looked toward the ceiling. "You've been hiding from your magic for years. Ever since your last years at Eton and your run in with . . ." She paused, tapping her lips in thought. "What was his name?"

"Malric Wrenne." Speaking that man's name left a foul taste in his mouth.

She snapped her fingers. "That's it. What happened was—troubling—and you've been hiding your magic ever since."

"It's safer that way. And it might be safer for Tatianna to do the same. Whatever she did—if she did anything—it wasn't intentional." He ran a hand through his hair. "That's what's troubling."

"Troubling?" Lilith tilted her head. "Because you'd rather believe she's dangerous... or because you believe you are?"

He didn't respond. He knew Lilith well enough to know he didn't have to. The fact that she knew him so well was unnerving, though. He couldn't control how or when others used his magic, which made him dangerous in his mind. Tatianna

Wylde's use of magic was too careless, unpredictable. He feared someone would use her, like he had been used.

Lilith sat back with a sigh, smiling like she'd won. "Careful, Archer. The fine-eyed Wylde may not need a spell book to cast a spell or steal your heart. But that doesn't make her dangerous, just unpredictable. Just like what happened in the past doesn't make you dangerous or likely to do harm to anyone."

He pushed his chair back and stood.

"I'm going for a walk." He nodded his head in a slight bow before walking towards the door.

"Of course you are," Lilith called after him. "If you see her, tell her hello from me."

He didn't respond. But he did glance once—just once—toward the west garden, where the ivy grew wild and the last traces of the moonlit ball still clung to the edges of the field where the willow tree branches danced in the wind, reminiscent of the spinning couples from the night before. He told himself his interest in Tatianna was nothing more than curiosity.

But the spell still lingered, warm beneath his skin.

As did his curiosity . . . that was where all the trouble always began.

Archer walked through the halls of the estate his friend had purchased. The portraits lining the hall seemed to follow his journey, their eyes tracking his every movement. The silk carpet muffled his journey as he crossed over into the west wing, the portraits changing to landscapes that did not track his passage. He opened the door and descended the stone steps of the west wing and crossed the dew-touched lawn with long, purposeful strides. The morning was unusually quiet—birds chirped at intervals, but even they seemed reluctant to break the hush that had settled over the grounds.

He took the gravel path that curved along the edge of the rose garden, where the hedges grew in controlled abundance and the air smelled of the early days of spring and secrets. The gravel crunched under his boots as he walked, each step a grounding reminder of the earth, solid and mundane, beneath all the glittering artifice that was the magical society.

No Tatianna.

Not that he was looking.

At least that's what he told himself. He was out walking to clear his head, nothing more. He didn't think magic could hang in the air for this long, and certainly not hers. But he could still feel it—ghostly and feather-light—coiled under his skin, near his heart, like the breath of a spell not yet spoken, therefore not yet active.

He shook it off and kept walking, rounding the edge of the meadow where the ball had taken place. In the daylight, the magic of the night before was gone. The hanging lights were stationary, no longer dancing in the breeze. Basically, it looked like the magic had evaporated with the rising of the sun.

A soft cough pulled his attention away from his thoughts and to the other side of the path.

His aunt, Lady Cordelia, stood there wearing a hat impressive in its size and decoration. She was pale and composed, just as he would expect. One gloved hand rested lightly on the shoulder of her daughter, Emelie. The girl looked thinner than Archer remembered—not much more than a wisp in a pale pink cloak, her skin almost gray and cheeks hollow despite the spring sun and crisp air.

"Mr. Thornfield," Lady Cordelia said with the faintest smile. "You walk early."

He offered a slight bow. "Lady Cordelia. Cousin Emelie."

Emelie gave a fragile curtsy, her legs trembling beneath her skirts. Archer politely ignored how her mother lifted her up from the crouched position.

"I find the air's clearer before breakfast conversations cloud my mind," Archer said, tone neutral.

Lady Cordelia's lips moved in an attempt to smile, but it didn't quite reach her dark eyes. "I suspect we all need a bit of clarity this morning. Emelie wished to see the flowers before the day grew too warm."

Emelie looked up at him, the sparkle in her eye a stark contrast to the pallor of her skin. Her voice was thin, so faint it was almost not audible. "The roses were humming last night."

Archer stilled. "Were they?"

She nodded. "You know, the flowers sing when spells go sideways. I thought everyone knew that."

"Emelie, darling—" Lady Cordelia squeezed her daughter's shoulder, a gently reproving glance flickered across her face.

"No, it's fine," Archer said, waving his hand as if the action could push her words away. He focused on Emelie, studying the girl. It appeared she knew things, but as far as he was aware, she rarely left her home. "She's not wrong."

Lady Cordelia exhaled quietly. "You'll have to forgive her, Mr. Thornfield. The fevers leave her . . . Weak and fanciful. She's had visions since she was very small."

"I don't doubt her," Archer said, and realized he meant it. "The world is stranger than it pretends to be. Why wouldn't roses sing when spells go sideways?"

He crouched so he could meet Emelie's eyes. "Did the roses sing for long?"

Emelie tilted her head. "Just a short while. They stopped when someone sang back."

A chill traced down his spine. What if there were two spells?

Lady Cordelia took her daughter's elbow in her hand, supporting Emelie's weight. "That's quite enough talk for now."

"Yes, Mama," Emelie whispered, casting one last longing glance toward the meadow.

Archer straightened. "If she ever wants company on a morning walk, I'd be glad to join her."

Lady Cordelia blinked, her expression caught between surprise and gratitude. "That's very kind of you, Mr. Thornfield."

He nodded once and turned, heading back toward the town, not yet ready to end his walk. He pondered Emelie's words. Running them through his head over and over again.

Until someone sang back.

A spell hadn't just been cast. Someone had answered.

And if he didn't find out what that meant soon, he feared the roses wouldn't be the only thing singing warnings before spring turned to summer.

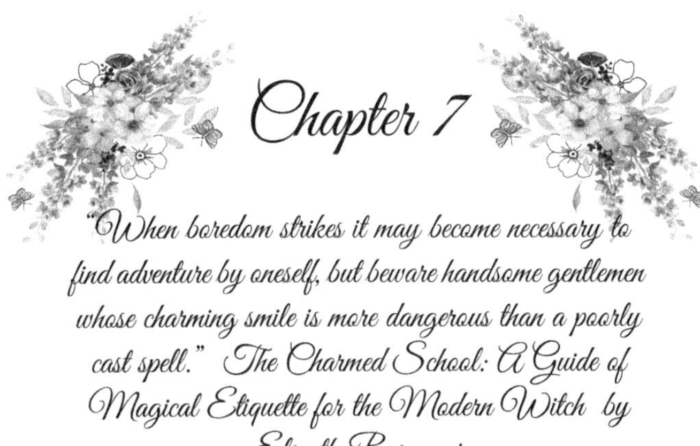

Chapter 7

The morning room was flooded with pale sunlight and the quiet tick-tock of the longcase clock in the corner. Tatianna slouched in her chair by the window, a book open in her lap, but her eyes weren't moving across the page. She stared blankly out the window at the quiet garden, one foot bouncing restlessly.

Effie sat across from her, posture immaculate, needlepoint in hand. Her silver thimble caught the light with each precise motion of her needle.

"This is terribly dull," Tatianna muttered, flipping a page she hadn't read. "Surely something exciting should happen on a morning like this."

Effie didn't look up. "Not every day can be as exciting as anticipating a ball, Tatianna. Some of us quite enjoy a bit of calm."

"I'd rather like a mild scandal. Or even a moderately interesting errand."

Effie raised one eyebrow as she pulled her thread taut. "If you're bored, you could always mend that hem you ripped climbing out the stable window last week."

Tatianna looked at her mother with something akin to awe. How did she know about the stable incident?

"Or—I could convince Leondria to bicycle into town, and we could picnic by the lake instead." A smile formed as she thought of various ways to make the day engaging.

As if she had summoned them, the door creaked open and all three of her sisters stumbled into the room in various stages of disarray. Leondria blinked against the light, her blonde hair still half-pinned, as if she had gone out the night before. Rhiannon's spectacles were askew, and she clutched a half-buttoned cardigan like it was her lifeline. Celestine had wrapped herself in a blanket and looked like a butterfly about to emerge from its cocoon, her dark hair wild, fluttering around her.

Tatianna straightened. "Good heavens. Did the three of you go to a ball last night and not invite me?"

Leondria sank into a chair, wincing. "Don't be ridiculous. I just . . . didn't sleep well. Too many dreams. I kept dreaming of the tinkling of bells throughout the night."

"You look as though you didn't sleep at all." Tatianna said, concern laced through her words.

Rhiannon rubbed her eyes. "I had the strangest dreams. Fog, fireflies, and—bells, I think? I can't remember."

Celestine yawned wide enough to make her eyes water. "I'm sure I was in bed sleeping, but it feels like I ran a marathon in my corset."

"Still tired from the night before," Effie said, lips pursing. "You shouldn't have stayed out so late at that ball. Moonlight frolics are all well and good, but they wear one thin quickly."

Tatianna looked at her sisters, their exhaustion was the complete opposite of how she felt. Yesterday she'd been tired from the night before, but today she was refreshed and bored. She stepped closer to Leondria. "Come to town with me. We'll ride bicycles, escape Mother's disapproving glances." She looked over at her mother. "And lunch by the lake. I'll even pack the good cheese."

She winked at her sister. Hoping her energy would help Leondria perk up a little.

Leondria shook her head, a small frown tugging at her lips. "I wish I could. I'm just . . . bone-tired, Tati. I need a rest."

"Rest? You've just come down from bed."

"I know," Leondria said softly, "but it feels like I didn't rest at all. I don't understand what's wrong with me. Perhaps we can go out later."

Tatianna hesitated, unsettled. It wasn't like Leondria to turn down going out for a bicycling adventure, even if she was tired. But she tried to shake it off. "Fine. But I shall have my adventure without you, without any of you." Tatianna pushed her chair back from the table and stood. She skipped out of the room, her tinkling laughter echoed in the room long past her departure.

Tatianna straightened her straw hat, the pink silk ribbon brushed against her cheek in the gentle morning breeze. Without much thought, she tugged on her kidskin gloves, the leather supple and cool against her fingers, but she knew they would keep her hands warm as she rode through the crisp morning air. She brushed her palms over the mint-green wool of her cycling costume, smoothing away invisible creases, and adjusted the pale pink collar of her shirt until it lay just so.

Her gaze flicked to her reflection in the window—only a glimpse—but it was enough. The shorter skirts made cycling infinitely easier, and she couldn't help but smile at how prettily her white leather boots peeked out from under the skirt, the mint-green lacy insets catching the light. They matched her suit perfectly, of course. It was a small, frivolous triumph, but one she would allow herself.

She nodded, satisfied with her choices and that she felt like a heroine in one of the novels Rhiannon always buried her nose in—independent, determined, with a hint of a rebellious nature—Tatianna swung her leg over her bicycle and pushed off, the crunch of gravel giving way to the soft hush of moss and dirt under her wheels.

The countryside opened before her in full spring splendor. She pedaled along the narrow track that curved gently through the meadow, a reddish-brown ribbon of earth likely worn by deer and the occasional fox. Wildflowers nodded as she passed—blush pinks, bright yellows, and soft purples swaying in her wake as she rode by. Butterflies flitted alongside her; blue, yellow, and black wings catching the sunlight like tiny bits of magic in the air.

The sky above was a pale blue, stretching wide with the promise of a beautiful day, unusual this time of year, and Tatianna couldn't help but breathe in the scent of honeysuckle and new grass. The mundane morning at home melted away behind her with every turn of the wheels. The sense of freedom helped push away her doldrums, but what she needed was something new, something a little thrilling, something unexpected.

Maybe Evangeline would be up for an adventure. A picnic by the lake. Or maybe a stop at the patisserie where they could gossip over strawberries and clotted cream. Something, anything, to shake the feeling that everything around her was just a little . . . off. She couldn't quite put her finger on it. Maybe it was the stillness in the air on a day that should be at the very least windy, if not cold and blustery, or how her sisters had looked so pale and worn, as if they hadn't slept at all.

But the sun was shining, and she had her favorite boots on as she rode down the lane with no one to tell her what to do. That had to count for something.

She crested a low hill and caught sight of the familiar bend in the road that led to the Duskmoor estate, Evangeline's home. The hedgerows rustled in a sudden breeze, and a lone hare darted across the road in front of her, disappearing into the field of wildflowers, impish as its fluffy white tail bounced away.

Tatianna gripped the handlebars tighter as she careened down the road. Her dark curls soon joined the ribbons on her hat fluttering in the wind, as her hair pins escaped into the wild.

Something tugged at the edge of her awareness as she moved closer to her friend's home—a shift in the air, like the prickly magic she'd felt recently, but couldn't quite place it.

As soon as she felt the magic, it disappeared, as if unable to exist near her.

Despite its absence, she pedaled just a little faster as she turned down the drive to her friend's home.

The gravel drive to Duskmoor crunched under her wheels as Tatianna coasted to a graceful stop in front of the ivy-covered house. She swung her leg over the saddle careful to not catch her boot on the rear fender and contemplated fixing her hair. Evangeline's mother was sure to find issue with her appearance, just like her own mother would. Looking up, she found the front door ajar, as if someone had left in a hurry or had been too tired to close it fully. That was unlike the Duskmoors. Evangeline's family prized order almost as much as Effie Wylde.

Tatianna propped her bicycle against the front column and climbed the stairs leading to the cracked open door. Before she could knock, the door creaked open wider, revealing a house-maid with tired eyes and a rumpled apron.

"Miss Wylde," the maid said, blinking like she was trying to chase away sleep. "Miss Evangeline is in the drawing room. She's—well, she's come down from her room, but not quite herself this morning."

Tatianna picked at her gloves, pulling them off one finger at a time. "Is she unwell?"

The maid hesitated, her gaze darting to the stairs before she dropped it again. "I shouldn't . . . just tired, miss. That's all."

That wasn't all. But Tatianna nodded and stepped inside and made her way to the drawing room. Something she'd done a hundred times before, but today every step she took on the floor coverings felt heavy.

The drawing room was cast in shadows, the normal cheerful pink wall coverings dull in the darkened room, the dusty blue curtains drawn as if someone's head ached and the smallest bit of light exacerbated the pain. The scent of lavender hung in the air—freshly sprinkled on the hearthrug, judging by the dusting of petals. The scent was meant to soothe anyone in the room. Evangeline reclined on a fainting couch, a heavy wool blanket thrown over her despite the spring sunshine.

Tatianna slowed as she approached her friend. "You look like you dueled a will-o'-the-wisp and lost. Are you ill?"

Evangeline groaned softly, turning her head toward Tatianna. Her hair was in loose, unbrushed curls and her normally bright eyes were rimmed with fatigue. "No. Not ill, at least I don't think so. I'm exhausted. I couldn't sleep. Not really. Singing filled my head."

Tatianna raised an eyebrow. "Singing?"

"And bells," Evangeline murmured. "So many bells. All night. Over and over. It was beautiful and sounded like the dancing of fairies and . . . I don't know. I feel like I've walked for miles in my dancing shoes, but I never left my bed."

Tatianna knelt by her friend, taking Evangeline's hand in hers. Evangeline's skin was cool, her pulse steady. But there it was again. Something in the air changed—it was the same as before where something felt not-quite-right.

"You dreamed of bells?" she asked gently.

"It was so real," Evangeline whispered. "I swear I *heard* them. And when I closed my eyes, I swear I could see lights flickering like stars in the forest. It was as if they called to me. In my dreams I followed them, Tati."

Tatianna's fingers curled against the embroidered edge of the couch. Her sisters had looked the same this morning. Exhausted. Like they had spent the night somewhere far away, instead of in their bed asleep.

"I came by to see if maybe you'd want to come to town," she offered softly. "Fresh air. A bit of distraction?"

Evangeline gave her a weak smile. "Today I think I need distraction even less than I need sleep. As much as I would love to come to town, Tati, today is not the day, maybe after I get more sleep."

Tatianna nodded once, lips pressed thin.

Something was happening.

And she was going to find out what.

After leaving her friend's side, Tatianna meandered towards town, walking her bicycle down a lane lined with cherry trees, the wheels crunching over fallen petals. She rounded a curve—and collided with a tall, fit statue in the middle of the path.

"Archer," she said, blinking at the man who stood in front of her. "I mean Mr. Thornfield."

He reached out, his hands clasped her elbows, steadying her. "Miss Wylde. Out for a ride?"

"Is it that obvious?" She glanced up with an arched eyebrow.

He dropped his arms. "Are your sisters with you?"

She looked down as she stepped back. She noticed his boots were scuffed and dusty, like he'd been walking for a while. "Not today. I'm trying to have an adventure, but everyone in town seems to have come down with a case of inexplicable exhaustion."

His brow furrowed. "Strange. I noticed a few guests appeared rather drained this morning. In fact, Lilith and Aisling were still in bed when I left for my walk this morning. It's as if everyone is under some sort of spell, even the townsfolk were quiet as I made my way through town."

They regarded each other in the dappled shade, the rustling of leaves the only sound. Neither noticed cherry blossom petals drifting down around them like soft rain falling on peaks and valleys of the countryside.

Tatianna swallowed, unable to hide the worry fluttering through her. She tilted her head to the side, trying to keep her tone light, when she finally responded. "Isn't it a little early for such ominous observations, Archer?"

"Isn't it a little late to be the only one not asleep on their feet?" he questioned, his tone sharp, but with less bite than the last time they had spoken.

She grinned up at him, a grin that didn't quite reach her eyes. His accusations had hurt, but more than that, she feared everyone was tired because of something she'd done. What if she had accidentally cast a spell, and it had made everyone in the town sleepy?

She looked down at her arms, where his hands still held hers. He noticed the direction of her gaze and let go as if scalded, then clasped his hands behind his back.

"Where are you off to on this adventure? Perhaps I should accompany you?" The words were out of his mouth before he knew their intent.

She shrugged. "It's up to you, but I must warn you I have no destination in mind and I wouldn't want to inconvenience you."

With a slight bow, he gestured for her to continue before falling in step beside her.

Tatianna swung her leg over the center bar and perched astride her bicycle, the wide saddle creaking faintly beneath her as she let the bike meander forward at a lazy roll. Her booted toe tapped the ground now and then like a dancer testing her next step, while the other rested comfortably on a pedal, ready to ride away at a moment's whim. The wheels gave a gentle hum, content to follow the rhythm of Archer's slow, steady stride beside her.

She swayed with each gentle lurch, a breeze tugging at the loose tendrils of hair beneath her hat. "I do believe I've invented the most inefficient form of travel," she mused aloud, her voice light with mischief. "Neither here nor properly there."

Archer chuckled, casting her a sidelong glance. "You seem quite determined to dawdle."

"Well," she said, eyes twinkling as she half-rolled, half-walked, "I did say I was set to have an adventure, dawdling is one of the best ways to find yourself in the middle of one."

He shook his head, but she caught the smile threatening the corners of his mouth. Maybe he didn't find her quite so insufferable as he'd stated the other night.

She glanced towards him. "Well, you may as well keep me company on my outing. It will prevent you from having to walk ominously in the woods alone."

Archer gave her a look. One she couldn't read.

"You're not afraid I'll lead you into danger?" He asked with a raised eyebrow, and for a brief moment he looked rather rakish instead of brooding.

"I can't imagine you leading me into danger. You're too cautious. You have to be impetuous to lead someone into danger."

He shook his head, but despite his reluctance continued to walk beside her. They turned off the lane onto a narrow path, overhung with wisteria. A breeze stirred the branches, sending pale blossoms dancing around them.

Archer caught a single flower out of the air. He paused for a moment. Tatianna waited, wondering what he planned to do with it. His hand reached out like he was going to put it behind her ear, instead he let it go, and watched as it drifted away on the breeze.

They continued down the path next to each other, both lost in thought. Tatianna debated whether or not to express her concerns, or to stay silent. It wasn't in her nature to keep her thoughts to herself, so it wasn't long before her words tumbled from her mouth, one atop of the other. "I'm worried. Everyone

I've spoken to this morning is . . . have not been themselves. Tired. Pale. It's like the ball wrung them all out, like damp linens. But it's been two nights, and they were all fine yesterday morning. At least my sisters were their normal selves."

Archer's brow creased. "Something happened in the meadow at the end of the ball. I think we both felt it."

Tatianna nodded. "The ball was beautiful, but I do think there was something, a shift like a spell being cast that didn't match the intentions of the night. But I thought it was just me being fanciful."

"You're always fanciful," he said with a sidelong glance.

"You say that like it's a bad thing."

"That was not my intention."

Their eyes met for a beat, and something unspoken passed between them—something curious, a little wary. Taking them back to the moment before Effie Wylde interrupted them, but she was afraid to even think about those feelings because of everything that had followed.

Tatianna looked away first. "Anyway, I think it's more than just fatigue. Leondria was a mess this morning. I'm surprised she even left her room, and Rhiannon said she had dreams about fog and bells. In fact, everyone I've talked to has mentioned bells. It's strange they are having such similar dreams."

Archer grew quiet. "Yesterday, when I was walking, I ran into Lady Blackthorn and her daughter, my cousin Emelie, and she told me the roses were singing the other night, that they always sang when a spell went sideways."

She stopped. "The roses were singing? I've never heard of anything like that."

"Neither have I, but she was adamant. I humored her, even though her mother tried her best to stop Emelie from sharing. I didn't think anything of it at the moment. But now…" He glanced at her. "Ever since the ball it has felt like the air's shifted, it feels strange even now, doesn't it?"

She swallowed and looked down at her fingers gripping the handlebars. "Yes. I believe you mentioned that your morning walk included the town center of Bramblewick?"

"Yes, why do you ask?" Archer's eyes followed the road as it disappeared into a copse of trees.

"I wanted to go shopping with my sisters or my friend Miss Duskmoor. But they're all too tired." She continued moving along the road with her inefficient way of travel next to him.

"Bramblewick was quiet this morning. There was nothing open when I walked through town, not even the bakery."

She continued looking ahead. "That's odd. Widow Merryweather always starts baking before dawn. Do you think this . . . thing . . . has affected more than our friends and family?"

He didn't answer. She wasn't sure she expected him to.

They continued in silence for a moment as a bird chirped overhead, cheerful and oblivious to whatever blight was affecting the town.

"Come on," Tatianna said, nudging the bicycle forward again. "Let's go to the lake. Maybe if we're lucky, it'll only be a perfectly normal cursed forest."

"You're making jokes," he said softly, shaking his head, bewildered.

She shrugged. "Of course, I am. It's either that or panic."

"And what does your instinct tell you?"

She looked at him, startled by the question. "My instinct?"

He nodded. "You strike me as someone who listens to hers."

"Actually, I usually ignore mine," she said with a half-smile. "Much to my own detriment."

"Maybe it's time to start listening."

She was quiet then, eyes thoughtful as the woods opened up and the lake shimmered into view—still and glassy, a little too calm.

Her instincts told her something dark was afoot, and that should they fail to act, matters would only worsen. Yet, she had no notion of what must be done, and so, with a determined lift of her chin, she resolved to think no more of it — trusting, perhaps foolishly, that by tomorrow all would be well.

Chapter 8

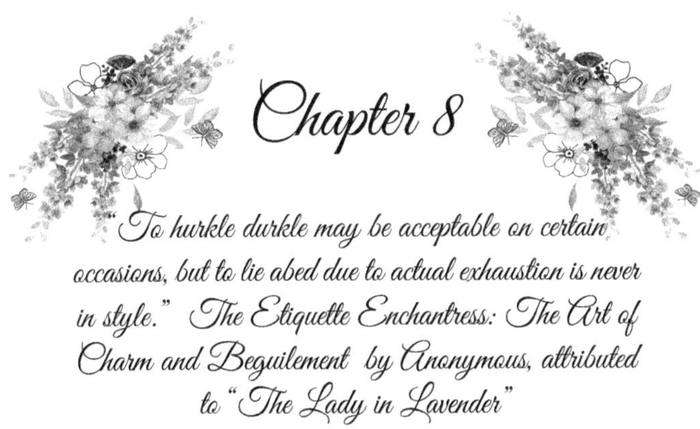

Tatianna hadn't been able to sleep. She tossed and turned beneath her linen sheets until they knotted around her feet. Her mind circling endlessly around the conversation she'd had with Archer. Every word, every glance between them replayed itself with maddening clarity. She went from wondering what he thought of her, and if his unreadable looks were actually interest, to analyzing what he related to her about everyone's exhaustion.

At last, the sky outside her window lightened, allowing her to give up on sleep and do something else. With an exasperated sigh, she flung back the covers and pulled on her dressing gown. Barefoot and silent, she crept from her room, careful not to disturb the sleeping household. Perhaps a cup of her favorite tea would soothe the restlessness that had taken hold of her.

She padded softly down the darkened corridor, her hand trailing lightly against the wainscoting, when a flicker of movement caught her eye.

Tatianna froze, half-shadowed by the grand staircase, she watched as her sisters—all three of them—stumbled in through the front door, dressed in splendid ballgowns she had never seen before.

Only—there was no ball. At least, not one she knew about. How dare her sisters go to a ball and not bring her along! What had she done to cause them to leave her behind?

She continued to watch them as they made their way up the stairs. Something was off. They moved strangely, as though walking through a dream. Their faces pale in the ghostly light seeping through the tall windows, the hush of dawn wrapped the room in a quiet, uneasy stillness. Leondria's hand trailed along the banister as she moved gracefully up the stairs. Celestine giggled faintly at nothing at all, stumbling with every other step. Rhiannon clutched a book against her chest like it was a lifeline, her eyes distant and unseeing.

And as Tatianna looked closer, her breath caught.

She could see a shimmer around them—something faint, almost invisible—a silvery mist that clung to their skin like the glistening of sweat after a vigorous reel.

Magic.

Old, wild, and unfamiliar. It reminded her of the specific moment at the ball when she felt a need for protection.

Tatianna's heart squeezed painfully in her chest. She stepped forward, whispering, "Where have you been?"

None of them answered. None of them even acknowledged her standing there.

They continued to drift up the stairs, silent and ethereal as celestial nymphs, each one disappearing into her room without a word, leaving only the faint scent of night air and magic hanging in the hall.

By late morning, the house was filled with golden light and the smell of fresh bread. Tatianna sat at the breakfast table, stirring her tea with more force than necessary, glancing up every time footsteps sounded.

Her mother looked up at her. "Tatianna, you're going to shatter your teacup if you keep stirring with such vigor."

She sighed. The words did not surprise, her mother always found fault with something.

"Sorry, Mama. I will attempt to be gentler in the future." She tried to sound demure in her response. Judging by the rolling of her mother's eyes, it didn't appear to work.

Her sisters entered the room one by one, looking rumpled and exhausted, as though they had not slept a moment. Leondria tried to hide a yawn behind her hand. Rhiannon blinked blearily at her tea, her normal book companion, laying listlessly beside her. Celestine slumped into her chair with barely enough energy to butter her toast.

Tatianna scrutinized each of them as they walked into the room, searching for any trace of the shimmer she saw this morning—but in the brightness of full daylight, it was gone, like morning dew evaporated away by the sun's rays.

Leondria looked at her through sleep glazed eyes. "Why are you staring at us like that? Is something wrong?"

"You're up early," Tatianna said, instead of answering her sister's question. She forced a lightness into her tone, one she didn't feel. "Did you sleep well?"

Leondria frowned at her empty plate. "I must have," she said, uncertainty laced her words. "I feel as if I had just shut my eyes. And my feet hurt as if I walked to London and back."

Tatianna leaned forward, intent on her sisters' answers. "Do you not remember last night or earlier this morning?"

Celestine looked confused, the magic that normally sparkled around her like a diamond in the sun, was dull, the expected shimmer muted. "And what of it? I was in bed all night, dreaming of those tinkling bells."

"Are you sure? You were dressed—for a ball. I saw the three of you come home right before dawn."

They exchanged bewildered glances.

"That can't be. We never left," Rhiannon said at last, her voice oddly flat. "You must have dreamed it."

Tatianna opened her mouth to argue, but the words caught in her throat. They truly didn't remember.

She watched as her sisters sat there, staring at their breakfast, not eating, like they were too tired to lift the food to their mouth. Rhiannon muttered her buttered toast spell. The knife wobbled before clattering back to the table. All four of them stared at the offending silverware, until Rhiannon picked it up and buttered her toast without the help of magic.

Tatianna sat back in her chair, her appetite now gone.

Something was wrong. Deeply, dreadfully wrong.

And she was the only one who seemed to realize it. The only one not affected by it. The only one afraid that she had caused it.

Tatianna began to rise from her seat, the confession of what she thought she'd done trembling on the tip of her tongue. She should tell her mother—Effie would know what to do, wouldn't she?

But as she glanced across the table at her mother, who was calmly threading her needle so she could work on her needlepoint, unaware of what was happening around her, a sudden, insistent feeling rooted her to her chair. Instinct, quiet but determined, whispered that speaking now would change everything—and not for the better.

Without proof, without understanding, she would only sound foolish. Worse, she feared she would put her sisters in even greater danger without knowing how or if she could fix it.

Tatianna swallowed her words like a bitter medicine, folding her hands neatly in her lap. She would wait. Watch. Listen.And next time—she would be ready.

Archer, back from his morning walk, found Aisling in the little library tucked into the east wing, curled into the window seat, her knees drawn up, a novel slipping from her hands. The late afternoon light brought out the strands of deep red in her dark hair, hair that seemed to float around her head like a storm cloud, emphasizing the fact that her face was pale and pinched with exhaustion.

He leaned a shoulder against the doorframe, arms folded, studying her. "You know, it's very difficult to maintain the illusion that you're the cleverest of us all when you're falling asleep mid-chapter."

Aisling cracked open one eye and offered a weak smile. "I'm merely . . . resting my eyes. Great minds require occasional pauses after all."

He stepped into the room, the soft thud of his boots on the rug announcing his approach. He knelt beside her, frowning slightly. "You've been running yourself ragged, Aisling. Even Lysander's noticed."

"And you know if Lysander notices, it must be dire," she teased, but her voice lacked its usual spark. "He rarely observes anyone other than the lady he is currently pining over."

Archer didn't smile. "I'm serious. What have you been doing to tire yourself so? Are you unwell? You're . . . thinner." He hated the rough edge to his voice, hated the gnawing feeling of helplessness clawing at his chest. He could fix so many things, and yet—if he didn't know what was wrong how could he fix it?

Aisling's hand found his and gave it a reassuring squeeze. "I'm just tired, Arch. The excitement of the ball . . . perhaps the change in the air. I'm just settling in after moving around. You fret too much."

"You're my sister. It's my duty to fret," he said, voice low. "If something is wrong, I wish you'd tell me."

For a moment, the only sound was the slow ticking of the clock and the slight rattle of the windowpane from the breeze outside.

Aisling's gaze drifted past him, out toward the garden, flowers swaying in the wind. "I can't explain why I'm so tired. But I promise you this—" She looked back at him, her eyes clear and solemn. "If the time comes when I need you, I will not be too proud to ask."

It wasn't enough. Not nearly. But Archer nodded, forcing a smile for her sake. "Good. Because whether you like it or not, little sister, I will always look out for you."

"And I find that oddly comforting," she murmured, settling back against the cushion. Within minutes, she had drifted into a light doze, the novel slipping once again from her fingers.

Archer retrieved it, replacing the dog-eared pages with a bookmark before placing it carefully on the side table.

He stayed a long moment, watching over her, heart heavy with a worry he could not name.

Chapter 9

"When instinct and propriety are in direct conflict, trust in the letter written in haste. It may carry the truth your heart already knows, but your mind has refused to acknowledge." To Spell or Not to Spell: Navigating Society When Your Temper is Enchanted by Lady Mirabel Northwick

Tatianna paced the dock, her bare feet silent despite the hard, worn wood beneath them. Her sisters had gone back to sleep after breakfast—if it could even be called sleep, she wasn't sure since she believed it was somehow magically induced. They hadn't stirred since collapsing onto their beds hours ago. She could still see their faces pale in the morning light, their movements clumsy and their magic troubled.

Tatianna sat down, letting her feet sink into the water while the rest of her remained dry. She chewed her lower lip, her arms folded tightly across her chest as she decided what to do next. She could go to her mother, but Effie would only scold her and fret. She would then insist on sending for the doctor, who would undoubtedly declare it a case of nerves or excessive exertion. He was quite worthless when it came to properly diagnosing any of them. She could say nothing at all, only hope—pray—that tomorrow would see her sisters returned to themselves.

But hope felt like a brittle thing this afternoon, hollow and fragile. And pointless. She knew something was wrong. Her sisters would not wake tomorrow well-rested. Her instinct said it was just going to get worse. She could not wait around for things to get worse, not if she could make it better.

And then there was Mr. Thornfield. Archer.

The thought of him brought a fresh wave of hesitation.

It was one thing to talk in riddles at a ball, to exchange wary words under the rustling of wisteria. It was another thing entirely to seek him out. To ask for his help. She didn't think he trusted her, so why would he help?

It would be bold. Improper. Dangerous, even, for her reputation at the very least, potentially for something else, she just didn't know what.

And yet—hadn't he been the only one who seemed to sense that something was amiss at the ball? He may have blamed her at first, but he hadn't seemed to the last time they met.

Hadn't his instincts matched hers, had he not sensed the same changes she felt? He even confirmed that he noticed similar behavior among his family and friends. He was the only other person truly awake and cognizant in a world that seemed half-asleep. Even now, as her sisters slept the day away, her senses pulled toward him.

She halted at her escritoire, her fingers drumming against the polished mahogany. Her heart thundered a warning: *This is improper, reckless even.*

But her instinct—that deep, sure part of her that had saved her more than once, when she deigned to listen—whispered back: *Trust yourself. Trust him.*

Before she could talk herself out of it again, Tatianna snatched up a sheet of paper. Her hand trembled slightly as she dipped her fountain pen into the ink well. A drop of ink fell to the paper before she lowered her hand, the nib scratching faintly as she wrote:

Mr. Thornfield,

I find myself in need of your assistance. There are matters I believe concern not only myself, but your family as well. Might I prevail upon you to meet me tomorrow at noon, behind the old castle ruins?

I trust you understand the need for discretion.

T. Wylde

She blotted the ink, folded the paper with care, and sealed it with a sliver of green wax.

She stood, letter in hand, but instead of rushing off to have a footman deliver it she lingered, as if one last protest might rise to the surface.

None came.

Tatianna rang for a footman and pressed the letter into his hand, her voice calm as she instructed him to deliver it to Archer Thornfield at the Covington Estate immediately.

As the door closed behind him, she sagged back into her chair, pressing her fingertips to her temples.

Now that the meeting was set in motion, she began to question the wisdom of bringing him in. He appeared to be the only one other than herself not affected by this . . . This Curse.

Archer was hiding in the estate's study, needing to be alone with his thoughts after seeing his sister in such a weakened state.

It was so unlike her.

Aisling was always effervescent in her energy, bringing smiles to everyone's face with her exuberance and wit. To see her pale and still, her vibrancy dulled to a shadow, twisted something deep and sharp inside his chest.

He sat slouched in a worn leather armchair by the fireplace, unaware that it was not lit, despite the chill in the room. One hand loosely gripped a book, long forgotten, the other raking through his hair in restless intervals, causing it to fall across his forehead in disarray.

The afternoon had dragged on in slow, aching minutes. The entire house was silent, as if it was the middle of the night, not the middle of the day. Which only caused the gnawing certainty that something was terribly wrong to become more prevalent—causing him to question whether or not he should call someone, but this was not something that could be fixed by a doctor, there was dark magic involved, he could feel it.

A sharp rap at the door made him jolt upright. His book thudded to the floor, reminding him he had been reading. He cursed under his breath and forced himself to stand. "Enter," he called, voice rough from hours of disuse.

A footman slipped inside, bowing slightly before extending a silver salver. "A letter for you, sir. Delivered most urgently."

Archer frowned. He retrieved the book from the floor and set it aside, incapable of letting it lie there waiting for someone else to take care of it.

He plucked the letter from the tray, noting the unfamiliar, feminine hand, its loopy scrawl simply spelled out: *Mr. Thornfield.*

The wax seal—a delicate shade of green that reminded him of wild thyme—already unusual enough to stir his curiosity.

He nodded his thanks, excusing the footman.

Once the footman withdrew, Archer broke the seal and unfolded the paper. His eyes scanned the brief message once, then again, slower the second time.

T. Wylde.

Her name alone was enough to send a peculiar warmth through his body—he wasn't sure if it was annoyance, intrigue, or something perilously close to hope. He brushed that errant thought away and sat to read her words carefully, feeling the weight of them settle against the raw edge of his worry.

Matters that concerned both their families?

Discretion?

The castle ruins—private enough for a meeting, but not without its own implications. Again, he pushed those thoughts away. It didn't matter that others used the ruins for clandestine purposes, only that it was private enough that they were unlikely to be seen.

Archer exhaled slowly, the paper crackling faintly in his grip.

He should refuse.

Or better yet, he should burn the letter, ignore it entirely, and focus on his sister. He looked toward the fireplace, realizing for the first time it was not lit.

But even as he thought it, he was already rising from the chair, moving toward the window where the last beams of proper sunlight slanted across the grounds as the sky took on the pink and orange hues of sunset. He looked toward the Wylde's estate somewhere off in the distance and knew he would meet Tatianna tomorrow.

Some deep instinct — that same instinct he had been taught to suppress — told him it was necessary, that their sisters' exhaustion was no mere coincidence, and it was all somehow related.

Tatianna Wylde had noticed something at the ball, as had he. But he wasn't sure they had noticed the same thing. But they both felt like the very air had shifted. It had to mean something.

And whether or not he wanted to admit it; he trusted her senses more than he had ever trusted his own, at least not since his time in school.

He tucked the letter safely into the inner pocket of his jacket.

By the time the clock struck noon tomorrow, he would be at the castle ruins, waiting.

Chapter 10

Tatianna stood before the narrow mirror in her bedroom, tying the ribbons of her straw hat beneath her chin with trembling fingers.

She told herself it was the briskness of the morning air seeping through the cracks in the house, not nerves, that made her hands unsteady. It was a lie. Her mother would never let cold air seep in. She would use a spell to stop it, but the thought comforted Tatianna, even if she knew it wasn't true.

On the dressing table beside her, lay the pen she'd used to write a letter in a rush of impulse and uncertainty.

It had been a risk, reaching out to Archer Thornfield so directly.

He was guarded—as wary as she of stepping into something they couldn't easily explain away with polite smiles and half-truths.

But this was no longer something she could ignore.

Not with her sisters drifting like ghosts through their days, and her own heart warning her that every hour wasted brought them closer to something terrible.

She gathered her skirts, choosing a sensible cycling costume in soft green wool with wild thyme embroidered exactly where the detailed accents were needed. She decided on sturdy boots instead of her more delicate boots since she didn't know where the day would take her.

There was no telling where the conversation might lead—or what they might decide to do, or not do, once they began searching for the truth.

Before she left, she hesitated a moment, glancing once more at the framed photo on her nightstand — her sisters, smiling, full of life and teasing laughter. The sight of it hardened her resolve.

She would figure out what was causing their exhaustion and she would stop it. She would protect them, even if it meant doing the most dangerous thing of all.

Trusting someone outside her family, someone she had just met and who didn't trust her.

Tatianna slipped quietly down the staircase, casting a spell with a wiggle of her fingers to keep her boots from clicking on the marble floors. She did not want to be caught, especially not by her mother, as she had not formed a plausible reason to be out before sitting down for breakfast. She flicked her wrist, and the door opened, allowing her to leave with no one the wiser. She mounted her bicycle and raced down the drive, the late morning sun caught the edge of her divided skirt as she disappeared into the waiting fields.

The path to the castle ruins was not a long one, but with every step, her heart beat a little faster, like a drum calling her forward toward a fate she couldn't yet name.

But she wasn't afraid.

Not yet. But she knew at some point she would be.

The ruins emerged from the wild grasses like remnants of a civilization long gone and almost forgotten. The crumbling stone parapets rose toward the sky, their jagged edges softened by creeping ivy and bursts of wild roses preventing them from making their final escape.

Somehow, the early afternoon light found its way through cracks in archways, stone walls, and empty windows, painting long, golden ribbons across the earth.

It was a place out of stories whispered late at night by firelight—where anything felt possible and everything felt magical. This haunting place of stone and nature was where Tatianna came to think, where she created tales of knights and princesses as she traced her fingers over the ancient runes carved into the stone walls of the lost fortress, worn from centuries of wind and rain.

She dismounted her bicycle as she approached what remained of the arch that once marked the entrance to the castle. She leaned her bike against a stone wall. A gust of wind pulled at the pins holding her straw hat in place, causing her to remove it and clutch it in her gloved hands.

There was no one in sight yet. Only the rustle of the breeze through the tall grass and the distant, sleepy chatter of dryads in their trees to keep her company.

She picked her way carefully across the uneven ground, the toes of her boots brushing fallen stones and delicate purple blossoms as she climbed over the roots of trees that had won the battle against the stone structures that had invaded their land.

A few cherry trees grew near the far wall, their petals floated down in slow, shimmering drifts, catching in her hair and clinging to the hem of her skirts.

She could almost pretend she was a heroine in a fairy tale—if not for the gnawing worry in her chest.

A soft crunch of gravel made her spin.

There, emerging from the shadow of a leaning tower, was Archer.

He was smoothing a piece of parchment—her letter; she realized with a flush—unfolding and refolding it as though uncertain what to do with it.

His coat, unbuttoned in the warmth of the midday sun, and his dark hair ruffled in the breeze, giving him a disheveled, almost roguish appearance that made her pulse quicken treacherously, even though this look was the antithesis of his practical nature.

For a moment they simply looked at one another, neither speaking, as the ruins seemed to breathe around them.

"You wrote to me," Archer said at last, his voice low and unreadable.

Tatianna gathered her skirts and stepped closer, the sunlight catching in her hair and casting a luminous halo around her. "I thought it best," she said, trying—and failing—to keep her tone light. "It seemed . . . unwise to trust chance encounters alone for something so important."

Something flickered in his eyes—something she could not read, gone before she could analyze it.

"Ahhh . . . practicality. Very unlike the reckless Miss Wylde I met under the willows."

Her lips twitched despite herself. "Even I can be sensible when the situation demands it. Although I do believe most would consider my actions the definition of reckless."

He offered a small, crooked smile—a rare and dazzling thing—before schooling his features back into their usual caution.

"Then tell me," he said, stepping nearer until the space between them was filled only with drifting petals and the faint scent of wild thyme and roses. "What has caused this reckless behavior? What danger are we standing in these ruins to discuss?"

Tatianna hesitated, her instincts warring with her upbringing—the part of her that said a lady never spoke of fears or secrets to a near-stranger, especially one who guarded his own so fiercely.

But she thought of her sisters' pale faces, their hollow eyes, the eerie silence that had fallen over the house.

She thought of the way the world had shifted at the ball, the way the magic in the air had felt brittle and strange.

She thought, too, of Archer's steady gaze the night they had first spoken—how he had not looked away when others might have.

Tatianna drew a breath, steadying herself.

"There's something wrong," she said softly. "With my sisters. With their magic. Maybe even magic itself. I can feel it . . . pulling at the seams."

The castle ruins seemed to still around them as she spoke. The breeze stopped rustling the grass, blossoms remained attached to the trees, and dryads ceased chattering.

"And," she added, voice just above a whisper, "I think it's only the beginning."

Archer's gaze sharpened at her words, but he said nothing.

Only the shifting of the wind, no longer still, coursing through the ruins, filled the silence between them—a low, sighing sound, as though the stones themselves were trying to join the conversation.

Tatianna twisted her gloves in her hands, the soft leather creaking. For all her boldness in writing the letter, in coming here alone, now that the moment was upon her, her courage wavered.

"What if . . ." she began, then stopped, biting her lip.

She watched as Archer's eyes caught the movement.

"What if what?" he prompted gently.

She dropped her gaze to the ground, watching a petal settle on the toe of her boot.

"When the magic shifted that night at the ball . . . I felt it." Her voice was low, almost lost to the sighing breeze. "I thought—just for a moment—that we needed protection. That something was wrong. I don't remember gesturing or casting a spell."

She swallowed hard, forcing herself to continue. "But then the very air seemed to change. It was subtle, but I felt it change and return to normal. And now . . ." she lifted her eyes to his, wide and shining with unshed worry, "Now my sisters are pale shadows of themselves. They barely speak, they barely eat. They don't remember where they've been at night. I can't —" Her voice caught. "I can't help but wonder . . . if I caused it."

The last words tumbled out in a rush, brittle and broken.

She clenched her fingers tight around her gloves, willing herself not to cry.

Archer stepped closer—close enough that she could see the faint gold flecks in his dark eyes, could feel the faint warmth of him in the cool afternoon air.

For the length of a heartbeat, she thought he might reach for her—might offer some physical comfort. The brush of a hand against hers, the slightest touch to anchor her. Deep down, she knew he wouldn't, because that would be truly reckless. So, she wasn't surprised when he only stood there, steady and unyielding, his voice low and certain.

"You didn't cause this, Miss Wylde," he said, offering no explanation.

"How can you know that? The other night, you all but accused me of doing something with my magic that could unintentionally do harm. What if that's what happened?" she whispered.

"There's something else. It smells and tastes different from your magic." He grew introspective before muttering. "This... this isn't your doing."

The conviction in his tone hit her like the moment sunlight breaks through mist and warms your face, and her breath hitched. She wanted to believe him—desperately.

"They've all returned home now. I don't know where they're going at night, but I saw them stumble to their bedrooms before dawn this morning, and yesterday," she said, voice still soft. "It's like part of them hasn't come home at all. As if . . . as if something's still holding on to them, forcing them to go out every night, but not remembering any of it."

Archer's jaw tightened. He glanced toward the crumbling archways, as if expecting someone to walk through. When no one did, he turned back towards her.

"Then we find out what," he said, his voice raspy. "Together."

Tatianna blinked at him. She hadn't realized how badly she needed to hear someone say it—that she wasn't alone. That someone else believed her, would stand beside her. She just hadn't expected it to be him.

A fragile smile ghosted across her lips.

"Together," she echoed.

Around them, a gust of wind stirred the cherry trees, sending another shower of petals cascading down—soft and silver-pink against the ancient stones. Tatianna felt like an ancient enchantment rooted deep within the ruins had blessed them.

For one fleeting, impossible moment, it felt as if the world had stilled—just for the two of them.

And though neither moved, though no hands brushed and no words of affection were spoken, something changed between them. It felt genuine and delicate, like the initial touch of spring following a harsh winter.

Tatianna exhaled, feeling lighter now that she had shared her burden with someone who not only believed her, but was willing to help her discover what was happening to her friend and sisters. Even with the relief she felt at not being alone, the enormity of what lay ahead weighed heavily on her.

Archer shifted, casting a thoughtful glance toward the sky, where the puffy white clouds looked like mythical creatures floating in the sky.

"From what you've said, questioning them won't work," he said, his voice low and cautious. "This spell or curse, whatever it is, causes them to forget where they've been. If we force them to remember, it could harm them—or worse, whoever's responsible might realize we're suspicious."

Tatianna nodded, her mind already racing as she paced a slow circle around one of the fallen stone pillars, her boots brushing through moss and fallen petals.

"We have to find out where they're going when they vanish," she said, her words gaining confidence. "It's the easiest way to figure out what's happening, and it could lead us to why it's happening."

Archer watched her. A glimmer of admiration flitted across his face as he listened to her plans.

"They return just before dawn," he mused. "It stands to reason they're being summoned during the night. Or they could be lured to wherever they end up."

Tatianna stopped pacing, tapping her finger against her chin in thought. "The next time it happens . . . we follow them. All we have to do is wait outside and watch for them to leave."

He arched a brow. "That simple?"

She smiled, the first genuine smile she'd offered him since the ball. "Sometimes simple is the best way to start."

Sunlight sparkled in her green eyes as she looked up at him, and for a moment, Archer forgot to breathe. He didn't want to be, but a part of him was captivated by her. She possessed a vibrant, almost frantic energy that didn't fit within societal norms. Her wild nature fascinated him.

He coughed lightly, dragging his attention back to the task at hand.

"There's one complication," he said. "If anyone discovers that we aren't under the same spell as everyone else, we could be caught and prevented from learning what's happening to everyone."

Tatianna's smile dimmed, replaced by determination. "I can be discreet. Plus, I'm an excellent actress. No one will be able to tell I'm not under the same spell as everyone else."

Archer's lips twitched, his serious nature fighting his need to respond, to laugh at her wit. "I don't doubt it, Miss Wylde. However, I'll still accompany you. No wandering off alone into the night."

The words came out sharper than he intended. It even sounded suspiciously like concern connected his words.

Tatianna tilted her head at him, something unreadable flashing in her eyes. "Of course," she said simply. "Together, remember?"

The weight of the promise settled between them — heavier than mere words should be.

Binding. Certain. Like a spell that could not be broken. Although this time she knew there was no spell, just the promise of their words.

Above them, the sun had dropped out of view, leaving only puffy clouds now tinged with pink, as a soft golden light flooded the castle ruins. The fallen petals now gleamed like scattered golden drops against the mossy stones.

Together they walked to the arched entrance to the ruin where Tatianna left her bicycle. She stopped to pick it up before turning toward Archer. She headed toward the path that would lead back to the cottage the hem of her riding skirt brushing against the wild grass.

Archer hesitated, then offered to walk her bicycle.

She glanced at it. A flicker of amusement and a deeper, unnamed, emotion crossed her face. She handed him her bicycle after just a moment of hesitation.

As they walked toward the town, neither spoke of what might come. But in the quiet, in the soft hush of footsteps, and the whisper of wind, a silent vow was made:

They would find the truth. And no matter what darkness lay ahead, they would face it together.

Chapter 11

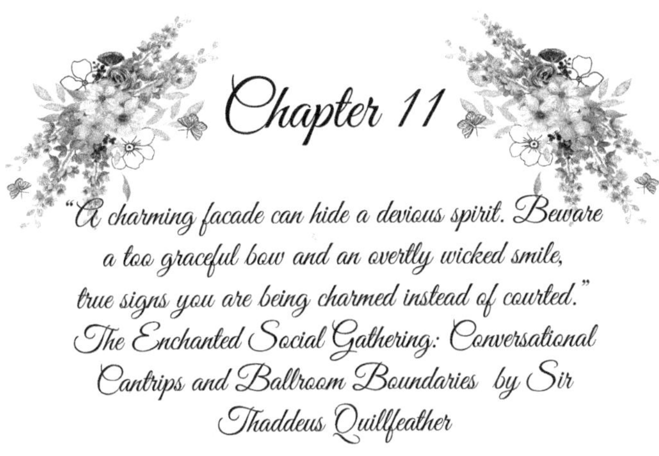

Archer matched his pace to Tatianna's, though it wasn't nearly as measured or refined as he might have expected. Her steps were quick, untamed, as if she moved not with calculation, but with conviction. It shouldn't have surprised him. Everything she did seemed touched by a kind of beautiful, reckless abandon.

They walked in companionable silence for a while, boots crunching gravel as they followed the worn footpath leading back to town. The evening sun clung to the horizon, not yet ready to rest for the night. The setting sun highlighting the silhouette of the local castle ruins—now mostly stone and ivy—loomed behind them like a memory.

Just as the lane narrowed into the hedgerow path that skirted the village green, a figure emerged from the bend ahead.

Archer slowed. There was something too smooth about the man's gait, too deliberate in the cut of his coat and too rakish in the tilt of his hat. He wiped his hand across his eyes, hoping the person he saw was a spectre, anything but the man that had ruined his life at school. Unfortunately, it was the one person he never wanted to see again.

"Wrenne," Archer said, his voice clipped. Tension formed between his shoulders as he stopped mid-stride.

Tatianna had no choice but to stop beside him. He could feel her eyes searching his face as he stared at the man approaching him.

"Archer Thornfield, what an unexpected pleasure," Malric Wrenne said, drawing out each syllable with the kind of casual cruelty that masqueraded as charm. "And with a lovely lady on your arm. I'm surprised to see you in the company of anyone, especially someone so enchanting." He looked at Tatianna and gave a slight bow. "You look familiar. Have I had the pleasure of making your acquaintance?"

Tatianna's eyes darted between the two men. She could feel the past humming in the air between them. There was no love lost, that much was clear—and it made her wonder what could have created such a rift.

"Tatianna Wylde." She offered her hand to the stranger, ever the polite daughter of society, no matter how much she wanted to discard its trappings. "Though I suspect you already know who I am."

He took her hand with fluid grace, the motion smooth, with practiced charm. Despite his debonair manner, there was a whisper of a chill at the back of her neck. He was undeniably handsome, with the polished elegance of a man well aware of his effect. She couldn't help but notice that there was something in his eyes—too cool, too calculating—and it unsettled her, although she couldn't put a finger on why. He nodded in a short bow, holding her hand a moment too long. Not long enough to provoke a reaction, but just enough to leave an impression.

"I have to admit you caught me, Miss Wylde. Everyone in town knows you and your lovely sisters," Malric said, a smile curving his lips, though it never quite reached his eyes. "Gossip drifts through Bramblewick like the soft scent of a lady's perfume in a crowded ballroom."

"Those are some pretty words, Mister . . . I'm sorry, I didn't catch your name." Her words lacked their natural curiosity, like she didn't actually care who she was talking to and wanted him to know it.

Archer looked over at the woman beside him. Her dismissive tone reminded him of her mother and the moment she interrupted them at the ball.

"Malric Wrenne, at your service." He bowed with a flourish.

Tatianna raised her hand to her mouth, almost hiding her scoff, but he still heard her. Clearly, Malric's flamboyant nature did not impress her.

Archer stepped forward, his movement almost imperceptible, just enough to insert himself between Malric and Tatianna without appearing obvious.

"I'm surprised to see you here. Are you still up to your old ways, using other's magic for your own benefit?" Archer asked. His tone mild, but every syllable was wrapped in ice.

Malric's eyes glinted. "Still pretending you're anything more than someone related to a family with magic? You wouldn't even be accepted to society without that connection."

The words landed like stones, sharp and familiar. A direct echo of Effie Wylde's diatribe the night of the ball.

Tatianna flinched beside him.

Archer didn't look at her, didn't dare. He felt her gaze on him, questioning, curious to discover if any of what her mother said was true.

"Careful," Archer said quietly. "The last time you touched what wasn't yours, you almost lost your place in society."

Malric's smile didn't waver. "And yet, here I am. Welcomed with open arms, while you're merely tolerated by those around you. It must be difficult to not have magic like everyone else."

"Gentlemen," Tatianna said sharply. "This is hardly the time."

Malric inclined his head, stepping back as if he had accomplished what he set out to do. "Of course. I wouldn't dream of interfering with your outing, Miss Wylde."

He tipped his hat and sauntered off, whistling.

Silence settled behind him like a fog.

Archer didn't move. He couldn't—not yet. His pulse still thundered in his throat. He clenched his fist, took a deep breath, then flexed his fingers, willing himself to calm down.

"Is it true?" Tatianna asked quietly. "What he said . . . about you and magic?"

He turned toward her slowly. There was no accusation in her tone. Just a question. No judgment.

"No," he said. Then, after a breath, "Not in the way everyone believes."

Tatianna's mouth tightened. "That's what my mother said about you. That you were only in society because of your aunt."

And there it was, the words that had hurt his pride only a few nights ago.

He nodded. "I heard."

She paled. "I didn't mean for you—"

"I know," he said, his words sharp as the memory returned to him unbidden, like a refrain from a half-forgotten song. "But I did."

Her lips parted like she wanted to say something, but the words never came. Instead, she looked away, silent for the first time, the wind catching a strand of her hair and sending it dancing across her cheek.

They continued along the path, neither one of them speaking. He wanted to hear whatever it was she had to say. But it didn't happen.

The hush between them deepened as they reached the low garden wall that circled her cottage. Ivy spilled over the stones. A curl of smoke rose from the chimney, the only sign of warmth in the otherwise chilly spring evening. They stopped just short of the gate.

She didn't look at him. Just stared at the ground, once again twisting her gloves in her hands. He waited, hoping the silence would end, open into something more—but it clung to them, unwilling to be broken.

The quiet, he knew, was unnatural for her. Tatianna Wylde was made of motion and thought and sudden bursts of laughter. This stillness felt like a mask, one she hadn't meant to put on, one she couldn't take off.

He cleared his throat. "Well."

She glanced up at him, just for a moment, then quickly away. "Thank you for walking me home."

"It has been my pleasure."

The words fell short of what he meant. He wanted to say more, say how he enjoyed watching her walk in silence, unraveling a problem that was resolving itself as he began to realize what she said to her mother at the ball might have very little to do with how she felt about him. But instead, he tipped his hat and stepped back onto the path.

Behind him, the garden gate creaked open.

"I'll see you later tonight." The wind carried her words towards him.

He turned to her. "Tonight."

She stood at the gate, the remnants of the sun casting an ephemeral glow around her, causing her to shimmer in the middle of the flower garden that led to the Wylde's cottage.

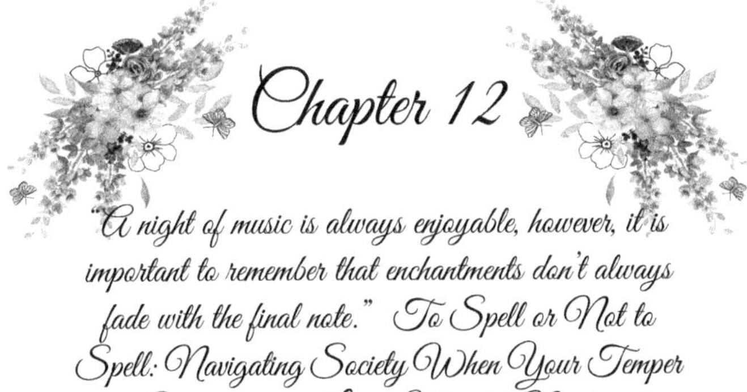

Chapter 12

Tatianna let the gate click shut behind her and stepped onto the gravel path, the fading light painting everything in soft hues of lavender and rose. She didn't know what to do with the knowledge that Archer heard her mother's judgmental words, or the fact that she said nothing to defend him. Knowing what he heard was almost enough for her to overlook what he had said about her later at the ball.

As soon as she walked through the front door, a flurry of activity surrounded her, servants scurrying this way and that—a startling contrast to the silent museum their home had resembled just this morning. She reached the door to their shared dressing room and pushed it open, only to be hit in the face by a swath of fabric and the scent of perfume and pressed violets.

"What in the name of all that's magical is going on?" she asked, tossing the fabric aside. To her surprise, no one responded as the frantic movement of her sisters continued without pause.

Rhiannon swept past her in a haze of silk and pinned curls, her gown reminiscent of wisteria covered in dew drops, sparkling in the morning sun. "Celestine, if you don't tame that spell, I swear you'll go to the musicale with one eyebrow!"

"I *like* the dramatic arch!" Celestine called from the hallway mirror using magic to perfect her eyebrows, her midnight-blue gown shimmering as if stitched with the night sky and star dust. Sparks crackled at her fingertips before she clasped her hands behind her back, mumbling an apology to the singed curtain.

Leondria glided across the room, a queen approaching her throne, another one of her golden gowns draped over her figure, catching the light and accentuating the curves of her body to perfection. "Honestly, do hurry Tati. We're expected at the Everett estate before half past. They have a proper string quartet, and I will not miss the opening number because you were too busy doing who knows what to get ready on time."

Tatianna blinked. "Wait—the musicale? That's tonight?"

Three heads turned in unison.

"You forgot?" Rhiannon's brows lifted. "That's very unlike you. You remember every social event because it's an excuse to get out of the house."

"I—well, yes." Tatianna shut the door behind her. "I was walking and... lost track of time."

"You've been gone an awful lot lately, never spending time with any of us." Leondria didn't look at her as she sat to pin her hair, arranging her golden curls with precision.

"Be nice Leondria, she's been spending time with Archer Thornfield, I assume?" Celestine asked, tone light, teasing.

Tatianna flushed, then shook her head. "It's not—never mind." She sat at her dressing table. "I would spend more time with the lot of you if you could stay awake during the day. This is the liveliest I've seen you since the ball."

Leondria gave her a measured look but said nothing as she draped a shawl over her shoulders, looked at herself in the mirror and grimaced before discarding it. "You have ten minutes if you still wish to come. Your dress is laid out in your room."

It was said so matter-of-factly, as if they hadn't been sleepwalking through life since the meadow ball. As if she hadn't watched them grow increasingly pale and weary with each passing day.

As if nothing at all was wrong.

Tatianna lingered in the room a moment longer, her fingers trailing over the carved wood of her dressing chair.

Ten minutes. She could ready herself in that amount of time. She stood abruptly and raced off to her room to change for the night's entertainment.

First, she would attend the musicale and afterwards, she would determine where her sisters were disappearing to every night.

The Everett estate shimmered like a dream spun from champagne and candlelight. The fairies had outdone themselves once again.

Tatianna stepped out of the carriage and into a world of gowns made with magic, tuxedos trimmed with velvet, and the lilting hum of string instruments filtering out into the garden. Laughter floated through the air like petals in the wind. It was exactly the atmosphere she had come to expect from events thrown at the Everette estate.

Her sisters, radiant as always, made their way to the reception line, taking their turn greeting their hosts. Leondria moved with her soft, but regal, confidence as she curtsied before the Everett family. Rhiannon murmured something about looking forward to the music selection before making a beeline for the library, and Celestine said her hello, then floated—quite literally for a moment—toward a group of charmingly rumpled poets near the garden terrace.

Tatianna held back, watching as her sisters appeared to be their normal, energetic selves for the first time in days. She couldn't help but smile, even if worry gnawed at the back of her mind. Deciding it was time to join the fun, she stepped forward. Her gown of mist and moonlight swirled around her feet as she moved and caught the lantern glow, causing her to look delicate and otherworldly. She tugged at her gloves, nerves pricking at her fingertips. Was she going to feel the same magic she'd felt in the meadow here? Would she find out tonight that the ripple of magic had affected everyone, or just those she was close to?

A familiar voice jolted her from her thoughts.

"Miss Wylde. You look"—Archer cleared his throat as he stepped beside her—"decidedly not lost in the woods tonight."

She looked up at him. He'd left his coat open, leaving the waistcoat underneath neatly buttoned, hair still somewhat windblown from earlier that afternoon. He looked handsome in his way—too serious, too observant.

"I'm surprised to see you here. It will not be a quiet evening," she admitted. "I almost didn't make it. I forgot the invitation altogether."

"Hard to imagine you forgetting an evening as extravagant as this." He glanced around at the crowd, the chandeliers strung between trees, the menagerie of vibrant dresses and perfectly rehearsed smiles.

She glanced around at the magically decorated outdoors, thankful the breeze had calmed and that the fairies had used an enchantment to ensure it was a warm spring night. "You're not enjoying yourself?"

Archer clasped his hands behind his back. "I prefer evenings where I'm not required to dance or make polite conversation about weather and trade policy."

"Ah." She leaned in, a sly smile danced across her face. "But there's no waltzing tonight, only music."

Their eyes met. The moment stretched. Only interrupted when a new melody began, a slow, haunting waltz that seemed to affect the weather as a gust of wind danced through the trees and stirred the lanterns above, making shadows flicker like lost souls searching for their home.

"I've been watching them," she said quietly. "My sisters. They're not . . . themselves. Tonight is the first time they've shown any enthusiasm for—well, just about anything. It's the closest to normal I've seen them for days."

"I've noticed the same thing with my sister," Archer replied, low and serious. "Aisling has been lethargic. Sleep-deprived.

Forgetful. Distant. Lilith isn't much better. And Lysander's been his cheerful self, but it seems subdued for some reason. He could just be concerned for his sister. When I returned home everyone was excited for this evening's entertainment."

Tatianna swallowed. "I still fear it might be me. That I did something to them without meaning to."

"You might have, but I no longer believe that to be true." His voice was steady. "And if it is something you did, we'll fix it. Although, I don't think you could do something diabolical, not on purpose, and definitely not by accident."

Her eyes met his as she tried to read what was behind his words. Part of her thought she should be offended that there was even a small part of him believed she could have done this. It was cold comfort to think everyone was cursed because of her and she didn't know how to fix it. For him to believe that could be true was bothersome, even if it was something that concerned her. Her thoughts were interrupted by a sharp, musical chime that signaled the start of the evening's performance.

"Shall we?" Archer offered his arm.

Tatianna hesitated, then placed her hand gently in the crook of his elbow. "Let's see if this musicale will reveal any secrets."

The area under a canopy of trees gleamed in soft candlelight, casting gentle golden halos across the stone steps and green grass. Guests spoke in murmurs, the scent of beeswax and rose petals drifted through the air. Tatianna stood near the back with Archer beside her, a polite smile on her lips, though her thoughts wandered far from the night's refined hum.

"I suppose we should count ourselves lucky," Archer said quietly. "At least it's not another ball."

She let out a small huff of amusement. "*You* may count yourself lucky. I'm hoping someone starts waltzing by the second interlude."

Before he could reply, the hostess rose and introduced the next performer. "Miss Emelie Blackthorn."

The rustle of skirts stilled. Tatianna's attention snapped forward. She could not recollect a time when Emelie had ever performed. The poor young woman had always been frail, too weak to do anything requiring exertion.

Emelie walked up to the concrete stage with a quiet poise. There was nothing dramatic about her entrance—no sudden gasp from the crowd—but Tatianna noted, with the faintest bit of surprise, that the young woman moved more easily than usual, her mother was not there to support her. In fact, her step was steady. Her color, though still delicate, held a touch of warmth rather than the pallor Tatianna associated with her.

Archer noticed too. "She looks . . . better," he said under his breath.

Tatianna tilted her head. "Yes. I don't think I've ever seen her perform. I wasn't aware she played."

Emelie sat at the pianoforte and played a gentle sonata, the notes shimmered like moonlight on water. Her fingers moved across the keys with a steadiness she normally did not possess. The notes were clear and expressive. It was beautiful, but not overly polished. She missed a chord or two, her tempo wandered off every now and then, and yet . . . everyone in the room quieted. A few guests leaned in. Not because of skill, necessarily, but the unexpected grace in her presence.

"She seems different, in better health," Tatianna murmured. "I mean, she appears to be a touch stronger, almost vibrant, but…"

Archer nodded slowly. "Could be nothing. Could just be good days and bad ones."

"True," she said, though something itched at the back of her mind. Not quite suspicion. Not yet. Just… a flicker of something not quite right.

When Emelie finished, the applause was polite but not thunderous. She stood, gave a demure curtsy, and left the stage without fanfare.

As the next performer was announced, Archer leaned closer. "I don't suppose it has anything to do with . . . everything."

Tatianna folded her hands at her waist. "No, probably not."

And yet, both of them continued to stare at where Emelie now sat with her mother, laughing, her cheeks rosy, something neither one of them had seen before.

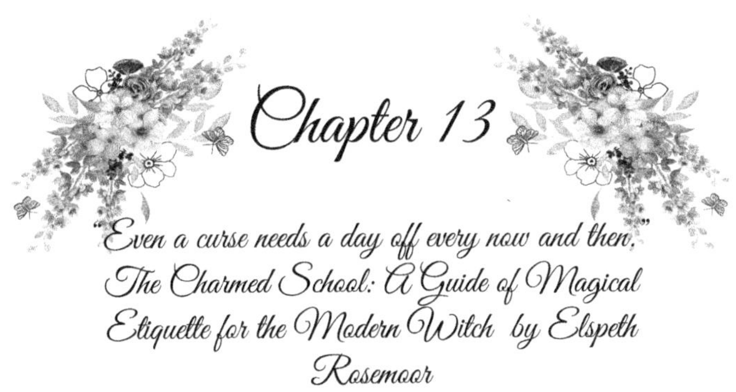

The final notes of the string quartet faded into silence, and a hush swept over the guests before applause swelled politely. Members of the quartet packed their instruments as the crowd stood and began to murmur their farewells, brushing off their gloves and collecting their cloaks. The moonlit night had grown cool, the faint scent of an upcoming rain threaded through the air.

Tatianna waited near the door as her sisters exchanged farewells with the Everetts, each one looking and acting like themselves. The excessive exuberance from earlier was gone, as was the shimmer of magic she was getting used to seeing hovering around them—tonight they were just a trio of young women, tired from a night out, laughing softly at some joke Celestine made under her breath.

"I don't know what unnerves me more, how unlike themselves they've been or how normal they are now?" she whispered as Archer appeared at her side. "What changed?"

He cast a quick glance toward Leondria, who stifled a yawn behind her gloved hand. "Maybe we're overreacting and it just took longer for them to recover from the ball at Covington Estate."

Tatianna shrugged, not convinced, but not sure what she could say to prove she was right. There were too many strange nights, too many missing memories. And everyone suddenly feeling fine tonight, even Emelie was just enough to stir up more questions for Tatianna without offering any answers.

The two of them bid farewell to their hosts before making their way down the gravel drive to the main lane. The moon hid behind heavy grey clouds, its glow cast faint silver shadows through the trees that bordered the road back to her home. They said little as they walked—what was there to say? If she was mistaken, and nothing was wrong, her concern was for naught. She had brought Archer into this for no reason.

The crunch of gravel underfoot and the soft rustle of leaves overhead filled the quiet space between them. At the gate near the Wylde cottage Tatianna paused.

"I'm going to stay up," she said softly. "See if they go out again."

Archer nodded. He didn't try to convince her she was over-reacting, that it would be better if they stayed home tonight like she expected him to do after this evening's entertainment.

"I'll wait by the gate, just in case. If they slip out on foot or by carriage, I'll make sure I remain unseen." He clasped his hands behind his back.

"Thank you." She hesitated, then added, "I'm not sure what will happen tonight. But if it's anything like the last couple of nights, my sisters will leave and return with no recollection of where they've been."

He turned to her, his gaze soft. "We'll figure it out."

They parted with a silent glance; she raised her hand as if she was going to reach out and touch him—instead her arm fell back to her side. But when their eyes met, they lingered there, warming the cool air between them.

Tatianna crept inside, closing the door behind her before she slipped off her shoes. She tiptoed up the stairs, shoes in hand, and slipped into her room to change out of her evening gown into something more appropriate for a night of watching and waiting. She made her way to her hiding spot in the silent house. There wasn't a single noise, not even the faint creak of floorboards or the sigh of a closing door as she moved about. She curled into the window seat with a shawl around her shoulders, eyes fixed on the hallway.

Midnight came.

Then one o'clock.

Then two.

But the doors to her sisters' rooms never opened.

In the pale light of dawn, as the shadows stretched longer until they began to fade and birds stirred, filling the air with their own magical song, Tatianna gave in to sleep, a single thought nagging at the edge of her weary mind:

Why was tonight different?

The house seemed to hold its breath as Tatianna suddenly woke with the realization she'd left Archer outside the entire night.

Tatianna raced to her room, threw on her coat, and laced her boots quickly. She slipped down the stairs, her bare hands gliding over the wood banister, gloves forgotten. She stepped through the door, her senses aware of every change around her. The air outside was damp and cool, clinging to her cheeks as she made her way down the garden path, the gravel loud under her feet in the hush of dawn.

A tall figure leaned against the gate at the end of the path, not much more than a silhouette in the silver mist. Archer pushed himself off the gate when he saw her, arms crossing over his chest. She hoped the motion was from nervous anticipation rather than impatience.

"You stayed here all night?" she asked, her voice soft enough not to disturb the sleeping roses. "I would have understood if you went home."

"As we discussed yesterday, we're in this together, whether we like it or not." His words were clipped, harsher than their conversation the day before.

She stared at him for a moment, deciding whether or not she should address his annoyed tone. She shook her head ever so slightly, it wasn't worth acknowledging, at least not right now.

"I watched the doors to their rooms all night. They never left," she said finally, pulling her coat tighter. "There wasn't a sound. Not a creak of a floorboard, or a sigh, or a giggle from one of my sisters. They were in their room, asleep all night long. They didn't go anywhere."

He looked down the lane toward the sleeping town. "I wonder why last night was different? Are you positive your sisters didn't just decide to leave you behind the last two nights?"

"I can't imagine them doing such a thing. And how does that explain your sister? She's been exhausted as well." She kicked a loose rock with the toe of her boot.

Around them the sky paled to a soft pewter, above them the edge of sunrise just beginning to stain the horizon with hints of peach and gold. A bird chirped somewhere in the hedgerow. Another answered it.

"I kept thinking maybe it's me," she admitted, her voice barely a breath. "Maybe I'm doing something without realizing it. Maybe my magic is pulling them into something. Maybe my mother is right, and I'm to blame because I never learned to control my magic properly."

Archer turned to her, something unreadable in his expression. "We've had this discussion. It's time to stop thinking that you did this. I don't believe you could ever use your magic to harm someone. Not after the time we've spent together."

"I don't know what to think. But I keep feeling . . . wrong. Like something's just out of reach, and if I could only see it properly, I'd know what's happening. And then I could fix it and they'd be safe. Why did my protection spell, as unintentional as it was, only work on the two of us? Why didn't I protect my family?"

His gaze flicked over her face, sharp and searching. "Tatianna, your magic—what little I understand of it—doesn't strike me as manipulative. If anything, it's protective. Not... predatory."

For a moment, he paused. "Besides," he added, with a faint curve of a smile, "if anyone is dragging people into trouble, it's far more likely to be my friends or my sister, and therefore me."

She laughed softly before she looked away.

"I suppose I'm not the villain in this story, then." She looked up at Archer with a lopsided grin.

"It would appear not," he said lightly, but the words didn't quite reach his eyes.

They stood together as the first true light crested the distant hills, washing the fields in the golden hue of dawn. Both of them lost in their own thoughts, neither one of them willing to voice those thoughts out loud. A comfortable silence filled the air between them, calming in its lack of awkwardness.

But that calmness, they both knew, wouldn't last.

Chapter 14

By the time Tatianna slipped back inside, dawn had long since brightened into full morning. She flicked her fingers at her boots, casting a spell so they made no sound against the marble tiles as she crept through the still house. Fatigue settled into every part of her body until her eyelids were so heavy she could no longer keep them open. She didn't even bother climbing into her bed—just curled under a wool throw on the chaise in her room, boots still on, and let her eyes drift shut.

When she woke again, it was to the faint sound of laughter.

For a moment, her sleep-fogged mind panicked, disoriented, unaware of where she was. She rubbed her eyes, and when she stopped, her room came into focus. Her canopy bed with its pile of pillows was in front of her. It all came back to her, waiting for hours for her sisters to leave, like they had the prior two nights, but they never left. Had the strangeness of the last few days all been a dream? The half-glimpsed returns at dawn, the foggy memories, the silence of last night?

She sat up and listened closely. She could hear her sisters downstairs. Their laughter was infectious, bringing a smile to her face. She heard them moving about. There was the chime of porcelain as they set their teacups down, the scraping of chairs against the wood floor, the gentle murmur of conversation. It all sounded . . . normal.

Tatianna washed her face and dressed quickly, twisting her hair into a simple chignon as she descended the stairs, even though she knew her curls would free themselves before long.

She found her sisters and mother in the morning room. Effie was at the table with a pot of tea and a plate of currant buns, Celestine flipping through a copy of the latest gossip rag, Leondria embroidering something in forget-me-not blue, and Rhiannon reading a new spell book with uncanny focus.

Everyone turned to greet her, more alert than she had seen them for days.

"Where have you been? You missed breakfast," Leondria said, motioning to the nearly empty dish of sticky buns.

"Did you sleep in?" Celestine asked, already reaching for the sugar bowl to prepare Tatianna's tea the way she liked it.

"I . . . suppose I did." Tatianna hesitated, unsure. "You all seem well-rested."

"I must have fallen asleep as soon as we arrived at home," Leondria said lightly. "I remember the ride home, Mama always insists we take a carriage despite it being close enough to walk. I must've collapsed into bed right away."

"That's so unlike you," Tatianna said, her gaze locked onto her sister. "You're normally buzzing with energy after a night out."

Leondria shrugged. "It's not so strange considering how tired I've been lately. I was ecstatic everyone felt well enough to attend last night."

"Yes, I'm so relieved you're feeling well today. We should do something. Maybe go shopping in town?" Tatianna asked.

"That sounds delightful," Leondria said. "But first, I think you should tell us how you got home, because it was not in the carriage with us."

Celestine handed Tatianna the tea. There was a gleam in Celestine's eye and a flush in her cheeks. She had the unmistakable look of someone who had a tale burning on the tip of her tongue.

Tatianna took a sip of her favorite breakfast tea and sighed, the warm liquid a familiar comfort when everything else was wrong. "Go ahead, I can tell you're dying to tell us something."

She glanced over at Leondria, who shook her head, the infinitesimal movement was enough to let Tatianna know her sister saw through her.

Celestine clapped her hands together. "Did you see him? The other new gentleman in town and he's so handsome."

"I don't remember meeting anyone new last night." She tapped her chin, trying to remember everyone that was at the musicale.

Rhiannon looked up. "I believe she's speaking of Mr. Wrenne. Celestine has spoken of little else since last night."

Her head snapped towards her sister. "Malric Wrenne? I met him earlier in the day."

"Isn't he handsome?" Celestine twirled and fell into a chair.

But before Tatianna could reply, she saw Leondria lift her hand to refill her teacup. The air shimmered faintly around her fingers as she whispered the incantation—but nothing happened. The pot trembled but did not lift. She frowned, tried again.

Still nothing.

Rhiannon glanced over and lifted her hand while muttering her own spell, attempting to levitate a sugar cube—only for it to rise half an inch before plunking unceremoniously onto her saucer.

"That's . . . strange," she muttered. "I've never had trouble with that spell." She shrugged, returning to her book.

Tatianna sat down slowly, watching them all, analyzing the aura of their magic.

They weren't tired. Not this morning. They weren't glassy-eyed or dull. This morning, they appeared normal.

But their magic—it wasn't the same. It was dimmed, like candles burning behind thick glass. Still visible, but not quite as bright.

And not one of them appeared the least bit unsettled by the change.

The Wylde family made their way into town with parasols open against the spring sun, their skirts swishing like branches of a willow tree in the wind. Tatianna took a deep breath of the crisp, cool air. She walked a half-step behind the others, allowing her to examine her sisters' behaviors and moods. They chatted and pointed out fabric in the general store's windows and millinery displays with delight. Everything appeared to be normal for the first time in days. With a shrug, she sped up a little and took Leondria's arm. If her sisters felt fine, she might as well enjoy her day with them.

Leondria suggested they stop at High Street Confectioners before they headed over to the bookshop to pick up another new spell book for Rhiannon. As they passed the dressmaker's, they nearly collided with a figure emerging onto the walk: Lady Cordelia and her daughter.

"Oh—my apologies, Mrs. Wylde," she said, dabbing at her brow with a lace-edged handkerchief. Her daughter, Emelie, trailed behind her in a soft violet day dress, looking pale and drawn—more like her normal appearance.

Gone was the flushed vibrance from the musicale. The dark circles were back beneath her eyes, and her frame seemed almost too light, too frail   as if the wind might blow her away.

"Lady Cordelia," Effie said with a polite, but cool smile. "What a lovely surprise."

"And your daughters look well this morning," Lady Cordelia replied with a thin smile, though her gaze lingered too long on Tatianna, as if she was trying to puzzle something out.

Tatianna didn't know what to make of Lady Cordelia's attention. Instead, she turned to speak with Emelie, compliment her on her playing the night before and ask if she was unwell—but before she could, a low voice cut across the walkway.

"Good morning to you Mrs. Wylde and to all your lovely daughters. I must confess I've yet to see so much beauty congregated in one place." Malric Wrenne stepped out of a shadowed alley between the row of shops with his usual catlike grace, all smiles and sharp jaw lines. He tipped his hat as if he was surrounded by the queen and her ladies, not on a sidewalk in Bramblewick.

Tatianna felt her stomach tighten. Even standing still, Malric gave the impression of someone about to pounce. It unsettled her, the way he appeared to be charming, but something in his eyes said he was hungry—for what, she didn't know.

"Mr. Wrenne," Effie said with a clipped nod, placing a protective hand on Leondria's shoulder. "A pleasure."

"Always," Malric said smoothly. His eyes flicked briefly to Emelie, then to Tatianna—and lingered.

"Mr. Wrenne, how wonderful it is to see you again." Celestine stepped forward, her arm extended.

His eyes darted between Tatianna and Celestine for a prolonged moment. A look of resignation flitted across his features before he took Celestine's hand with the flamboyance of a rogue. Tatianna saw his wicked smile did little to discourage her sister's blossoming affection.

"These bracelets are quite lovely and unique," he said, his eyes alight with curiosity.

She giggled. Before she could respond, another voice interrupted the moment.

"There you are, Tati . . ." The person cleared their throat. "Miss Wylde."

Tatianna turned to see Archer striding across the street with Lysander and their sisters, Lilith and Aisling. Both ladies, in slate blue walking suits, were laughing over something Lysander had said—but went quiet when they saw the group standing before them.

Tatianna caught Archer's expression—a flicker of unease, a quick glance at Malric.

"Good morning," he said, a touch too formally, his face a mask of polite indifference.

"Quite the gathering," Lady Cordelia murmured, her tone as unreadable as Archer's expression.

"Coincidences do make for the best stories," Lysander offered with a grin, moving to the spot next to Leondria.

His head bent towards her sister's, and for a moment they were so focused on each other, Tatianna felt like she was intruding just by watching their interaction. Their tête-à-tête did not last long though.

Malric smiled. "Though some stories are better left untold."

The silence that followed settled over them like an itchy wool blanket in winter, where one wanted to be rid of it, but to do so would risk catching a chill.

"Ah yes, quite so." Lysander, unable to handle the silence, couldn't help but speak. "We should take advantage of this happenstance and combine our outings into one. What do you say?"

Tatianna's fingers itched. She glanced at Emelie, who looked as though she might faint at any moment.

"I'm afraid we've finished our shopping for today and must be on our way. Emelie needs to rest after last night." Lady

Cordelia took her daughter's arm and pulled her close. Emelie stumbled before leaning into her mother more and more with every step they took. Tatianna continued to watch their journey until they disappeared into the local apothecary. She turned to her mother, to find they were all looking at her with one question in their eyes, quietly pleading for her to accept Mr. Goldvale's invitation.

Instead, Effie looked over at Archer and sniffed in disdain. "I'm afraid we already have a prior commitment at the Gilded Kettle and are unable to gather on a whim. Mr. and Mrs. Featherstone would be quite put out if we were not there on time."

The look her mother gave Archer as she spoke made Tatianna ill. She opened her mouth to speak, but Effie was already steering her daughters towards the tearoom, the sweet shop long forgotten after such an awkward meeting. Tatianna hung back, following her sisters but lingering in the back of the group as they crossed the street. She watched Archer murmur something to Lysander and then cross the cobbled street towards her. Lysander, looking crestfallen, gathered Lilith and Aisling and led them towards Brambles and Butter, the local bakery where the widowed Mrs. Merriweather baked croissants that had the power to end a feud.

"Do you have a moment?" he asked, his voice low enough that only she could hear.

Tatianna nodded, grateful her mother's distaste hadn't stopped him from talking to her. The tightness in her chest hadn't eased since Malric appeared, and for some unknown reason there was no one she trusted more right now than the quiet man before her.

They slipped down a side lane, away from the bustle of the main street. The sounds of the happy shoppers faded behind them. The narrow street was lined with climbing ivy and old stone walls, warm from the sun. Archer walked beside her in silence until they reached a quiet little square with a bench beneath a budding cherry tree.

He turned to face her. "I thought after last night, Emelie would look less sickly."

"She was so vibrant last night, at least for her," Tatianna said, perching on the bench. "But this morning she looked worse than I'm used to seeing her. Why perform if it's going to cause such exhaustion?"

Archer nodded, running a hand through his hair. "I don't know. Add it to the growing list of things that don't sit right in this town."

"And Malric . . ." Tatianna voice's quivered with unease.

His jaw tightened. "He always has a way of turning up where he's not wanted."

"I don't like the way he looks at people." She looked at him. "I'm afraid Celestine has developed an infatuation for him."

"If you can, I would keep her away from him." Archer gave a humorless smile. "He's not to be trusted."

"I doubt telling my sister that would do any good. She's headstrong." Tatianna folded her gloved hands in her lap, staring at the cobbles.

"I feel like that's a common trait among you and your sisters," Archer said.

"Speaking of my sisters—this morning they tried to use magic, and it didn't work. I don't think that's ever happened to them before." Tatianna looked down at her hands, willing them to stay still. Her mother compared her to a bird flapping its wings whenever she was agitated, which was not the impression she wanted to give right now. Tatianna hesitated, then continued, "What if . . . what if whatever is causing them to disappear at night is also taking their magic?"

Archer's eyes met hers. "Most people have hiccups with their magic at some point. Are you sure this isn't one of those times?"

She didn't answer right away. "No, but it's never happened to them before. And two of them in one morning? Seems like too much of a coincidence," she said finally. "And I can't stop thinking about the night of the ball. About the way things have felt ever since . . ." She remembered she was supposed to be having tea. "I'm sorry, I have to go, my mother will be wondering where I've ran off to."

He stood, offering his hand to assist her. "Whatever this is, we'll figure it out."

"You still believe me?"

"There's something going on here," Archer said. "We need to unravel what it is."

She turned to look at him, startled—but before she could reply, a breeze stirred the cherry blossoms above them. White petals fell gently between them, like snow catching the sunlight.

It felt like a promise.

Chapter 15

"When taking tea, one must never rattle one's cup on its saucer. If incapable of not committing such a faux pas, magical intervention is required." Magic, Manners, and Mishaps: A Collection of Essays compiled by Mrs. Peregrine of Bramblewick Ladies' Academy for the Magically-Inclined

Tatianna stood outside the Gilded Kettle taking in a deep breath. She paused for a moment to adjust her gloves, smoothing her features into practiced composure. She was sure her cheeks were still a touch too pink from her walk with Archer, but she hoped no one would notice. Feeling her features settle into the mask she wore for most of society, she pushed open the painted green door, causing the bell above to give a polite chime.

As always, the cozy tearoom smelled of lavender and honeyed scones with the faint essence of Earl Grey tea, the scent floating in the air like a feather on the breeze. The open windows' lace curtains stirred faintly in the breeze, while the clinking of china accompanied the gentle murmur of conversation like a well-rehearsed symphony.

Mrs. Featherstone, her ever-present violet shawl draped over her shoulders, gave her a knowing nod from behind the counter. "Bit late to be joining the party, Miss Wylde."

Tatianna smiled faintly. "Just taking in the morning air before enjoying a cup of your famous Earl Grey tea. Who's winning today, you or Mr. Featherstone?"

"That's not even a question, love," Mrs. Featherstone said with a smile. "I am, of course. I only let Mr. Featherstone think he has a chance of brewing a cup of Earl Grey as good as mine, but everyone else knows mine is the best." She tapped the side of her nose before turning and taking Tatianna to her family's table.

Her mother sat at their usual table by the window, surrounded by delicate white and lavender teacups and a towering arrangement of violets decorating the table. Her sisters were already seated, each looking as demure as they could in their pastel day dresses—Tatianna knew it was all an act, especially for Celestine. Leondria was the most ladylike out of the four of them; it came naturally to her. Rhiannon was too bookish to ever be considered ladylike. Even now, she had a book hidden in her lap under the table, which occupied all her attention. She was quiet, which could not be said about Tatianna or Celestine.

Effie Wylde set her teacup down with an audible clink. "There you are. I was beginning to wonder if you'd wandered straight into the lake. Or perhaps you were off with Mr. Thornfield again? Despite the discussion we had about him at the ball."

Tatianna met her mother's gaze evenly, careful to keep her tone light. "Hardly. Just needed some fresh air to think."

"About what, I wonder?" Effie's tone was mild, but Tatianna knew it well enough to recognize the thread of warning beneath.

"Your sisters have been here nearly a quarter of an hour. You almost missed the lemon curd entirely."

"I'm sure I'll survive." Tatianna slid into her seat and accepted the cup Daisy passed her with a genteel nod to thank her. Her eyes flicked over her sisters—chatting, nibbling, smiling. After days of seeing them exhausted, she should have been happy they were acting normal, but she couldn't shake the feeling of trepidation that had settled in her stomach.

"Were you thinking about last night's musicale?" Effie prompted. "It seems to be the talk of the town."

"Not particularly." Tatianna stirred her tea slowly, watching the cream swirl. "Just thinking how odd things have felt since the ball."

Effie's eyes narrowed. "The only odd thing is the amount of time you're spending with that young man. I do hope you're not making a spectacle of yourself and developing an attachment to him. You mustn't confuse affection with suitability, Tatianna. He simply isn't your equal."

"Yes, Mama, you've made your opinion quite clear," Tatianna replied too sweetly. "At least I've been able to leave the house during the day the past few days, even if it means making the acquaintance of that young man. Not everyone at this table can say the same."

A beat of silence followed, broken only by the faint clatter of cutlery on porcelain. Outside, cherry blossoms danced in the breeze.

Effie tutted and reached for another scone. She slathered it with clotted cream before looking at Tatianna. "You've always had a flair for drama, my dear. But there's no need to drag your sisters into it."

"She's right, Mama, we've been stuck at home, so lethargic that Rhiannon hasn't even picked up a book until today." Leondria smiled before taking a sip of her tea.

Tatianna returned her sister's smile, who winked back at her before picking up the last cucumber sandwich from the three-tiered tea tray.

"Are there any more sandwiches?" Tatianna asked, changing the subject with a brightness that felt a touch too forced. There was no use dwelling on her worries now. For the moment, things seemed—if not perfectly right, then at least pleasantly ordinary. And she intended to enjoy this fragile illusion of normalcy while it lasted.

Content with her decision, she took the last cucumber sandwich Leondria passed to her and tried to enjoy it as the late afternoon light slanted through the windows of the Gilded Kettle, casting a warm glow across polished teapots and lace-draped tables. She wanted to continue with their shopping excursion, instead she sat across from her mother, feigning interest in a half-filled cup of Earl Grey tea while trying not to fidget under her mother's reproachful glances. Leondria, poised as ever, was delicately folding a napkin into a swan as if she'd done it a thousand times. Rhiannon still sat with them, absorbed in whatever she was reading, while Celestine had convinced their mother to let her go to the ribbon shop to find some new trim for a bonnet she wasn't happy with.

The door chimed, and in swept Aisling Thornfield, bright-eyed just like she had been when they met at the ball, her arm looped casually through that of Lilith Goldvale—tall and poised. The two of them were a picture of modern elegance in their tailored linen walking suits and wide-brimmed hats.

"Misses Wylde," Aisling said with a lilting warmth, offering a smile as she approached their table. "How fortunate we are to find you here."

Lilith's eyes sparkled as she set down her parasol. "We were just talking about the two of you this morning and thought after a day in town, we simply could not bear a dull evening. We were hoping you would join us."

Tatianna raised an eyebrow. "What did you have in mind?"

"A night of parlor games," Aisling answered with a grin. "At the Covington Estate. Nothing too grand—just a few friends, a bit of charades, and the Minister's Cat, and we'll hang up garden lanterns strung like stars. You must come."

Leondria glanced at their mother, who looked from Aisling to Lilith with a cautious smile before nodding her approval.

"I suppose that would be suitable," Effie said. "Provided you return before midnight."

"Oh, we'll have you home long before the carriages turn into pumpkins," Lilith teased lightly.

Leondria smirked. "Then we'd be delighted."

As the women chatted and tea was refreshed, Tatianna couldn't help but feel the edges of something stir beneath the simple invitation—a whisper of curiosity and something deeper, something threaded between polite smiles and parlor parties.

Once again, the Wylde sisters' dressing room was a whirlwind of silk and laughter as the sun slipped beneath the horizon. Sometimes this was Tatianna's favorite part about going out: getting ready with her sister and best friend. Leondria stood before the mirror, pinning a sprig of fresh lavender into her carefully curled hair, while she fussed with a line of stubborn buttons at the back of her gown.

"Will you help me with these buttons?" Tatianna said, her voice half-muffled as she twisted to reach the last buttons and failed. She stomped her satin slippered foot on the carpet, groaning when her fit didn't properly illustrate her frustration.

Leondria muttered a spell and flicked her hand towards Tatianna. The buttons that had stubbornly been fighting her obeyed her sister's magic in an instant, leaving Tatianna standing in her contorted position.

She blew curls out of her eyes as she dropped her arms by her side. "Did you cast a spell to button my gown? Mother would be so disappointed that you used magic for such a mundane task. She would have told you to call a servant."

Leondria shrugged. "The servants are busy with dinner for the others. I didn't want to bother them. I'm actually surprised you didn't do it yourself."

Tatianna needed to change the subject. She didn't want to discuss why she hadn't, at least not yet. She didn't know enough and saying something would just cause her sister to worry. "I'm really not sure how you convinced me to go tonight."

"It's not like it was difficult. I think all Lilith had to do was mention parlor games," Leondria replied, unruffled. "And because you like Aisling. And perhaps because a certain brother will also be in attendance, and despite your protests, I believe you like him as well."

Tatianna rolled her eyes, but the tips of her ears turned pink. "I'm only going because I knew it would make you happy."

Leondria smirked. "Then I expect we'll both leave satisfied. I intend to enjoy the company—I very much enjoyed conversing with Mr. Goldvale at the musicale. I hope we have a chance to speak tonight. He is quite clever and shares my interest in the stars."

Tatianna gave her a sidelong look. "That's the second time you've mentioned him this week. Are you hoping for your acquaintance to develop into something more?"

Leondria only smiled and swept towards the door. Her perfume lingered in the air as a reminder of past adventures and secrets.

The Covington Estate glowed softly against the twilight, its windows gleaming like floating lanterns as the sisters walked up the steps to double doors that were a breathtaking design of glass and wood so intricate it was clear only magic could have created such splendor. When they reached the top step, the doors swung open. Standing in the opening was a tall, stiff figure so formal it could only be the butler. He escorted them to the drawing room, their heels echoing throughout the foyer as they walked across the black-and-white marble floor, the staccato sound punctuating every step they took.

Aisling greeted them with delight in the drawing room, where clusters of guests mingled about the room. The scent of beeswax polish, cardamom tea, and scotch lingered in the air. Gentle piano music drifted from the far end of the room.

"Wylde sisters!" Lilith beamed. She grabbed their hands and pulled them farther into the room with a theatrical gesture. "We're just beginning a round of charades—but first, a proper turn about the room, don't you think?"

Tatianna linked arms with her without hesitation, grateful for a moment to settle in before jumping into the game. They moved in a slow circle near the periphery, commenting in whispers on the floral arrangements. The staff had outdone themselves. Then there was Lady Finchley's towering, feathered hat—she actually put a finch on the hat. And one couldn't help but notice the particularly aggressive tea-drinking posture of Mr. Rookwood.

Across the room, Archer leaned against the fireplace mantel, watching them with a faint smile playing on his lips.

"Taking a turn about the room, are they?" he remarked to Lysander, who had just joined him with two glasses of scotch.

"Seems they've read their Austen," Lysander replied with amusement. "Though I daresay Miss Wylde carries it off with more spirit than Miss Bennet ever did."

Archer said nothing, but his gaze lingered on Tatianna—her cheeks flushed with laughter, her curls catching the light like spun copper.

"She looks happy tonight," Lysander observed.

"She does," Archer murmured. "I hope it lasts."

When they finished their turn about the room, Tatianna made her way to her sister, who sat on the settee talking to someone she had yet to meet, all while casting longing glances towards the fireplace.

After proper introductions, Tatianna nudged her sister's shoulder. "You know, you could just walk over there. I dare say he would be happy to talk to you."

Leondria raised an eyebrow. "What makes you think we haven't already conversed tonight? Besides, the games are about to begin."

Tatianna shook her head, about to comment that now was the perfect time, but her sister proved to be correct, and the games began in earnest. Aisling divided them into teams, separating Tatianna and Leondria, claiming they would have an unfair advantage. Tatianna moved to the other side of the room to join her other team members. Charades began with Mr. Goldvale attempting an elaborate mime that no one could decipher until Leondria correctly guessed *Oliver Twist* and earned a chorus of delighted applause. The game progressed on, each person's pantomime more amusing than the one before. Spirits were high, laughter filling the room as any worries were forgotten in the pure silliness of the game. When Lilith called for a brief intermission, Tatianna flopped beside her sister on the settee, breathless from laughing at her friend Evangeline's attempt at portraying a washerwoman.

"You're very good at this," Tatianna said, nudging her sister.

"It's all the times we've played at home." Leondria tilted her head, watching Lysander as he took a seat beside the piano to take his turn. "He's rather good at it, too."

Tatianna followed her gaze and smiled to herself. "You like him."

Leondria didn't deny it. "He listens when I speak. And he doesn't seem to care that I prefer astronomy to embroidery. In fact, he also enjoys astronomy."

Tatianna reached for her hand and gave it a quick squeeze. "Then he's already more worthy of you than most."

Her sister smiled at her and made her way over to the piano.

Later in the evening, as guests lingered in clusters to sip spiced wine and play the Minister's Cat, Tatianna found herself catching Archer's gaze across the room. For a moment, it felt like a thread had drawn tight between them. But then he looked away, murmuring something to Lilith that made her laugh.

She wasn't sure what unsettled her more: the way his absence left a space she was suddenly aware of—or the way her sister was beginning to fill her life with things that didn't include her. She shook both thoughts away. If Leondria was indeed falling in love, it was a reason to celebrate, not get caught in doldrums.

The night air wrapped around them like a light shawl, soft with the scent of spring—earth, lavender, and a hint of woodsmoke from hearths being lit early against the breeze. Crickets chirped from the hedgerows, willow branches waved in the wind, and dryads chattered as the Wylde sisters walked the winding path back towards their cottage, their slippered feet crunching over gravel and scattering cherry blossoms. These sounds combined to create the quiet overture of their midnight stroll.

Tatianna kept her hands tucked into her cloak, her mind still half in the parlor, where Archer's glance had flickered towards her again and again, but he had stayed away from her the entire night, aloof and unapproachable to everyone but his close friends and his sister. After everything they'd been through, why would he keep his distance from her the entire night? And why, after nights of disappearing into the night, was everything suddenly back to normal again? Leondria had even been able to use her magic getting dressed this evening. Nothing made sense to her.

"I think he enjoyed himself," Leondria said, her voice light but purposeful.

Tatianna blinked, pushing her chaotic thoughts away. "Who?"

"Lysand . . . Mr. Goldvale." Her sister's lips hinted at a smile, but it was her voice that carried the warmth of one. "I believe he rather liked the games tonight."

"I would say he enjoyed all the games, including the one that you're playing." Tatianna tilted her head, nudging her shoulder against Leondria's. "You're allowed to show him you're interested, you know. No one expects you to be composed at every moment."

"That's where you're wrong," Leondria said, though without bitterness. "Composure is what makes them listen. I speak softly and keep my hair well-coifed."

They walked a few more steps in silence. She didn't agree with her sister, but Leondria was very much their mother's daughter in many ways.

"I noticed the way he looked at you," Tatianna murmured, almost teasing.

"And I noticed the way Archer looked at you," Leondria teased back.

Tatianna gave a snort of disbelief. "He was simply watching the festivities, but refusing to join. It was quite apparent he was avoiding my company."

"No, he was watching you, observing you. There's a difference." Leondria paused beneath an overgrown willow, where the breeze tugged its silver leaves around them like a curtain. "He watches you like he wants to understand you, but doesn't quite know how."

Tatianna didn't answer right away, her mind drawn back to the night they had met, and the swing hidden beneath a tree, just like the one hiding them now. Remembering how, in that moment, they had almost kissed, and she would have let it happen if her mother hadn't found her.

The wind tickled her curls. "I'm not sure I understand myself lately. Everything feels . . . off."

"You mean the magic," Leondria said quietly.

"And so much more," Tatianna admitted. "There's something happening here. It started at the ball. I feel like we're all characters in someone else's story, dancing and sipping tea while someone else is pulling the strings. I mean, look at how, for a moment, Emelie looked healthy for the first time ever, as far as I can recollect. And then there's the exhaustion that took over the town. Not to mention just this morning, both you and Rhiannon struggled with a simple serving spell."

They stood a moment longer, the willow creaking softly above them.

"I believe you're correct. I feel like there's something on the edge of my memory, but every time I try to focus on it . . . it disappears," Leondria said simply. "There is something happening here in Bramblewick. I want to help anyway I can."

"Thank you for believing me. For now, that is help enough." Tatianna reached for her sister's hand, and this time didn't let go until the lake glinted into view, the windows of the Wylde cottage golden in the distance.

Behind them, the town of Bramblewick slumbered peacefully—unaware there was a nefarious darkness in their midst.

<h1 style="text-align:center">Chapter 16</h1>

The fire in the grate had burned down to glowing coals, casting amber shadows against the shelves and dark paneling of Archer's favorite room, his study. He sat in one of the leather wingbacks, a glass of whiskey warming in his hand, untouched as he stared into the coals, brooding. The house was quiet—too quiet compared to the revelry just hours before, even if it was logical, since everyone else had made their way to bed. Normally he would revel in the solitude, but tonight he was on edge and he could not explain why.

He swirled his drink slowly, watching the golden liquid catch the firelight. Laughter and light conversation echoed in his mind. He could still see his sister and Tatianna laughing together over some shared secret as if they had been friends their entire life. Then there was Tatianna: he hadn't been able to take his eyes off her, and her eyes kept coming back to him. A glance here, a hesitation there. It was like being at the ball all over again, before her mother's interruption.

He frowned. Her smile had been bright, and her laughter infectious. Tonight, it was as if she had let go of all her worries. Tatianna had been fully present—laughing freely, twirling through parlor games and tea-stained conversations, relishing every second spent beside Leondria.

A creak in the hallway pulled him from his thoughts. He set the glass down and crept to the door, peering into the corridor just in time to see a flash of Aisling's skirts at the top of the stairs, followed closely by Lilith's unmistakable silhouette.

He waited. Counted a few heartbeats.

Then he followed.

The manor was still, but not asleep. The hush of velvet wall coverings and the judgmental gazes of the portraits lining the hall pressed in on him as he moved towards the staircase. Making his way down the stairs, careful not to make a sound as his feet fell on the carpeted steps. Outside, the garden was bathed in silvery moonlight. Mist drifted over the lawn like restless spirits out for an evening stroll.

He kept his distance as his sister and Lilith slipped through the wrought-iron gate at the edge of the property and onto the path. Not towards the town. Not back towards Lysander's house. Not towards the main road.

Towards the woods.

Archer's brow furrowed as he followed, ducking behind hedgerows and fence posts, his boots making the slightest of noise on the packed earth as he skirted the gravel path. They passed the Wylde family's ivy-draped cottage. He paused as a flicker of movement caught his eye.

Three figures—Leondria, Rhiannon, and Celestine—gliding like sleepwalkers across the lawn, dressed in ballgowns made with magic, their hair unbound and gleaming in the moonlight.

And behind them . . . Tatianna.

She wasn't sleepwalking.

She was trailing after them, still wearing her gown from this evening, her posture wary, but determined.

A strange chill passed through Archer, sharper than the night air. He'd thought his unease earlier was just nerves or discontent after keeping his distance from Tatianna all evening, but now it was clear it had been something else. He had sensed that something was going to happen tonight. Something he hadn't expected. Even though he had believed Tatianna when she said her sisters were disappearing at night, a small part of him held on to the thought that it wasn't true. Now, it could no longer be denied as they both followed their entranced sisters to some unknown destination.

As the figures vanished into the trees, a gust of wind stirred the cherry blossoms still stubbornly clinging to the low branches. Pale petals drifted down, reminding him of all the moments he and Tatianna had been together.

Archer stepped onto the road, heart pounding, and followed.

He didn't know what they were walking into, but he knew one thing with certainty: he wasn't going to let her go into it alone.

Archer kept to the shadows, each step measured and silent as he followed the drifting forms ahead, all while keeping an eye on Tatianna. She moved with purpose, but something about her posture—the tension in her shoulders, the way she kept glancing over her shoulder towards him, as if she could feel his presence.

She didn't see him. Not yet.

Moonlight spilled through the trees that arched over the path in silvery puddles, and the mist clung low to the ground, curling around the trees with purpose, its path not caused by nature, but by whatever was leading the women. Somewhere in the distance, an owl called—a soft, mournful sound that echoed the strange ache growing in his chest.

He should have said something earlier. Warned her. Asked the questions he'd kept neatly buttoned beneath his waistcoat and polished smiles. Admitted that all of this felt familiar in a way he couldn't name. And if he was honest, the thought of remembering—of truly knowing—terrified him.

A branch snapped beneath his boot.

Tatianna whirled.

Her eyes found his immediately, wide with surprise—and something sharper. A flare of fear that quickly cooled to annoyance.

"So, it is you— You shouldn't be here," she whispered, stepping off the path to meet him. Her voice was low but urgent. "You'll ruin everything."

He raised his hands in mock surrender. "Then I'm in good company."

She huffed, but it lacked heat. "I'm serious, Archer."

"So am I. Aren't we supposed to be doing this together?" His eyes flicked to the fading forms of her sisters in the distance, then to the direction where Aisling and Lilith had vanished. "You weren't the only one with restless company tonight."

"I had to follow them." Tatianna's brow furrowed. "They're all going to the same place."

He nodded. "If I remember correctly, the ruins are that way."

She crossed her arms, pressing them tightly against her ribs. "You think I should have stayed behind? That I'm meddling?"

"No," he said quickly. Too quickly. He didn't think she was meddling, she was putting herself in danger though. He took a deep breath, then continued, his tone more even: "I think you're the only one who's asking the questions no one else wants or knows to ask."

Hearing his words, her gaze softened, but her voice stayed brisk. "Well. Are you going to follow me around all night, or are you going to help?"

Archer gave her a crooked smile. "Lead the way, Miss Wylde."

Together, they slipped through the underbrush, keeping a careful distance from the figures ahead. The castle ruins loomed in the distance now—ancient stones caught in moonlight, tangled in vines and time, shrouded in mist and mystery.

And moments before they reached the crumbled outer wall, Tatianna's hand brushed his—the slightest touch, the faintest sweep of fingertips—he wasn't sure it was intentional, but it was enough.

His eyes caught hers, and for a moment, they stood there. He didn't say anything. Neither did she.

The silence that stretched between them as the mist surrounded them was not uncomfortable.

A breath held in anticipation of something more.

A step taken together—into whatever answers awaited them beyond the veil of mist.

Chapter 17

"An enchanted ball might appear to be the beginning of an exciting adventure, but to spend the night waltzing with a handsome gentleman is sure to cause whispers, that being said, the whispers may be worth it if the gentleman is handsome enough." The Etiquette Enchantress: The Art of Charm and Beguilement Beguilement by Anonymous, attributed to "The Lady in Lavender"

The forest had fallen unnaturally silent as they walked through the gap in the crumbling outer wall of the old castle. Even the night birds seemed to hold their breath.

Archer kept close to Tatianna as they moved beneath the dripping branches of cherry trees that had claimed the courtyard, their blossoms luminous in the night's light. Up ahead, their sisters drifted through the mist like wraiths in fine gowns, the luminescence of an ethereal ball blooming before them.

It emerged slowly—like something unfolding from the earth itself. A grand hall that should not exist, wreathed in ivy and moonlight, suspended in the clearing where nothing but rocks and ruins should have stood.

Tatianna's breath caught. "It's a glamour," she whispered. "Layered and old. How did I not feel this when we were here before? The magic is everywhere—it's almost impossible to breathe it's so thick. Magic isn't supposed to feel like this. It's too intense."

Archer glanced at her, concern warring with the knowledge he had to let her continue on this journey. "Your protection spell—it's holding?"

She nodded, clutching his hand. "For now."

They stepped over the threshold together. The moment they entered, the air shifted—like walking through water—and they emerged somewhere otherworldly, more vibrant and more mystical than the place they had just left. The entire town seemed to be there, gliding across the dance floor in dreamlike awe, their eyes vacant, their expressions peaceful.

Tatianna and Archer remained focused and clear-eyed as they stood on the edge for a moment, taking in everything around them.

The ballroom shimmered before them like a dream stitched together from stardust and forgotten fairytales.

Soft orbs of floating light hovered around gilded chandeliers, casting ripples of gold and violet across the intricate marble floor. Musicians—that appeared to be made from the mist that led everyone to this spot, none of them quite solid—played on a dais strung with ivy that sparkled with silver. Music drifted through the air—light and playful, filled with the tinkling laughter of ringing bells. It was all too perfect.

Dancers swirled in pairs, laughing with empty joy, their feet gliding perfectly in rhythm. Every movement felt exaggerated, graceful, too precise. Tatianna's eyes darted from one couple to another, each one dancing in a dream they couldn't wake from.

"They don't even blink," Archer murmured. "Look at Leondria."

Tatianna did—and her stomach twisted. Her eldest sister, naturally graceful, moved with impossible grace, but her expression was faintly off: her smile too wide, her eyes too bright. Her expression was a frozen mask worn to convey how she should feel in this moment.

"I don't think any of them realize they're here," Tatianna said, her voice almost impossible to hear over the music. "They're dreaming. Or made to feel like they are."

A dancer passed too closely, and Tatianna pulled Archer into motion, blending into the steps of the waltz.

"Smile more blankly," she whispered through a stiff-lipped grin. "You're thinking too hard." Tatianna's hand rested lightly on Archer's arm as they twirled among the bewitched crowd, trying not to draw attention to the clarity in their eyes.

"Don't draw attention," she murmured, one hand on his shoulder, the other fitting easily into his palm. "We need to stay inside this enchantment if we're going to learn anything."

Archer's lips quirked into a rueful smile. "You just wanted to dance with me."

She gave him a warning glance. "Behave. And stop counting, it makes your dancing overly stiff."

She felt him let out a deep breath and relax. When he did, his arms tightened around her, pulling her close enough for their legs to brush as they waltzed.

And in that moment, despite everything—the danger, the unease—there was something electric in the way their bodies moved together. She could feel the strength in his hold, the steadiness of his breath, the warmth of his skin even through his gloves.

"I could get used to this," he said softly, his voice just a shade too serious.

She should look away. This wasn't why they were here. This wasn't a real dance, and they weren't truly courting. Everything about tonight shimmered with illusion. And yet—whatever this was between them felt real.

Too real.

Her gaze found his, and she didn't look away.

They stopped moving, as if the magic itself were holding its breath. The music faded. He leaned closer, and this time, she knew—it was going to happen: the kiss her mother had so rudely interrupted before, the one that had haunted her ever since. His lips hovered just a breath from hers. Her eyes fluttered shut.

And then the music began again.

A laughing couple spun too close, bumping into them, jolting Tatianna back to the moment—back to the truth.

This was still a lie.

But the way her heart pounded in her chest? That felt like the only honest thing in the room.

Tatianna pulled Archer back into the dance. Her gaze darted across the crowd, tracking their sisters as they moved with other dancers, eyes glazed, mouths curled in perpetual delight. Aisling floated past on the arm of a handsome stranger, her laughter tinkling like wind chimes—but her pupils were too wide, her movements a fraction too slow.

They needed to find out more about the enchantment, and it wasn't going to happen on the dance floor.

"We need to search the hall or the ruins, whatever this is," she whispered in his ear.

He nodded, his cheek brushing up against hers. They moved as one, weaving through the dancers like threads in a tapestry, each footfall carefully timed, each expression painted with the right amount of blissful vacancy. At the edge of the dancers, she grabbed his hand and darted into the shadows. To her right she spotted a staircase. Unsure if it was real or an illusion, she took a chance, dragging Archer behind her. At the top she looked out over the hall, a flurry of brilliant colored ballgowns circling on the dance floor below them.

And that's when she saw them.

The runes.

Carved into the marble, half-hidden beneath the swirling hems, glowing faintly with each pass of the dancers' feet were interlocking symbols.

Her breath hitched.

"Archer," she whispered, pulling him to the balustrade so he could see. "The floor."

His eyes flicked down. "Runes. Old ones."

She knew those runes. She had seen them once—buried in the margins of her grandmother's spell book, labeled only with a warning regarding the potential dangers of the spells between its bindings.

Not enchantment. Entrapment.

"Archer," she said lowly as she stared. "The floor. It's a circle, and runes are all circular. A containment spell, I think. Maybe more than one."

He followed her gaze, catching only a flicker of the markings as dancers spun and skirts flared. "You're certain?"

"No," she said, "but it's familiar. Too familiar. This isn't just a ball. It's a ritual. We need to go back to the dance before whoever cast this spell finds us."

They raced down the stairs. Archer swept her into his arms, leading her through the dance.

Tatianna was happy to follow his lead because her mind wouldn't let her focus on the steps. She counted the symbols. She marked the placement of the lights. And she began to wonder: if this was a spell . . . who had cast it? And to what end?

"They're only part of the spell. Anchoring it, maybe amplifying it." Her heart began to race. "This isn't just enchantment. It's a tether."

Archer's jaw tightened. "So they're not just attending a ball. They're being held here."

Tatianna nodded slowly, eyes scanning the dancers. "For what purpose? It can't be because someone likes to watch people dance. There is definitely something much more devious afoot."

Chapter 18

The enchantments faded until all that was left were the ruins of the old castle. The great hall they had spent the witching hours in had disappeared like mist in sunlight, leaving only the fading moonlight as it turned to dawn and the rustling of wind through the cherry trees. Archer and Tatianna followed the winding path back towards the Wyldes' cottage. Ahead of them, their sisters walked, still lost to whatever held them at the ball, each of them missing their normal vivaciousness and vitality. Normally, their laughter danced like fireflies on the air after an evening like this—lively and bright. But tonight's dance wasn't real, and their noiseless walk home only illustrated that further. It was clear something wicked controlled tonight, and it had not yet revealed itself.

Neither of them spoke for a long while. The faint glow of morning had a hush to it, the kind that settled as one reflected on something extraordinary. Tatianna clutched her cloak tighter against the breeze, though it wasn't the cold that made her heart flutter.

She glanced down at her feet with a rueful laugh. "I've worn straight through the soles of my shoes."

Archer looked over at her. "That does not surprise me. We danced for hours."

"We had to," she said lightly. "Or we would have been caught."

"I was not complaining. I'm sorry the night has come to an end." He sounded almost wistful.

She didn't ask what he meant. The spell between them—real or not—had left a trace. And though they walked in silence again, it was a silence rich with everything they left unspoken.

When they reached the edge of the estate, Tatianna paused. The house glowed softly in the distance, the sound of her sisters' steps trailing off as they disappeared inside. She opened the gate and stepped through. Stopping, she turned back to him.

"I know it wasn't real," she said quietly, not looking at him at first. "The dancing. The magic. This—I don't know— But it still felt like something." Her eyes darted to his face as her words trailed off.

Archer's jaw tightened, and his gaze dropped to the gravel. "It was something."

She nodded, a small smile playing at her lips despite herself. "And now my shoes will never be the same."

"Neither will I," he said, almost too softly to hear.

But she heard him.

And this time, she didn't look back as she walked towards the door—because she knew he was still watching her.

Morning came slowly, filtering in through gauzy curtains with a pale gold light that seemed too gentle to wake anyone. Although it was still early, the house was unusually quiet—no clatter of breakfast plates, no chime of teacups, just the occasional creak of floorboards and the distant murmur of a servant moving about in the hall.

Tatianna sat cross-legged on the floor of the small attic reading room, dust motes swirling in the light around her as she cracked open another leather-bound tome. Her fingers were smudged with dust and ink, and a growing stack of rejected books surrounded her like the stones of a fallen fortress.

She'd never gone to sleep.

After slipping off her ruined shoes, she'd crept upstairs instead of going to bed, driven by the need to find out where she had seen the runes before. The need percolated in her, stronger than a cup of coffee. It forced her to keep searching one book after another, driving all thoughts and feelings of exhaustion away. The runes etched into the floor of the glamoured ballroom were ever present in her thoughts—sharp and precise, almost as if burned into her memory.

She paused her search of books and grabbed a blank paper and pencil. She sketched the runes, her pencil moving across the paper with sharp, decisive strokes until every symbol was there, laid out before her eyes once again. Sighing, she could breathe again. The urgency of finding the meaning of the runes was still there, but it no longer pressed on her in the same way.

Her grandmother's spell books were older than most in the house, stored away in a lacquered chest behind the reading room bookshelf, forgotten until now. Some of the pages were brittle, others still faintly smelled of lavender and smoke. They felt important. They felt like they should have held the answers.

But they didn't.

Tatianna turned another page, skimmed a passage on warding charms, another on elemental weaving. Still no runes. No clue to what kind of spell could enchant an entire place—an entire gathering—and still leave her and Archer untouched.

She sighed, brushing a curl from her forehead, leaving a trail of dust in her fingers' wake. Her hands trembled from lack of sleep.

A soft knock came at the doorframe. Rhiannon peeked in, bleary-eyed and wrapped in a shawl. "You're up already?"

Tatianna nodded, closing the book on her lap. "Couldn't sleep."

Rhiannon stepped inside and sat beside her without a word, leaning her head on Tatianna's shoulder.

Tatianna sighed. "If I could just figure out the meaning of the runes, I might be able to figure out why you, Leondria, Celestine, and so many more keep running off to a ball every night. One that leaves you and your magic . . . exhausted, for lack of a better word."

"I don't remember going anywhere last night." Rhiannon's voice was quiet, sleepy.

"I know." She stroked her younger sister's hair. "But you've noticed your magic is off, haven't you? And you're always tired? I think the runes are at least part of what's causing it."

She pushed her sketch of the runes over so Rhiannon could see it.

Rhiannon nodded, her cheek rubbing on her sister's gown. "My buttered toast spell hasn't been consistent at all. You believe it's all related to these runes?" She picked up the paper.

"Yes, I thought maybe I'd find something," Tatianna said quietly, "in Grandmother's old books. Something about these runes. But there's nothing."

"There will be," Rhiannon said, more out of faith than certainty. "Maybe I can help you look."

Tatianna nodded again, but the silence between them carried her doubt. The dance was over, but the spell wasn't broken. If anything, it had grown stronger—just out of reach.

"Of course." She grabbed a stack of books and set them in front of her sister.

When Rhiannon didn't respond, she looked down at her. Relaxed hands, deep rhythmic breathing. She was asleep. Her sister, who loved books on spells more than anything, had fallen asleep even with the prospect of searching through them looking for a specific spell. An activity that normally would keep her awake at all hours of the night couldn't even stop her from falling asleep right after she had awakened.

She needed help. And if it wasn't here, then she would have to go somewhere else to find it.

Archer hadn't even taken his second sip of coffee when the bell rang.

He glanced towards the front door from his seat in the study, the cup paused halfway to his lips. The house was still draped in a muffled hush of early morning—most of the staff moving quietly, as though afraid to disturb any of the home's occupants still sleeping off whatever enchantments lingered from the night before. His own thoughts had yet to settle. He hadn't slept.

Not after the way she had looked at him on the dance floor. Not after the almost-kiss that had nearly undone him.

The door opened down the hall, and footsteps echoed briskly across the marble. Then a familiar voice—impatient, determined.

"I need to speak with Mr. Thornfield. Now, please."

Archer stood before he could think, abandoning his coffee entirely. By the time he reached the front hall, she pushed her way past the butler and was looking into the drawing room—wind-flushed cheeks, curls cascading down her back, a worn satchel slung over one shoulder, and her cloak trailing behind her, somewhat longer on one side, like she hadn't taken the time to fasten it properly. Tatianna Wylde, burning with purpose.

"Tatianna," he said, halting before he ran into her.

She turned towards him immediately, her green eyes bright with urgency. "We have to go."

He blinked. "Go . . . where?"

"To the library," she said, already stepping forward, pushing past the butler again who continued to follow her around the foyer. Needless to say, the servant still looked mildly scandalized by her entrance.

"We can start with the one in town. Or we can go straight to the next town over, Quillmere, and talk to my friend Nigel. He works at the Hall of Arcane Histories. He might know where the book I'm looking for is located. The Hall specializes in rare grimoires. And they have a collection of archived family spell books in addition to other research materials. I've seen the runes before last night, Archer. The ones on the floor of the ballroom. I know I've seen them before."

Archer caught her by the elbow, not roughly, just enough to still her. "Slow down. You think this spell book and the runes are connected?"

"I don't think," she said. "I know."

There was fire in her now, the same strength he'd seen every time she talked about saving her sisters, when she would set her shoulders against fear and confusion and still moving forward. But now there was desperation, too—a thread of exhaustion that made his chest tighten.

"I couldn't sleep, so I went through every one of my grand-mother's old books this morning," she said, quiet now. "There was nothing. But I remember a volume she used to borrow. A blue spine, silver clasp, margin notes in her handwriting. She said once it belonged to a former archivist at the library; I can't remember which library, though. Maybe it's the one here, or maybe it's in Quillmere. I'm sure that's where I've seen the runes."

Archer didn't hesitate. "I'll ready the carriage."

She blinked, just once, maybe surprised by his quick agreement. "You'll come with me?"

"Of course I will. We agreed to do this together," he said. "I meant it then, and it is even more true now."

Tatianna's eyes searched his for a moment. He didn't know what she was looking for, but whatever it was, she must have found it. The longer she searched, the softer her gaze became. There was something, maybe hope in them that hadn't been there the night before. Seeing those runes had narrowed her purpose, given her something to focus on. And he intended to be by her side every step of the way, aiding her in her search. Not only did he want to help her, but finding answers affected his and Lysander's sisters too.

She nodded once. "Thank you."

Archer turned, calling for his valet to prepare for travel, but as he did, a single thought rose like a fog across his mind—sharp, unrelenting.

If she figured out the mystery behind the runes . . . how close were they to unraveling everything? And would discovering the truth destroy whatever was growing between them?

Chapter 19

The bell above the door chimed with cheer, which was utterly at odds with the tension humming beneath Tatianna's skin. She sneezed, her body having already had its fill of dusty tomes, but here she was, in another room where dust-motes danced in the shafts of sunlight that spilled through the tall windows, illuminating rows of sagging shelves too old to creak anymore. The only thing keeping them from cracking was a strength spell that shimmered like chain-mail.

"This won't take long," Tatianna murmured as they entered. Every time Rhiannon came to town, she insisted on stopping at the library, so now Tatianna had memorized where every section was during the many hours she'd spent walking around the small building. She moved towards the arcane section with brisk determination, already tugging off her gloves.

Archer followed, quiet, watching her like he always did. It had become something she could sense, his observant gaze that steadied her overwrought nerves.

He stopped when she did, leaning against the shelves while she searched.

The library's spell books were mostly surface-level: local hedge witch diaries, herbals and potions, a few grimoires with overly elaborate covers, but very little substance. There wasn't a single book that discussed runes.

"I know I've seen those runes before," she muttered, running her fingers along a cracked spine. "But not here."

"I believe you," Archer said, though his voice sounded distant.

Then came the unmistakable voice, slithering through the quiet like a blade wrapped in silk.

"Well, well. If it isn't Lady Tatianna Wylde and her ever-brooding shadow."

Tatianna stood, her posture stiff and unwelcoming. Archer gritted his teeth, his jaw tensed before he even turned toward the intruder.

Malric Wrenne stood in the aisle, dressed impeccably in a deep green coat, a too-knowing smile playing on his lips. "Researching spells at the local lending library?" he asked. "Charming."

"What are you doing here?" Tatianna asked, not bothering to hide her distaste.

"Oh, I occasionally check in on the locals," Malric replied breezily, picking a book off the shelf and flipping through it without looking at it. "You never know what little treasures you'll find buried in small towns."

"I'm surprised you find anything here worth your time," she said, folding her arms.

"I find you fascinating, my lady." His eyes flicked to Archer. "Both of you."

Tatianna's scowl deepened, but Archer's silence was stonier than usual.

Malric's gaze lingered a moment longer, and then he bowed ever-so-slightly. "Well. Do enjoy your reading." And with that, he disappeared down another aisle, his footsteps soundless.

They stayed where they were, silent until they heard the bell's cheerful chime and the click of a door shutting.

Tatianna let out a breath. "I don't trust him. There's very little I know about him, but he makes my skin crawl."

"You are not alone in your distrust," Archer said, voice rough.

"But..." She looked towards the shelves, suddenly uncertain. "You don't think he's involved, do you? Celestine is rather taken with him. Maybe I should warn her away. Not that it would do any good. She's as headstrong as the rest of the Wyldes, myself included."

Archer didn't answer. There was a stillness in him now, a quiet withdrawal. His shoulders hunched, folding inward like he was trying to vanish beneath the weight of something unspoken.

He reached out, steadying himself against a bookshelf. His hand trembled.

"He did so much more than use my magic," he whispered.

Tatianna stopped her rambling and turned. "What?"

Archer's eyes were distant. "I always knew he used my magic without my consent. But it was so much more than that. He . . . he used me. My magic. Twisted it. I trusted him—we were boys—but he knew what I could do, and he took it."

Tatianna stepped closer, her voice soft. "What did he take?"

"I don't know," Archer murmured, pain flickering behind his eyes. "I only remember the aftermath. Lying in the field. I thought I was going to die."

She touched his arm. "But you didn't."

"No," he said, blinking hard. "But part of me stayed in that field. And since that moment, I've let everyone believe I don't have magic."

The morning had grown warm while they were inside, the kind of still, soft heat that settled gently over the cobblestones and brought out the scent of blooming wisteria. There was no breeze as they walked back to the carriage in silence. The quiet between them was thick now—not uncomfortable, taut. Waiting.

Archer felt stretched thin—too many nights without sleep, too many half-buried thoughts scratching at the edges of memory, too many unanswered questions.

Tatianna walked beside him, fingers fiddling with the button of her glove, lips pursed in thought.

He felt her glance more than he saw it.

He could feel the questions burning inside her, hovering on her tongue as she practiced the words in her head. Trying to find the right arrangement that didn't feel intrusive. But she must not have found them. And he didn't offer any words as an answer to her unspoken questions. He couldn't.

Not yet.

The memory sat raw in his chest, it felt tight, like something ancient and cold had cracked open inside him.

The burst of power rushing out of him, like a dam had broken, the echoing silence afterward. Malric's hand on his shoulder—almost gentle—as he'd drained him. The way the light had dimmed all at once, as if the world had closed its eyes to what was happening. Or maybe it was just his eyes closing, not possessing the energy to keep them open. Whatever it was, he was abandoned on that field, helpless, alone.

She finally spoke.

"You said you thought you were going to die."

"I did." He did not elaborate.

A beat.

"Why didn't you tell anyone?" Her question was quiet, her voice steady and soothing.

"I tried. The only person who believed me was Aisling." His voice came out quieter than he'd meant. In that moment, his entire body burned, like salt poured on an open wound, one he believed had closed long ago. "By the time I made it back to school, the rumors had already spread. I'd been reckless. That I'd overreached."

Tatianna slowed, turning to face him. "But you weren't reckless."

"No." He met her gaze. "Just naïve."

The truth settled between them. He could see the weight of what he had just told her behind her eyes—the anger, the sympathy, the instinct to fix.

"You're not that boy anymore, Archer."

He wanted to believe that. He wished he did.

But before he could say it aloud, she stepped back and looked down the road. "We need to go to Quillmere. That book—the one with my grandmother's notes—it's there. It has to be."

Archer nodded, relieved she'd changed the topic of conversation. "Then we go."

She offered him a small smile, faint but real, and for a moment he could breathe again. This—being with her, working side-by-side—it made the past fade away, at least momentarily.

As they turned down the path, he stayed a step behind her, watching the way sunlight caught in her hair, how her shoulders set with resolve. He didn't know what they would find in Quillmere. But for the first time in years, he didn't feel like he was running from his past.

He was walking towards something.

Towards her.

Tatianna had returned home after the visit to the library. As much as she wanted to hop into Archer's carriage and leave without a word, she needed a change of clothes at the very least. And it didn't feel right to leave without telling any of her sisters where she was going. Especially since she needed one of them to lie to her mother and convince them she was traveling with Evangeline.

So now, she stood in front of her trunk, trying to decide how many traveling cloaks one might need when chasing cursed magic across counties. Two seemed reasonable, but was three excessive?

She sighed, sending the second cloak to her trunk with a decisive flick of her wrist. This wasn't just a trip for answers anymore—it was something else, something laced with the edge of purpose. Archer's revelations had rattled her. Not because she didn't believe him—she did, fiercely—but because of how much he had never said.

He had nearly died. And only his sister had known.

A soft knock at her bedroom door made her turn. Leondria leaned in, her expression unreadable. "You're really going, then?"

Tatianna looked up at her sister—noting Leondria, the dark circles under her eyes, and the pallor of her skin—and Tatianna nodded. "I have to. The book's there. I remember seeing it with Grandmama—an entire margin full of her notes on protective runes. I think it's the same spell work from the ball. I know you don't remember the ball or disappearing almost every night, but you are, and so are Rhiannon and Celestine. It's even affected Aisling and Lilith."

Leondria stepped inside, smoothing her hand down her skirt. "I know—well, I don't actually know, but I believe you. Quillmere's not exactly welcoming to strangers though."

"Neither are most places with answers," Tatianna replied. "And Nigel is there; hopefully knowing him will ease our way."

There was a pause.

"Will you be safe with him?" Leondria asked quietly, trying to hide a yawn.

Tatianna hesitated. "Yes. Of course I will."

She didn't mention how she'd felt when they had almost kissed. Or the way Archer had looked at her that morning when she had barged into his home— She definitely didn't mention the ache in her chest when she saw how he looked at her. She didn't say that she trusted him, perhaps too much, or that some foolish, starlit part of her wanted to believe in him entirely. All of that had to wait. For now, she had a spell to unravel.

"I'm not going far," she added gently. "It's only the next town over. I should be back late tomorrow, or the next day, depending on how long it takes to find what I'm looking for."

Leondria nodded, then leaned forward to kiss her cheek. "Bring us something interesting. A relic. Or a scandal."

"I'll do my best." She started to walk away, but stopped. "Try to keep Celestine away from Mr. Wrenne. He's not a gentleman to be trusted."

Leondria nodded. Tatianna hoped the warning wasn't too late.

With her satchel slung over one shoulder and her cloak clasped at the neck, Tatianna headed downstairs. With a quick flick of her fingers, her trunk followed her to where Archer was waiting by the front gate, one hand resting on the handle of a small leather case. He glanced up as she approached, offering a nod that felt heavier than usual—until he saw her trunk floating behind her.

"Ready?" he asked.

"As I'll ever be."

"Are you sure you packed enough?" he asked with the lop-sided smile that made her heart flutter.

She rolled her eyes. "I can go back and pack more."

She gestured at the trunk, and it floated to the back of the carriage, where it stayed as the leather straps tightened around it. She magically ensured it was secured for the trip before offering him her hand.

They started towards the carriage, the early spring breeze tugging at the hem of her dress as he helped her up. Quillmere loomed ahead—wild and wood-bound, tucked between rivers and hills—and at its heart, the Hall of Arcane Histories where Nigel waited, and hopefully, so did answers. Soon Bramblewick would be behind them. She could only hope the stories of Quillmere were greatly exaggerated.

But even now, as she sat next to Archer in his well-appointed carriage, something buzzed beneath her skin. A warning. Or perhaps anticipation.

Because the truth wasn't buried. It was waiting.

And Tatianna intended to find it.

Chapter 20

"If you have a trunk for the trip, what's in your satchel?" Archer asked, curiosity getting the better of him.

She smiled at him from across the carriage. The rhythmic clopping of hooves and the wooden wheels crunching against the dirt road made a kind of music all their own.

"Wouldn't you like to know?" she teased. The tension that lived beneath her skin hadn't vanished, but for a moment, she reached for the levity that used to come so easily.

Sensing her need for something lighter, he played along. "I do. But if I'm prying, I suppose I'll have to suffer the suspense a little longer—hopefully not forever."

Her smile lit the interior of the carriage. "Then I suppose I'd better put you out of your misery. I intended to share the contents with you anyway."

She opened the satchel with a flourish, revealing a careful array of parcels and wrapped bundles. "I brought snacks."

Archer leaned forward, his eyes taking in the assortment of goodies with amusement. "Is that a whole wheel of cheese?"

She nodded, clearly proud of herself. "And I brought three types of biscuits. I wasn't sure which kind you liked. Plus, I have dried fruits, candied ginger in case one of us suffers from travel sickness, and two jars of honey. One lavender, one orange blossom. Oh—and tea. Obviously."

"Obviously," he echoed, smiling despite himself. "Planning to feed an entire regiment?"

"I wasn't sure what kind of food Quillmere would offer. The stories of the town leave much to be desired. And besides," she added, her voice softening, "sometimes a good snack can fortify you better than a spell."

There it was again, that flicker of the old Tatianna—clever, prepared, shining through the worry with stubborn hope, the Tatianna he met in the meadow before everyone she loved was threatened by an unknown person who cast an unknown spell.

He watched her wrap the food back up, her movements slower now. Her shoulders sagged with the weight of too many unanswered questions and too many sleepless nights. As she tucked the last jar into place, she gave a little sigh, then leaned against the cushioned corner of the carriage seat.

"We'll find something," he said quietly, unsure whether he meant the book, the answers, or simply peace. "We always seem to, don't we?"

She gave a sleepy smile, eyelids heavy. "I guess . . . it's not always what we're looking for though."

The rhythm of the carriage changed subtly as they passed into a shaded stretch of road, the dappling light and rolling wheels lulling the interior into a soft hush. Rain drops hit the roof of the carriage, adding to the orchestra of their travels. Tatianna blinked once, twice, then let her eyes close.

Archer didn't speak. He just watched as her breath slowed and steadied, her face relaxing for the first time in days. One hand slipped free from her cloak, resting open beside the satchel, palm faintly glowing with the after-resonance of spent magic. He resisted the urge to touch it.

Instead, he leaned back and turned his gaze to the window. The trees of Quillmere's outskirts whispered past, and across from him, the woman who had shaken loose something long buried inside him finally slept.

The carriage jolted to the left, and Tatianna slipped off the seat. He caught her and pulled her close to his side, holding her in his arms so she could get the rest she so desperately needed.

The carriage wheels clattered over cobblestones, slick with rain, sending up the occasional splash of water as they passed under wrought-iron gas lamps and drooping lilac trees. Quillmere emerged through the misty rain like something from a dream   its rooftops uneven, its chimneys tall and spindly, and every shopfront painted a different faded pastel. The scent of parchment, ink, and blooming rosemary hung in the air.

Inside the carriage, Tatianna slept, her head snuggled into the crook of his shoulder, one hand tucked under her chin, the other rested on his chest, fingers splayed. Archer had tried to rest, but his thoughts kept pace with the horses, each clop of their hooves sending another thought through his tired brain. The runes. Malric. Her hand slipping into his as they danced in the glamoured ruins. The near-kiss he hadn't been brave enough to finish, no matter how desperately he wanted to.

He glanced at her again. Peaceful. Still.

The carriage slowed, turning down a narrow lane lined with low stone walls and curling vines. Up ahead, nestled between a cloistered garden and a green-domed observatory, stood the Hall of Arcane Histories. The government building's grey stone façade was weathered but proud, the stained-glass windows glinted with symbols older than the town itself. The building looked more like a grand old library than a government hall, but Archer supposed that it was more a library than anything related to the government.

The carriage jerked slightly as it came to a full stop. His arms tightened around her, preventing her from slipping.

"Tatianna," he said, voice low, reluctant to pull her from sleep.

She stirred at once. Blinking up at him, she straightened, eyes widening as she took in their surroundings and her location in his arms. "We're here?"

He nodded. "We are. I thought we might stop for a room, get settled first—"

"No," she interrupted, already reaching for her cloak. "We go straight to the Hall. If Nigel has my grandmother's books, or knows anything about those runes, I want to see him before he disappears behind some locked archive."

Archer hesitated. "You haven't even eaten. You fell asleep before partaking of the feast you packed."

"I'm not hungry," she said, though her stomach rumbled faintly in protest. "We'll get food after we talk to Nigel. Come on."

Before he could argue, she'd swung the carriage door open and stepped down to the cobblestones. He followed, waving off the footman who reached for their bags. "We'll be back for those," he said.

Tatianna's gaze swept over the building as they approached the heavy wooden doors. "This is the place," she murmured, almost to herself. "I can feel it."

Archer opened one of the arched doors for her, and together, they stepped into the cool hush of the Hall.

The Hall of Arcane Histories opened into an awe-inspiring vaulted foyer of dusky pink marble and polished oak, lined with floor-to-ceiling shelves holding tomes both ancient and new. A narrow catwalk circled the room's perimeter, offering access to each level of shelves. Magic hummed in the air—wards woven into the very stone, protective enchantments slumbered behind elegant carvings of mythical beasts, blossoms, and runes Tatianna half-recognized. Light filtered through stained-glass depictions of sorcerer scholars, casting fractured rainbows across the inlaid floor. A spiral staircase twisted upward, its steps winding past each level through enchanted gates that shimmered faintly in the glow. The faint scent of incense mixed with parchment and leather wafted through the air.

No one greeted them at the door. Instead, a bell chimed somewhere in the distance, but otherwise, the hall was quiet.

Tatianna glanced around, eyes narrowing with focus. "Research chambers will be through there," she said, gesturing towards a narrow archway off the main corridor. "Archives tend to be east-facing. Better morning light."

Archer raised an eyebrow. "You sound like you've spent your life in places like this."

She offered him a sly smile. "Have you not had the pleasure of conversing with Rhiannon? She's dragged me to so many libraries I've lost count. My general distaste for spells normally leaves me with nothing to do but wander around. I've discovered most libraries have many things in common: one of which is their layout."

They passed under a paneled ceiling and deeper into a maze of corridors, where the scent shifted—more dust, leather, and parchment now, less incense. The halls grew quieter, the silence heavy, as if the knowledge contained within the walls had its own gravity.

Just as they turned a corner past a row of shelves marked Siren and Merfolk Histories: Cross-Referenced, a man in a navy waistcoat, rolled up sleeves, and a bow tie nearly collided with them.

"Well, now!" he exclaimed, steadying himself. His eyes widened behind his round, wire-rimmed glasses when they landed on Tatianna. "I see you've arrived safely, Miss Wylde."

Tatianna blinked, trying not to laugh at the librarian's owl-like appearance. "Yes—it's so nice to see you again, Nigel, although I wish it was under better circumstances."

"I've heard there are some unique going-ons in Bramblewick," he said, smiling, delighted to be recognized. "Miss Wylde, your older sister, I believe, sent word ahead you would be arriving. And if I may say, you have *excellent* timing. There's a fresh pot of tea in the scrying room, and I've just uncovered a rather interesting collection on corrupted protective wards. Although, I believe you're looking for something specific?"

"The runes," Tatianna said, serious now. She pulled the drawing of the markings out of her pocket. "They were carved into the ballroom floor—well, the illusion of one. I know I've seen them before. I think in the margins of one of my grandmother's books."

Nigel nodded, already walking briskly ahead, muttering as he walked past the stacks. He snapped. "Ah yes, we'd best start in the Etheric language collection. This way—"

They followed him down two more winding halls and up a different spiral staircase. Tatianna's fingers itched with anticipation as they entered a warm, dim room where the air was thick with dormant spells, and recently disturbed dust danced like embers.

He led them to a glass cabinet and pulled out a thick, leather-bound volume with a worn sigil on the spine. As he set it on a reading desk, the cover gave a faint shimmer—as if waking up—before it settled into the blue she remembered so vividly.

"This belonged to Adalina Wylde, yes?" Nigel asked.

Tatianna nodded, reverent as she opened the book. Inside, her grandmother's notes curved in scrawling script around sketched diagrams where she had translated the runes and speculated on the spells the symbols could carry out.

Archer leaned over her shoulder as she flipped through the pages—then stopped.

"There," she said, her finger landing on the pattern from her sketch. "That's the one. The exact design from the ballroom floor."

Nigel hummed, adjusting his glasses. "Curious thing. You're not the first to ask about this book recently."

Tatianna looked up sharply. "I'm not?"

"No," Nigel said slowly. "A woman came through just a few weeks ago. Stylish. Demanding. I remember she asked very specifically for this volume—she spent quite a few hours with it before leaving. It's been out for cataloguing ever since. In fact, we just got it back yesterday."

Tatianna and Archer exchanged a glance.

"Did she leave her name?" Archer asked.

"I'm afraid not," Nigel said, frowning. "But she knew what she was looking for. That's for certain."

Tatianna's heart picked up pace. "If she wanted this book, then she must be the one that's doing all this—the ball, the runes, everything."

Archer nodded grimly. "Which means we're at least on the right trail. Even if we are still two steps behind."

She nodded in agreement. "We have to figure out what this spell is being used for. Unfortunately, I'm terrible at written spells."

She stood with the opened book cradled gently in her hands, her eyes tracing the circular lines of the runes inked into the yellowed vellum. The scent of old paper and lavender ink stirred something in her memory—something important, she knew it, but it was just out of reach.

She looked up at Nigel, who watched her with quiet curiosity over the rim of his spectacles. "Would it be possible," she asked, "to make copies of these pages? Just the ones with the runes. I want to study them, but I don't want to be a bother."

Nigel blinked once, pondering her words, then smiled, pleased with her instincts. "Of course, I know just the thing," he said, snapping his fingers. "We have a copying charm that leaves the originals untouched. It will take just a few minutes. If you'd like, I can also give you a reference sheet to help you determine the meaning of the older runic forms. Some of these predate standardized spell weaving."

"That would be perfect, thank you." Tatianna exhaled, her tension easing a fraction. She gently passed the open book back to him, her fingers lingering for a moment on the edge of the page.

Nigel took the tome and moved towards a nearby worktable beneath a leaded glass window that cast rainbows around the room that reminded her of fairies dancing. "I'm just going to work over here. This charm takes up a decent amount of space," he said cheerfully. "You may want to have a seat yourselves. This will take a moment—and you both look like you've had a week of rough nights."

Tatianna gave a soft laugh that didn't quite reach her eyes. "You don't know the half of it." She lowered herself into an armchair, eyes focused on the shelves in front of her as her fingers tapped the desk in a staccato rhythm. "This is progress. These copies will allow us to study the spell, see if the structure of the spell gives us any clue as to what kind of magic we're dealing with."

Archer stood quietly beside her, his arms crossed, his gaze fixed on the sketch of the runes as if trying to remember something long since forgotten .

Chapter 21

"Should a lady find herself accompanied on a magical errand by a man who listens more than he lectures, she is advised not to let him go." Magic, Manners, and Mishaps: A Collection of Essays compiled by Mrs. Peregrine of Bramblewick Ladies' Academy for the Magically-Inclined

Tatianna stood, drifting towards a velvet-upholstered bench under a window. She let her eyes rest on the dust dancing in the sunlight that filtered through the leaded glass. Archer followed, sitting beside her close, but not too close, his hands loosely clasped in front of him.

For a moment, neither spoke, both too occupied with their own thoughts.

"You've been quiet," she said, not accusing, just observing. Her voice was soft, carrying only to him.

Archer didn't answer at first. "Because memories long forgotten are rushing back, but I don't know what's real or my imagination."

She tilted her head. "The spell? Or before, when you were at school?"

He nodded. "I'm trying to remember more from before . . . to determine what I don't remember. What's my recollection and what was shaped by someone else's will. It's like parts of my past lives in the thick fog of dawn, and every time I try to look too closely, I only see shadows walking away in the mist." He paused, fingers tightening. "And Malric is always there, somehow. Smiling like none of it mattered."

Tatianna's heart clenched. She resisted the urge to reach for his hand. Instead, she leaned in a little closer, bumping his shoulder with hers. "We'll sort it out. We're already starting to. One tiny piece of the puzzle at a time."

He gave a faint lopsided smile, a smile she was starting to look forward to seeing.

"You make it sound simple," he said.

"No," she said, the teasing tone dropped from her voice. "But I'm not leaving you to do this alone. Remember, we agreed, we're in this together."

The silence that followed was warmer. It no longer felt as fragile as blown glass.

Just then, Nigel approached with a tidy bundle of parchment. He handed it to Tatianna with reverent care, as though he was passing along something far more delicate than mere copies.

"These are your pages," he said, then added thoughtfully, "There's something odd, though." He took off his glasses, scratching his head with the earpiece. He opened the book and set it on the table before gesturing for Tatianna and Archer to join him. "The ink used in this section is not original to the book. It can't be, see here . . ." He pointed to something only he knew to look for. "Older ink and pens never left lines that precise. Current writing tools leave much cleaner lines. This first part was written in the early 1800s. The ink gives it away: look at how it has little lines that move away from the lettering like a spider web. But this ink is newer. It doesn't do that at all, probably added in the last twenty years."

Archer frowned. "At the very least, that means someone modified the spell."

"Or trying to hide something in plain sight," Nigel agreed. "Either way, I don't think anyone was supposed to discover the addition."

Tatianna opened her mouth to ask another question, but Nigel had already turned back towards the desk with a distracted murmur, "Strange how the other woman asked for the exact same pages . . ."

"Other woman?" Archer echoed, but Nigel was already halfway down the row of shelves, waving a hand over another stack of books. The books took to the air and flapped their way to the shelves they called home. Nigel hummed as he kept walking, his mind clearly elsewhere.

Tatianna watched Nigel, then looked over at Archer. "I wonder who else was here looking for this book. Do you think she cast the spell?"

"Maybe." He didn't sound convinced.

She shoved the pages into her satchel. "Let's take these to the inn. I need nourishment and a nap. Then, we can look at these pages with fresh eyes and figure out what these runes are used for."

Archer offered his arm. "Come on, then. We've got pages to pore over, a mystery woman to identify, and hopefully, a room with more than one chair."

"And maybe a window that doesn't rattle in the wind," she added with a tired smile.

They stepped back into the light filtering through the great doors of the Hall, parchment bundle secured, questions multiplying with every step.

After being turned away from three inns, they arrived at the last acceptable inn in Quillmere, the Fox and Fern. The place looked like something plucked from the pages of a well-worn storybook—half-timbered, ivy-covered, and glowing warmly in the early twilight. Lanterns swung gently outside the door, casting a welcoming golden light across the cobbled path.

Tatianna leaned against Archer as they stepped through the door, exhaustion creeping into her bones now that they'd gone from one public house to the next after leaving the Hall. She clutched her bag to her chest, wanting nothing more than to be able to sit somewhere for the night and sleep. Even if that was an unlikely scenario.

Archer held the door to the Fox and Fern open for her. She stepped through the arched doorway and couldn't help but sigh. Inside, the inn smelled of spiced stew, cinnamon baked apples, and wood smoke. A rosy-cheeked innkeeper greeted them with a wide smile and ink-smudged hands.

"Room for two?" she asked cheerfully, already reaching for a key.

"Yes," Tatianna said at the same time Archer muttered, "Two rooms, if you've got them."

The innkeeper blinked at them, then laughed. "Ah, young travelers. I'd give you as many as you like, but I've only one room left. Festival season, you know. You're lucky to get that."

Tatianna felt Archer go still beside her. She turned to him, arching a brow. "Unless you want to sleep in the stables . . . After all, this is the only inn we haven't been to, and it does have a room available. Unlike all the others."

"As charming as sleeping on hay might seem, a room with a fireplace would be preferred," he said dryly, then sighed and nodded to the innkeeper. "We'll take it."

The room was small but charming, tucked into the eaves with low beams and a little window overlooking a trickling stream. There was just enough room for a small table and two chairs tucked into the corner near the fireplace, which already had a crackling fire in it. The bed was wide and covered in a patchwork quilt in soft blues and greens, taking up almost every inch of space in the cozy room.

"Well," Archer said as he set his satchel on the writing desk, "at least it's not a cot."

Tatianna set the parchment bundle down on the table, laying out the pages next to each other. "We'll figure out the sleeping arrangements later. I want to look through these pages before I forget what Nigel said. Are you any good at reading spells? I'm quite terrible at it. At least, I'm terrible at casting spells from spell books. Maybe I'll discover that I have a natural talent for discovering a spell's purpose, even if my magic refuses to cooperate with the written word."

He leaned against the doorframe as she chattered, words spilling out of her mouth like water over a cliff. He watched her pull out a notebook and uncork a small inkwell. "You're avoiding the inevitable, you know."

She glanced up. "The spell?"

He grinned faintly. "The bed."

Her lips quirked, but she didn't take the bait. "You snore, don't you?"

"Only when cursed or nearly murdered," he said. "So, odds are decent I won't tonight. Unless you have plans I don't know about."

She shook her head and laughed softly, her eyes warm. "Just try not to steal the covers, Mr. Thornfield."

His heart gave an unexpected lurch at the way she said it—light, teasing, but with something deeper threading beneath it. He wondered if she had intended her words to sound that way. Not that he should be thinking about that right now.

They had a spell to unravel, a mystery woman to identify, and secrets still curled in the shadows between them. But for now, there was candlelight, quiet pages, and the growing tension of proximity.

And one bed.

By the time Archer returned from downstairs with a tray balanced in one hand—laden with warm bread, two bowls of spiced stew, a wedge of soft cheese, and a pot of tea—Tatianna already had written half a dozen pages of notes, most of which were crumpled and tossed onto the floor. The copies Nigel had made for them were spread across the table and pinned beneath smooth river stones she'd conjured from her satchel.

She barely looked up when he entered. "Thank you," she murmured.

She stacked a few pages, making room on the small table for the tray. Archer set the food between them while Tatianna continued to study the different spells in front of her, reaching for a slice of bread without breaking her focus.

He pulled his chair closer and leaned in. Candlelight flickered over the ancient symbols and scrolling penmanship, while the faint shimmer of magic danced along the ink as if the paper knew it held the secrets to a spell.

Tatianna tapped one of the diagrams with the tip of her pen as she looked over the sheet of runes Nigel had given her. "It's a siphoning spell. I'm certain of it now."

He frowned. "Siphoning what? Magic from others?"

"Yes, but . . ." She trailed off, flipping through the pages, her brow furrowed. "It wasn't malicious. At least, not originally. The way this is designed—look here, see this sequence?—the magic wasn't stolen just to steal. It was meant to sustain someone whose body rejected their own power."

"Someone allergic to their own magic?" Archer asked, brows raising. "I didn't even know that was possible."

She nodded. "My mother told me about a great-aunt of ours who was so inflicted. I never knew if she was telling the truth or trying to frighten me in to only using spells. This great-aunt was very much like me." She shrugged. "I was always told careless use of magic would eventually cause my body to reject the power, and it would make me ill, unbearably so. I would be weak, eventually so weak I wouldn't be able to fight it, and the magic would consume me."

Archer stared at her, eyebrow raised. "And your mother told you all this to force you to use spells?"

She nodded. "I convinced Rhiannon to research it for me. While it is true that a person's body can reject their power—develop an allergy, as you so succinctly put it—there are no ties to the way in which a person uses their magic. But Rhiannon discovered that a potential cure was to siphon magic from others—carefully, deliberately—you could stabilize them. Maybe even heal the person completely."

He glanced at the pages filled with symbols, careful hand-drawn lines, the margin notes in spidery script. "Then why did it affect your sisters so much more than anyone else?"

"We don't know for sure my sisters have been affected the most. My friend Evangeline has barely been seen out and about since the ball in the meadow. Your sister's been unwell too, but she's not one to use magic for daily tasks." She tapped the table with her fingers, drumming a staccato beat. "Something must have gone wrong when the spell was cast. Something more than my protection spell," she said. "Something has shifted the balance, so the spell is taking too much from certain people, or maybe it's everyone. I've watched as their auras have dimmed—not to mention when Rhianon and Leondria couldn't use their magic properly." Her eyes darkened. "Someone must be taking too much. Whether by accident or design . . ." Her words lost shape around a yawn. The adrenaline of discovery gave way to the exhaustion she'd been holding at bay all day. Her pen dropped onto the parchment, and she blinked slowly at the glowing runes.

Archer watched her head dip forward, chin brushing her shoulder as sleep finally won. A smile touched his lips, soft and fond. He rose from his chair, stepped quietly to her side, and scooped her into his arms.

She murmured something incoherent and nestled instinctively closer.

"You're relentless," he whispered, cradling her like something precious. "And far too tired to be up solving ancient curses and the mysteries surrounding them."

He laid her gently on the bed, pulling the quilt up around her shoulders and brushing a loose curl from her cheek. For one lingering moment, he studied her face in the lamplight—strong, stubborn, radiant, even in sleep.

Then he bent and pressed a kiss to her forehead. "Sleep well, Tatianna Wylde."

Before climbing into bed himself, Archer built a divide down the middle of the bed with extra pillows, creating a barrier between them. Not because he feared himself, but because he respected her. Their situation was precarious enough without making her worry that some impropriety had occurred.

He settled on top of the covers, arms folded behind his head, listening to the crackling of the fire and the steady rhythm of her breathing.

Sleep didn't come easily. Not with secrets still coiled in his chest.

Not with memories creeping back like shadows just out of reach.

Not with her inches away.

Chapter 22

Morning light filtered through the window, illuminating the room with its golden glow. Tatianna sighed before throwing her arm over her eyes to block out the sun's rays, which were rudely interrupting her slumber. She burrowed deeper into the bed in her attempt to escape its persistence when her backside bumped into something solid.

She pried one eye open and gazed upon a room that was unfamiliar to her. Momentarily lost, she opened both eyes, and everything came flooding back. This was a room at an inn, and she was not alone. Pushing herself up on her elbows, she looked at the man lying next to her.

Archer lay atop the covers, his cloak wrapped around him like a makeshift blanket, one arm thrown over her waist, a soft line of concern furrowing his brow even in sleep. Between them, pillows. Apparently, he made a barrier between them last night after she had drifted off to sleep. It hadn't held up as well as he probably thought it would. Somehow, despite his precautions, she'd ended up in his arms.

She stared at him a moment longer than she should have, her heart flip-flopped just thinking about his need to not overstep any further than what had already occurred. The impropriety of sharing a room would destroy her reputation if it were ever discovered. But that hadn't stopped him from trying to protect her. And something about that simple boundary, that quiet respect, made her chest ache.

Tatianna slipped from the bed, careful not to disturb him. She stood, shivering, and instantly regretted leaving the cocoon of warmth his body had created. She sighed, grabbing her cloak and pulled on the outer layer with quiet efficiency. She didn't wake him until she'd washed her face and pinned back her hair, leaving most of it cascading down her back.

"Archer," she said, nudging his boot.

His eyes fluttered open. "You didn't leave," he murmured, blinking up at her.

"Not yet. But you better hurry and get ready or I might just have to leave you if you're going to lollygag around." She glanced out the window. "We've a long ride ahead, and I'd rather not spend half of it arguing about whether or not we should stop for breakfast."

A wry smile curved his lips as he sat up. "Then I'll have to bribe the coachman to pack food for the road."

She gathered the papers from the table as he went about his morning ablutions. It wasn't long before they were packed and headed downstairs to begin their journey home.

The road curved through golden fields and budding orchards as the carriage rocked gently beneath them. Bramblewick was still a few hours away, but the shadows had already begun to move, elongating as the sun moved lower in the sky. Clouds formed overhead, heavy and grey, and the breeze carried the early scent of rain.

Tatianna folded the pages, placing them on her lap with a sigh, glancing sideways at Archer. "We have to talk to Lady Cordelia. I believe she's the woman Nigel mentioned. You do agree, don't you?"

Archer shifted in his seat, gaze fixed on the countryside slipping past the window. "I think suspicion and truth are not always the same thing."

"You didn't answer me."

He exhaled through his nose, folding his arms. "No, I don't think you're wrong, not necessarily. I think you're too close to be objective. And rushing to an accusation is not the wisest course of action."

"I think her daughter is the key," she said, ignoring the slight warning in his voice. "Something's wrong with her. She's always been sickly, but never like this. And Lady Cordelia is always attentive, but now she's . . . desperate. This spell—it's not about power, not entirely. I think she's trying to save Emelie."

"And in doing so, she's hurting others." Archer's tone was controlled.

Tatianna nodded, excited to have a theory. "Exactly. That doesn't make it right. But it makes it human."

Before he could reply, the carriage gave a violent lurch, tossing them towards each other. Archer braced his arm across her shoulders as they slammed back against the seat.

The carriage ground to a halt.

The driver's voice called back apologetically through the partition. "Beg your pardon, sir, miss! One of the axles has given out—I'll need to walk to the nearest town, or maybe there's a farm that has replacement parts, or at least a spare cart, so I can get you back to town. Might be a couple of hours at least."

Archer glanced at Tatianna, who was already peering out the window.

"Well," she said with a wry smile, "at least it's a pleasant spot to be stranded."

They gathered their satchels, wrapped their cloaks tighter against the wind, and stepped down into a quiet patch of overgrown grass. Ahead stood the moss-covered remains of an old stone church, its windows long shattered, ivy crawling over its half-collapsed walls. The tower stood, proud and lonely against the sky.

Archer took the coachman aside, and they discussed something quietly. He handed the driver a handful of bills, then returned to her side.

"This feels like we've walked into a very cursed fairy tale," Tatianna murmured, eyeing the ruins with wary amusement.

Archer chuckled. "Don't say that aloud. The dryads will start humming."

They wandered inside the fallen walls of the stone church, the quiet of nature wrapping around them. Birds chirped in the rafters above. A tree had grown where the altar must have been in days gone by, roots snaking through old flagstones; its branches swayed in the breeze brushing up against a stone wall as it moved. It was a place touched by time, forgotten by civilization, but not by the natural world.

"I vote for a picnic," Tatianna said suddenly, pulling a cloth bundle from her satchel.

"I'm afraid we don't have any more food. We already enjoyed the meal I had the coachman procure for us," he stated, disappointed he wasn't prepared for this unplanned stop.

Tatianna smiled at him, opening her bag so he could see inside.

"You brought more food?" he asked with a raised eyebrow. His lips twitched upward as he fought his need to smile.

"I always bring food." She winked at him. "You never know when you'll be abandoned beside a crumbling ruin in the middle of nowhere."

They settled on a sun-dappled patch of grass near the open wall; the air filled with birdsong and wind through the leaves. Tatianna spread the blanket and set out a modest feast: a loaf of bread, berries, slices of cured meat, a small jar of fig jam, and a wedge of honeyed cheese.

For a time, they ate in companionable silence, the tension of the morning softening under the sunlight. Archer asked her for stories about her and her sisters' escapades. She complied, enjoying talking about her family, exaggerating some of their shenanigans just so she could see his lopsided grin. She inquired about his sister and friendship with the Goldvales. His stories were amusing, and it wasn't long before the sound of laughter echoed faintly through the trees.

Eventually, Archer leaned back on his elbows. "So. If you are to confront Lady Cordelia, what will you say to her?"

Tatianna nibbled a berry thoughtfully. "I'll tell her we know that the spell was meant to heal, but it's hurting people. I'll give her a chance to tell the truth."

"And if she doesn't?"

Tatianna's eyes met his, clear and calm. "Then we stop her."

"And if it's not her?" His quiet words were almost carried away by the breeze.

She glanced up, her expression quizzical. "Then I continue to search for the culprit. I can't stop until I know my family is safe. Whoever is doing this has to be stopped."

A gust of wind tugged at her curls, and Archer caught a loose strand, tucking it behind her ear with absent care.

"You're braver than I am," he said softly.

She tilted her head into his hand. "I don't think that's true. I just think I'm too stubborn to be afraid for long."

Her eyes fluttered shut as they lingered in the warmth of the moment. It felt like the world held its breath around them, or maybe it was just the sprites and dryads silent as their sanctuary was disturbed.

The soft hush of wind moved through the ruined chapel. It was the kind of breeze that made the leaves whisper secrets and the grass bow gently to passing clouds. Their meal had long since dwindled, crumbs clinging to napkins and jam-stained fingers, but neither of them moved to pack up.

Tatianna lay back against the blanket, hair fanned across the mossy stones, her gaze lost in the clouds that raced across the sky above them.

Archer watched her for a long moment, admiring the way the golden light painted her in warm tones and how a moment of peace softened the lines around her eyes. She looked more like the lady he had met in the meadow, more herself than she had been in days.

"You're staring," she said, voice barely above a murmur.

"I am," he admitted with a shrug.

She sat up and turned her head towards him. "Are you going to kiss me properly this time, or do we need a third interruption?"

A faint, self-deprecating laugh escaped him as he pushed up from his reclined state, but he leaned in all the same. Their lips met in a kiss that was no longer hesitant or stolen in shadow. It started sweet, gentle until he swiped his tongue across her lips before drawing her lower lip into his mouth and nibbling on it. When she gasped at the tingling sensation, he took that opportunity to deepen the kiss, and his tongue swept into her open mouth and danced with hers. The kiss was deep, slow, aching with all the weight of what had been unspoken for too long.

When her hands found his collar and his fingers brushed the edge of her waist, the world around them blurred until there was only this moment, this ruin, this hush.

His gentle touch became firmer, pulling her closer to him. Her hands worked their way upward until her arms wrapped around his neck and her fingers tangled in his hair. They kissed for an eternity that passed in a blink of an eye. Archer pulled away, and her arms fell to her side. She followed his movement for a second with a pout, until she felt his lips on the side of her neck, under her ear. He moved from her neck to her ear. She sighed as her body came alive. Every part of her tingled, craving more, wanting whatever came next.

Her fingers stumbled with his tie as she clumsily attempted to untie it. He noticed her movements, taking it off as he moved back to kissing her lips. The tie gone, she worked on his shirt buttons until it gaped open. She went to touch his bare skin, but stopped.

"Can I . . . Is it okay?" Her voice trembled as the words tumbled from her mouth.

Archer caressed her cheek. "I believe I'm supposed to be the one asking that question."

She laughed. "The answer to my question is yes, it's okay, and yes, you can."

He took her hands in his and put them on his chest, then let go. Even with all her time in the sun, her skin was pale compared to his. She caressed his chest, moving her hands down to his abdomen, running her fingers over the hard ridges of his body. He took in a shaky breath, weaving his fingers into her hair before his mouth crashed down on hers.

She kissed him back, her arms circling around his waist under his shirt. It wasn't enough for her to touch him; she wanted his hands on her. He must have read her mind, because his fingers flew over her back, slipping the pearl buttons through their loops until her bodice was gaping open. She slipped it off and tossed it to the side, leaving her covered in only three layers instead of four. Frustrated, she flicked her fingers and more clothes came off, leaving her in just her undergarments.

Archer laughed when he noticed her clothing folding itself in a neat pile next to them. He shrugged off his shirt, followed by his pants, leaving them in a rumpled mess next to her clothes.

Her eyes looked over his body, taking in everything she saw. After a moment of intense perusal, she grabbed him, pulling them both to the ground. He braced himself, keeping the full weight of his body off her before his hand wandered to her waist, caressing her curves. He rained kisses on her from her mouth to her neck and lower. Relishing each unfamiliar sensation, she waited in anticipation of what she would feel next. She sighed as his hand moved lower; she felt its warmth through her cotton pantaloons. His hand skimmed over her thigh until he found the gap in her undergarment.

A jolt of electric sensation coursed through her as he touched her in the most intimate of places. His fingers moved, stroking back and forth, until one slipped inside her, causing every nerve in her body to come alive. Her back arched as the sensation built, stronger, uncontrollable. It took over her entire body. Her toes curled as a dam broke inside her. He held her as her body trembled from everything she'd just felt.

"Are you okay?" he murmured into her hair.

She tilted her head up. "That was . . . I don't know . . . There's more, isn't there?"

He nodded. "There is."

"I want the more."

"You're sure?" He tilted her chin until their eyes met.

She nodded. His lips met hers once again. Gently at first, but desire, already sparked, grew to a burning fire in mere moments. This time, when his fingers found her center, there was a new urgency. As the tension in her built, his fingers were replaced by his length. She felt him press into her, there was a brief twinge of discomfort as her body adjusted, but it passed quickly as the feeling of him sliding in and out of her caused everything she had just felt to return, but stronger, more intense, until her body convulsed as wave after wave of ecstasy crashed through her.

He was right there with her, experiencing his own shattering orgasm at the same time as Tatianna. What passed between them in the remains of the old church was both gentle and fierce, an expression of something deeper than desire. No illusions, no enchantments, no curses. Just two people choosing one another in a moment of quiet between the chaos that consumed them.

Later, they lay in the grass, tangled and half-dressed beneath Archer's cloak, the scent of crushed wildflowers around them, the sky now streaked with pink.

Tatianna traced slow circles on his chest. "I wish we could stay here longer."

"I know," Archer said softly.

But reality had already begun to gather at the edges of their consciences. The sound of hoofbeats approached along the road, slow and deliberate.

They sat up. Tatianna flicked her fingers, and they were fully dressed once again. They stood, and Archer looked down at her, tucking her hair behind her ear just in time for the driver to emerge from the trees, leading a replacement carriage.

"Sorry for the wait," the coachman called. "Had to borrow from the cooper's yard. Should get us back to Bramblewick without further delay."

Tatianna nodded, squeezing Archer's hand once before rising.

As they settled into the fresh carriage and rolled back onto the road, silence hung heavy between them—not awkward. Just full.

"I want you to know, if you need to use my magic to break the spell, you have to do it." He turned towards her, grabbing her hands. "Promise me you will."

She looked at him, thoughts racing through her head. "I don't know. What if I can't control when to stop and I use all your magic, just like Malric did?"

"I trust you." He turned back in his seat, their fingers still interlaced.

And as the road curved back towards Bramblewick, towards truth and confrontation, they sat hand in hand in the growing dusk—two people no longer running from the past, but ready to face whatever came next.

Back to Bramblewick.

Back to truth.

Back to whatever storm was waiting for them.

Chapter 23

The sky had already deepened to indigo by the time the carriage rolled back into Bramblewick, gas lamps casting warm halos of light along the cobbled streets. The comforting sight of home didn't soothe Tatianna as it normally would, not when her mind spun with spell diagrams, half-translated runes, and the weight of a mystery that had yet to be solved.

The carriage came to a slow stop in front of the Wylde's cottage gate. Archer jumped out first, then turned to help Tatianna down from the carriage. She hesitated as her body brushed his, reliving the moment at the ancient church, before stepping away from him, fingers lingering on the sleeve of his coat.

"We have to find a way to undo the spell," she said quietly. "If we're right about the siphoning, then everyone who's trapped at the dance every night is in danger of losing all their magic and potentially their life."

"I know," Archer replied. "And I meant what I said earlier. If my magic can help—even if it's just to amplify yours—I'll gladly give it."

She looked up at him then, surprised by the steadiness in his voice. "I'm not sure I can do that to you."

A shadow crossed his face, but he pushed through it. "Then we'll find another way to stop it. Together. But I promise, this time, I refuse to run from what I can do."

They parted just outside the cottage—Tatianna heading inside to see her sisters, while Archer lingered at the gate, fingers brushing the edge of his sleeve where magic still hummed faintly from the journey.

Inside, the parlor was aglow with light. Leondria sat in her armchair, one leg crossed tightly over the other, an untouched cup of tea growing cold in her lap. Rhiannon sat next to the fire, a forgotten book open in her lap. Celestine lounged on the settee, cheeks flushed with something more than just warmth from the fire. The three of them were silent, lost in their own worlds.

"You're back!" Celestine said, sitting up straight as Tatianna entered. "I was starting to think you'd run off with him."

Celestine's magic still vibrated around her. Anyone that didn't know her well would say she was her normal self. But Tatianna noticed dark circles around her eyes, the way her excitement was muted.

Tatianna blinked. "Run off with—Archer? No. Of course not." She paused. "Wait, why do you look so . . . pleased with yourself?"

Celestine's smile was dreamy, with a touch of self-satisfaction. "Malric called on me this morning."

That brought Leondria's head up sharply.

"He said he enjoyed our conversation at the musicale and couldn't wait to continue our acquaintance," Celestine continued, tracing her fingertip along the embroidery on a throw pillow. "He brought me flowers—peonies. Apparently, he remembered they're my favorite. Isn't that the sweetest?"

Tatianna frowned, setting down her bag. "He remembers a lot of things, doesn't he?"

Celestine waved her off. "Oh, don't be like that. You're always suspicious of anyone charming. Just because he isn't brooding like your Mr. Thornfield doesn't mean he's wicked."

"He's not that brooding," Tatianna muttered under her breath, unheard by anyone.

"He's thoughtful," Celestine went on, eyes unfocused. "And he listens. I told him about Emelie and he seemed genuinely concerned. How she was so much better the night of the musicale, but the next day she seemed more sickly than ever."

Tatianna's spine went rigid. "Do you think he's involved with Lady Cordelia?"

"He didn't say he was. It seemed like he was very concerned about Emelie's health. And he asked a lot of questions about our magic. About you, even."

Leondria finally set down her teacup. "And that didn't strike you as strange?"

"He's *interested*, Leondria. That's not a crime."

"No," Tatianna said slowly, unease crawling up her neck, "but asking about all of our magic . . . That's not normal."

Celestine narrowed her eyes. "You're overreacting."

"Maybe." Tatianna crossed to the fire as her body turned cold, warmth that she didn't feel licking her face, her thoughts were miles away. "Maybe not."

Celestine didn't acknowledge her words—her attention wandered back to the peonies, which now sat in a vase on the side table.

Tatianna looked at Leondria, questions in her eyes. Her sister shrugged, even though concern was etched on her face. Leondria was worried, without knowing what Tatianna knew about Malric. Would Leondria tell her to warn Celestine or would her advice be to stay silent, knowing Celestine would do the opposite of whatever she was told?

Sighing, unable to listen to her sister expound on why Malric was such a dashing gentleman, Tatianna made her way upstairs to her room. She needed to get away from her sister before she exploded. Alone now, she flopped onto her bed, finally allowing her to focus on her own thoughts. Her mind drifted back to the remnants of the church and what had conspired there.

"What has you smiling like a cat that got into the cream?" Leondria asked, jolting Tatianna out of her daydream.

She fingered the edges of the lavender quilt her grandmother made for her, feeling the ridges created from row after row of loving stitches. It brought forth the memory of her hands on Archer's body and warmth flooded her cheeks.

"Now you have to tell me what happened: you're as bright as a strawberry. I've never seen you turn such an alarming color because of an errant thought." Leondria leapt onto Tatianna's bed, her normal sense of propriety set aside in the privacy of this room. "Tell me everything."

And so Tatianna did: she recounted everything that had happened over the last few days, but instead of focusing on the spell and her sisters' disappearing, she talked about Archer, how much he's helped her, supported her, and how she felt things for him she had never felt before. The two of them drifted off to sleep while giggling like girls talking about boys. It was one of those moments the two of them would always cherish.

The market square buzzed with late-morning activity. Stalls brimmed with fruits, vegetables, and cut flowers; the scent of fresh bread wafted from Brambles & Butter. The Wylde sisters strolled arm in arm down the cobbled lane, tired, but they refused to stay home. So now they were here, each of them attempting to comport themselves as if nothing was wrong. Leondria presented her normal self, elegant and composed; Celestine, radiant with mischief; Rhiannon, lost in some fictional world; and Tatianna, half-distracted, searching every face they passed.

She wasn't sure what she expected—Lady Cordelia cloaked in shadows, or Emelie stumbling through the street like a ghost—instead, Malric stumbled across them.

He emerged from the doorway of the Gilded Kettle with the ease of someone at home wherever he was, a pastry box tucked under one arm and a charming smile plastered across his face.

"Well, if it isn't the four loveliest blooms in Bramblewick," he said smoothly, bowing slightly with a grin that sent Celestine into a fit of giggles.

"Mr. Wrenne, you are too kind," Celestine purred, brushing an invisible bit of lint from her shoulder. "We keep bumping into you. It's starting to feel like fate is pushing us together."

"I was just thinking the same." His eyes flicked between them all, but lingered too long on Celestine—and then, pointedly, on Tatianna. "I like to believe fate has a hand in throwing us together."

Tatianna's jaw tensed. "Some might say fate, others might say you're always showing up where you don't belong."

Celestine *tsk*ed. "Tati, must you? There's no need to be rude."

Malric raised an eyebrow, amused rather than offended. "I assure you, I belong everywhere I go. And I go only where I'm invited."

"Do you?" Tatianna's eyebrow arched, her words sharp beneath a calm surface.

She wanted to say more. She wanted to ask about the spell book and its interesting notes. About Emelie. About what Archer told her and what he wouldn't tell her and everything she suspected. But to do that would mean dragging truths into the light that didn't belong to her—truths tied to Archer's past, his pain, and his magic. So, she smiled tightly.

"Well, Bramblewick has always been terribly hospitable, welcoming every lost soul that comes its way."

Malric gave her a slight bow, as though they'd exchanged pleasantries and not unspoken accusations. "I'd say it's even more so today."

"Are you staying in Bramblewick for long?" Celestine asked, twirling a lock of hair that had escaped from pins around one finger.

"Hard to say. I hadn't planned to stay long, but something about this town makes it difficult to leave."

Tatianna's heart beat like a warning bell in her chest. She needed to warn her sister, even if it meant divulging Archer's history.

"Well, if you do stay," Celestine said with a smirk, "perhaps you'll let me show you my favorite view in town."

"Careful, Celestine," Leondria muttered under her breath.

But Malric only smiled, not hearing or ignoring her sister, that same predatory glint in his eyes. "How could I refuse?"

Tatianna's hands clenched inside her gloves. *Not here. Not now.* The market was too public, her knowledge too fragile, and her accusations only half-formed. She couldn't accuse Malric without unraveling Archer's past—and he hadn't given her permission to do that yet, especially not in such a public place.

So instead, she said nothing.

But her silence felt dangerous.

Tonight she would warn Celestine. Hopefully it wouldn't be too late.

The Wylde sisters left Malric behind and set out to return home as the sun slipped low behind Bramblewick's rolling hills. Tatianna lingered behind her sisters, only half aware of her surroundings. She had hoped to run into Archer today. After so many days with him, her day felt incomplete without some interaction, especially after yesterday. She smiled, a quiet smile meant only for her. Until she saw them.

Lady Cordelia, upright and austere as ever guided Emelie down the walk towards the apothecary. The younger girl looked worse than before—her steps dragging, her skin ashen, her frame nearly lost in a heavy cloak. Her eyes barely opened.

If the spell is meant to heal her, Tatianna thought, *why is she getting worse?*

She hurried to catch up with her sisters, even more distracted than before. She barely noticed the golden light that kissed the eaves of their ivy-draped cottage and cast long shadows over the flowering hedgerows. The cozy warmth of her home did little to ease the tightness curling inside Tatianna's chest.

She lingered behind her sisters at the gate, glancing one last time down the village lane. She couldn't shake the image of Lady Cordelia and Emelie as they walked inside the apothecary. The vision of Emelie, a ghost of her former self, haunted her through supper, through the strained conversation with Leondria about Celestine's infatuation, and all the way up to her room—until she found the letter.

It lay on her pillow, its seal unbroken.

Her mother stood stiffly by the window, arms crossed. "You've received a letter," she said, her tone clipped.

Tatianna crossed the room and picked it up, her heart leaping and sinking all at once.

"I don't suppose you'd care to tell me why a young man with no magic and a family that merely tolerates him, is writing you letters?" her mother said.

Tatianna didn't look up. "Mama, you don't know what you're talking about. Especially when it comes to the Thornfields."

Her mother's eyes narrowed. "You're a Wylde, Tatianna. You have responsibilities. You don't get to go traipsing off on magical whims with someone beneath your station."

Tatianna turned slowly to face her. "He's not beneath anything. And maybe you should worry less about who's writing letters and more about what's going wrong in this town. What's happening to your daughters every night. But you're more concerned with appearances than you are an actual danger."

Her mother opened her mouth to speak, but Tatianna cut her off.

"No, I don't want to hear it. I'm not being fanciful, it's not all in my head, the danger is real and if you were paying attention, you would know I'm not making things up."

Before her mother could respond, Tatianna slipped the letter into her pocket and left her room. Silence followed her as she made her way to somewhere in the cottage she could read the letter in peace, away from the judgmental eyes of her mother and the insipid giggling of her sister. Their library. No one would think to look for her there.

She read the letter in the quiet comfort of the library, surrounded by shelves that once belonged to her grandmother, filled with spell books, both old and new. The flickering lamp cast shadows across the inked words.

Tatianna,

There's more I should have told you. But it wasn't until recently that I allowed myself to remember everything about that day at school.

Years ago, at the boys' school I was sent to, there was a student whose magic was…untamed. Beautiful, but volatile, some might have even called it wild. We became friends, since neither of us possessed the type of magic society considered normal. Then Malric befriended the two of us, said he could help. I trusted him immediately in the way only the young do, before trust has been betrayed. I never suspected that he wasn't a friend, that he only kept us close to use us. But that's exactly what he did. He used my gift—my ability to amplify others' powers—to siphon that boy's magic. Not to save him. Not to help him. He just wanted to take it for himself. All of it.

The boy survived, barely. I . . . did not. Not really. Yes, I am alive, but Malric left me there, unconscious, my magic completely drained. After that moment, I became a shell of my former self. I blocked the memory out. The pain, the guilt. I only told Aisling, and then only part of it. I forgot how to trust others. I didn't remember it clearly myself until you said the spell was a siphoning one. Then, piece by piece, that day came back to me.

I should have told you sooner. I was afraid you'd see me the way I see myself, as unworthy as your mother says I am.

But now you know everything. If you want to discuss further, meet me at the castle ruins at dawn.

Forever yours,

Archer

Tatianna sat perfectly still.

The words blurred in front of her as tears welled in her eyes. She attempted to blink them away, but one fell onto the letter, obscuring his name. The steady, pounding ache in her heart drowned out everything around her. How could he have kept this from her? After everything—after what they'd shared. How could he not warn her about Malric? How could he keep secrets from her after the picnic?

She didn't know whether she was more furious or hurt.

A knock jolted her back to where she was. The once cozy surroundings now were closing in on her. She needed air. Her mother swept in without waiting for permission, brandishing a crumpled note.

"She's gone. If you and Leondria hadn't tried to push her away from him— Whatever is she thinking!"

Tatianna took the crumpled paper. Her stomach dropped.

Don't wait up. I've found love and won't be back. — Celestine

"Foolish girl," Tatianna muttered.

Her mother sniffed. "She's run off with that charming boy you refused to accept."

Tatianna clutched the note, heart hammering. Malric had her sister.

And she feared she knew exactly what he was going to do next.

Chapter 24

Mist clung to the morning like a memory that wouldn't let go, curling around the shattered archways and broken stone of the castle ruins. Dew sparkled across the wildflowers that had claimed the ancient flagstones reflecting whatever light the water drops could find, causing the petals to shimmer under the heavy morning mist, and somewhere in the distance, the forest creatures sighed as the rising of the sun roused them from their nightly slumber.

Tatianna stood at the edge of what turned back into the great hall of the castle every night, her cloak drawn tightly in an effort to keep the morning chill at bay. Her sisters had returned home an hour before, stumbling through the front door with silver-silken leaves in their hair and no recollection of where they'd been, just like every other night.

She had not asked either sister. She'd simply known they didn't remember a thing.

Celestine was still gone. And Malric had been the last one seen with her. Tatianna knew her sister was in his hands, and his only intention was to steal her magic.

The spell was getting stronger every night. The curse was spiraling tighter. If it wasn't broken soon, everyone in town was at risk of losing their powers.

And she—*they*—had missed it. All because *he* wasn't honest about his past.

She heard footsteps behind her, but didn't turn.

"Tatianna," Archer called, his voice warm, a little breathless as he crossed the uneven stones to her. "You're here early. I wasn't sure if you—"

He stopped behind her, close enough that she could feel the familiar heat of him. She wanted to lean into him, seek comfort in his arms. She hated that she wanted those things, that he still affected her. Even after he had kept secrets from her, secrets that led to her sister's disappearance.

"I've been thinking about yesterday," he said gently. "I know you've been quiet, but I thought maybe . . . after everything, we could finally—"

He touched her arm, his movement featherlight, tentative. She turned towards him but didn't pull away, so he stepped closer, cupping her cheek. His head dipped towards hers.

She pulled back her arm and slapped him.

The sound cracked through the ruins like a spell being broken.

Archer staggered back, hand flying to his face, stunned.

Tatianna's voice shook as she glared at him. "You *knew*. You knew what he was capable of. You knew what he did to your friend—and you still didn't tell me!"

She waited for him to say something, anything.

He didn't answer. He didn't move.

"My sister is *missing*," she spat, eyes bright with fury. "And you—what were you doing? Waiting until it was convenient to mention that Malric is a predator who uses other people's magic like kindling? Her magic is just like your boyhood friend, the one Malric almost killed."

"Tatianna—" His voice was low, hoarse. "I didn't remember it all until—"

"Until I figured out it was a siphoning spell. You had all day in the carriage to tell me. You waited too long!" she shouted. "How could you trust *me* with everything else? With your magic. With *you*. But not this? If you told me when you remembered, I could have stopped her. I would have done more."

He lowered his gaze, hands falling to his side. "I didn't want you to look at me the way I look at myself."

She blinked hard, once, and shook her head. "Don't you dare make this about you."

He flinched like she'd hit him again.

"I thought we . . ." Tears filled her eyes, threatening to overflow. "I believed that we . . . That you . . ."

"I do . . . ," he started.

A single tear trickled down her cheek.

"I can't look at you right now," she whispered. "I *won't*."

She turned and walked away, every step brittle with pain.

She left him there, standing alone among the ruins, the silence folding in around him like a punishment earned.

The mist rose higher, and he watched her disappear into it.

Archer didn't move for a long time.

The mist thinned as the sun crawled up over the hills, casting fractured light through the crumbled arches and tree branches. Morning had come. Tatianna was gone. And he remained rooted where she had left him, as though her fury had turned him to stone.

The sting on his cheek had long since faded. But the ache in his chest—*that* was only just beginning.

He ran a hand over his cheek, then dragged it through his hair, the gesture doing nothing to calm the raging storm of emotions inside him. What had he expected? That he could bury the truth in silence, tuck it behind good intentions and half-formed excuses, and she'd simply forgive him?

That she wouldn't feel betrayed by his silence? That his silence wouldn't have consequences?

It wasn't just that he'd failed to tell her what Malric had done in the past or what he had allowed to happen through his silence. It was that he had opened up, just enough for her to trust him without actually earning it in full, then betrayed her by keeping silent. Letting her walk towards danger with only part of the map, just because he'd been too afraid of what could happen if she knew the truth.

And worse, it wasn't only his fear that had stopped him from opening up; it had been his pride. He couldn't handle having her look at him like everyone else did. His pride kept him from trusting her, and yet he had asked her to trust him, not with words, but with his actions.

He thought of how her eyes sparkled when they danced, the way she smiled when she forgot to be worried. The teasing voice in the carriage, the soft exhale as she fell asleep surrounded by new theories and possible answers. The way she'd trusted him with all of her.

And he had shattered it by hiding, not only from her, but from himself.

He remembered how she'd looked just now—*not* angry, not just angry.

She looked wounded.

Like he had broken something delicate inside of her. And not the kind of delicate that meant weak, but the kind that meant precious. Finely spun. Irreplaceable.

He'd made her *breakable.*

And no apology in the world could undo that. It would take so much more than words if there was any hope of earning her forgiveness.

Archer looked up, fists curling at his sides. If he let this be the end, if he let her carry the burden of his silence alone—then he deserved to lose her.

But he wasn't going to let that happen. He needed to be a better man, to prove to himself he wasn't the person society thought he was, the person he had always believed himself to be.

There was only one thing left for him to do now: fix what he had destroyed. Even if it cost him everything.

He turned away from the ruins, eyes hard with purpose. He didn't know how he was going to do it, but he was going to find Celestine and stop Malric.

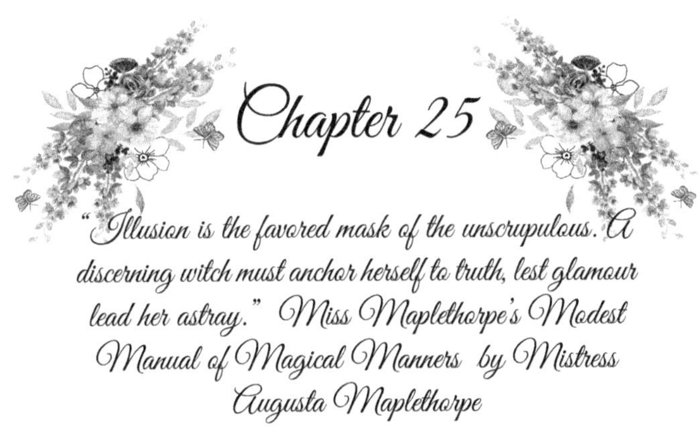

Chapter 25

The ruins shimmered in the moonlight, the glamour thick in the air, infiltrating the ruins like smoke drifting through the broken stone and skeletal arches. Tonight's cursed ball had begun—music drifted through the air from everywhere and nowhere all at once. Laughter echoed from the walls of a castle that no longer stood. Until the shimmering stopped and the castle suddenly stood in front of Tatianna.

And she stepped into it, alone.

The protection spell she had recast this morning hummed through her body, becoming more and more noticeable with every step she took. It served as a reminder to stay cautious of her limits. Of *why* she was here.

To find Celestine. To stop Malric.

Not to get swept away by the magic that was everywhere.

Couples filled the dance floor, spinning and twirling in timeless elegance. Their faces illuminated by floating chandeliers that were just more things that didn't actually exist. The scent of night jasmine and forgotten longing filled the air. She reminded herself that none of it was real—except for the danger.

She slipped through the hall, looking at each face as they danced and twirled past her, each fluttering gown and tailored coat. She searched for a glimpse of Leondria's golden curls or the familiar tilt of Rhiannon's chin. But the crowd shifted like water, constantly moving, and more than once she nearly lost her bearings as she made her way around the dance floor.

She turned towards the dais, expecting to see the spectral musicians that had been there before—and froze.

Across the floor, near the edge of the illusion, where it frayed into reality and the ruins showed through, stood Malric.

And—*Archer*.

Her breath caught.

Unlike everyone else here, they weren't dancing. They were *arguing*—or at least Malric was. His normally charming face twisted in fury, gesturing wildly. Archer's posture was tense, shoulders squared, fists clenched at his sides. Whatever his response was, it was quiet. Controlled. But there was a wildness in his eyes she had never seen before.

She stepped forward instinctively. "Archer?" Her heart leapt in her chest, pounding uncontrollably. She wanted to go to him, prevent whatever emotional pain being around Malric caused him.

But just as she moved, a smiling couple whirled between them—a blur of silks and enchantment—and when they passed

. . .

They were gone. Vanished like smoke in the wind.

She spun, searching every face in the crowd, heart racing, but they were not among the couples dancing—just people trapped in the illusion and moving to the music, and the relentless ache in her chest of knowing she might have imagined it; they could have been part of the glamour. Or worse: they had seen her, he had seen her, and they left.

Her pulse hammered. Archer had no protection spell—if he was here, he was vulnerable. And Malric . . . Malric couldn't be trusted.

A horrible thought wormed itself into her brain. *What if Archer wasn't arguing with Malric? What if he was helping him?*

She pressed a hand to her mouth and her other to her corseted waist as waves of nausea threatened to make her sick. She took a small step back, one arm extended to steady herself, and breathed deep. Could she really have misjudged him so completely? She didn't know what was real anymore. The spell made everything uncertain—made *everyone* uncertain.

Except Celestine. She had to find her. Wherever Malric was hiding her.

And until she did, she'd keep her heart guarded just as fiercely as her magic.

Tatianna turned deeper into the illusion, the music swirling around her once more.

Archer stepped through the veil of glamour into the ruins with a grimace. The stones glowed faintly beneath the enchantment, reminding him to be mindful of what really was there and what was an illusion. He heard the musicians pick up their instruments and start playing; the music drifted towards him. While the sound was beautiful, it was loud, too loud. He couldn't help but wince as it invaded his head like a memory from a place he never meant to return to.

He didn't come here for the dance. Not that he went anywhere to dance, but that was not the point.

He came for *him*. To confront the man who had affected his life for too long. It was time to put a stop to it all, to save this town, and hopefully himself along the way.

Malric stood at the edge of the glamour, shimmering as he stood at the edge of reality and illusion. It did not surprise Archer that Malric was as poised as ever, his coat immaculate, and his dark hair shining under false candlelight, as if he was part of the curse instead of the person manipulating it.

As if he hadn't *ruined* lives, as if he wasn't still ruining lives.

Archer stopped just short of him. Everything inside him urged him to punch the sardonic smile off Malric's face. While the action would be satisfying, it wouldn't solve anything. He was here to find Tatianna's sister.

"I doubt you're surprised to see me," he said, glaring at the man in front of him.

Malric bared his teeth for what might pass for a grin, but the warmth of the expression never made it to his eyes. "You've always been predictable, Archer. I knew you would be here as soon as Miss Wylde's sister disappeared. You're just like a dog, eager to earn its dinner."

A flicker of rage caught behind Archer's ribs. "You're doing it again, this time to an entire town."

"I'm sure I have no clue what you're talking about." Malric picked at his nails as if he had better places to be, more important people to talk to.

"You drained my magic and took all from someone else who counted you as a friend. Left both of us there to *die.* Used me and my powers against my will to rip magic from someone who couldn't even protect himself. And you never once looked back."

Malric tilted his head, waving a hand to dismiss Archer's words. "That was a long time ago. One would think you would be over it by now."

"Not me, and I doubt anyone else you've done this to has forgotten what you did," Archer said, stepping closer. "I remember what it felt like. You coming back into my life made me remember."

"Oh? I thought you'd buried all that nicely. Along with your spine."

Archer's hand twitched at his side, a current of magic rising in response to his fury. He forced it down; his magic was still too easy to turn against him. "You're hurting people again, aren't you? The spell. The siphoning. Emelie. And now Celestine. Who else, Malric? How many more?"

Malric's smile sharpened. "You think you understand what's happening here? You don't. You never did and you never will. You still think magic's a tool. But it's a currency. And some of us know how to spend it wisely."

Archer's voice dropped. "You're killing Emelie."

"Don't be dramatic," Malric snapped. "She's *surviving*. Because of me. Because of what we've done. You think she'd last a week without other people's power?"

"You're delusional, lying to yourself. Emelie had one good day." Archer clenched his fists. "This may have started with helping her, but now it's about you and how much you can take."

Malric smiled. "Turns out I can take quite a bit, and Emelie doesn't need that much to keep her alive. Can you imagine your own magic turning on you?"

Archer surged forward, nearly chest to chest with him now. "And what about Celestine? Where does *she* fit in?"

Malric blinked, and for the first time, there was a crack in the mask. "She came willingly."

"It's not willingly if everything she knows about you is a lie," Archer said. "Ask yourself, does she know who you are? What you're capable of?"

"Neither does Tatianna," Malric said with a sneer. "Does she?"

That cut deeper than Archer expected. "She knows more than you think she does."

A movement caught the corner of his vision. A flash of familiar hair. *Tatianna.*

But the moment he turned, a couple danced past, spinning in a blur of color and magic. When they cleared, she was gone—and so was Malric.

Archer stood alone beneath the illusion, heart pounding, the ghost of Malric's words still clinging to him like ash.

Does she? She knew everything now, but did she believe him?

"When a gentleman comes to the rescue and admits his folly, it may feel like he has cast a forgiveness spell, but fear not, this is no magical enchantment, instead it is his actions and words begging for forgiveness. Causing him to become more a danger to your heart than any spell ever cast." The Etiquette Enchantress: The Art of Charm and Beguilement by Anonymous, attributed to "The Lady in Lavender"

The house was too quiet. That awful kind of quiet that comes only when something is terribly wrong. Her sisters' teasing banter couldn't be heard throughout the home. Their laughter, something that was constantly present, was completely absent.

Tatianna stood at the kitchen window, looking outside. Dark shadows emphasized the tired bags under her eyes, the pallor of her skin highlighted her freckles. She looked like a ghost of her former self, standing there, fingers tightening around a chipped teacup. Her sisters were still asleep—or whatever one would call sleep induced at the hands of a curse. It wasn't natural or restful. Leondria hadn't stirred in hours, her breath shallow and her skin pale. Rhiannon had muttered something about glittering masks and shadowed music before falling into another unnatural sleep.

The magic from the ball was draining them. Had been draining them for days. And so far, she had failed to find a way to stop it.

She needed to find Celestine, save her from whatever nefarious plot Malric intended on carrying out. She needed to stop whatever spell was doing this. She needed—

A knock startled her from her thoughts. The pounding didn't sound urgent, but it was quite insistent. As much as she wanted to ignore whoever was there, the continued sound informed her that was not an option.

She opened the door and froze.

There in front of her stood Lady Cordelia, elegant even in her weariness. Her eyes were sunken, her gloves wrapped around shaking fingers. She clutched her shawl as if it were armor.

"I need to speak with your mother," Lady Cordelia said, sounding like she was on the edge of breaking. Everything about her was brittle, barely holding on to her composure.

Tatianna straightened, blocking the doorway. "She's not here at the moment. And even if she were, I'm the one you want to speak to."

Lady Cordelia's eyes narrowed, and her cheeks turned a splotchy pink.

"I know what you've done," Tatianna continued quietly. "I know about the siphoning spell, the magical ball. About Emelie. About Malric."

For a moment, Lady Cordelia wavered—then, as if her spine crumpled from the weight of her secrets and fears, she sagged forward and stepped inside, almost falling into Tatianna. She led the powerful matriarch into the parlor, the air thick with words yet to be spoken.

They both sat. Neither spoke at first. Tatianna watched Lady Cordelia pick at her skirt from across the room. She wasn't going to speak; she wasn't the one looking for help for a situation she created.

"I never wanted this. I had a plan. It would save her, and no one would ever know what happened. But he's taken over, twisted it into something I can no longer control," Lady Cordelia began, hands twisting in her lap. "When Emelie was born . . . her magic was wrong. It turned on her, unraveled her from the inside. I tried everything—healers, scholars, fairies, and so much more. And then I found a reference in an old journal. A theory. A spell."

Tatianna's voice was soft. "My grandmother's spell book. She'd written a spell to siphon magic from others. To keep someone whose magic had turned on them alive."

Lady Cordelia nodded. "But I couldn't do it alone. As powerful as I am, I don't have enough magic. I needed help, but there wasn't anyone to ask." She looked up, her composure cracking. "They would've said no. They would've let her die."

"How would you know? You never asked." Tatianna crossed her arms, not offering the woman any sympathy.

Lady Cordelia lifted her hand to her lips, as if she was holding back a sob. "Why would they help me? If anyone knew about my daughter, they would treat her the same way they treat my niece and nephew."

Tatianna understood why she thought no one would help her. Her mother was a perfect example of how society looked at people without magic.

"So, you turned to Malric Wrenne."

"I didn't know what he was," Lady Cordelia whispered. "Not truly. At first, he helped. She seemed better. But then the spell—it kept needing more. And more. And now... now she's fading again."

Tatianna's heart thudded painfully. "Because he's not just using it to help her. He's using it for himself."

Lady Cordelia nodded miserably. "He's taken control of the spell. It's no longer helping Emelie heal; instead, he's taking the power for himself. I can't stop it. I don't even understand the spell anymore. Everyone in town is growing weaker. You've seen it. It's happening to your sisters. *You* know."

"I do," Tatianna said. Her voice shook. "And my sister is missing. She's with him."

Lady Cordelia's eyes filled with tears. "He has to be stopped. But I don't know how to stop him, not now that he's gained so much more power."

The door clicked shut behind Lady Cordelia, and Tatianna leaned against it, pressing her forehead to the wood. Her fingers trembled at her sides.

The truth had tumbled out of Lady Cordelia like shattered glass, sharp and glittering—too dangerous to hold, too jagged to make sense of yet. Emelie, the spell, Malric. And worst of all, Tatianna had no idea what to do next. She needed time to think, to breathe, to—

A knock.

She froze.

Not again. She couldn't handle much more today. Not after everything Lady Cordelia had revealed.

She opened the door and her breath caught.

Archer stood on the threshold, as dark and brooding as the day they met, cradling Celestine in his arms. Her bracelets were gone. Her wild hair hung limp over his arm. Her skin, once flushed with mischief and spark, was pale as moonlight.

"I found her," he said, voice hoarse. "She's alive, but—he took everything from her, all of her magic. Just like before, with my friend."

Tatianna stepped back to let him past her, stunned, unable to put any words together. Archer carried Celestine inside. He laid her gently on the sofa, brushing a hand over her forehead.

"She followed him willingly," he said, as if confessing a crime. "But she didn't understand what he was. What he does. He used her, Tatianna."

"I know," she whispered.

Archer's jaw clenched. "I should have told you everything sooner. But I didn't want to remember. I *couldn't* remember. I thought it was fear. Cowardice. But I think . . . I think part of it was a spell. Something Malric did to me, to make me forget. The moment you told me what the spell was, it cracked something open. I saw it all. Remembered it all."

She didn't speak. Couldn't.

His voice broke. "It's my fault. If I'd told someone when it happened—if I'd stopped him—it might have been different. I let him go free, and now your sister . . ." He looked at Celestine like she might disappear. "It's all my fault."

"No," she said sharply, then softer, "It's his. You were a boy. He was the one who stole someone else's magic. He chose to twist. To hurt. He did it then, and he's doing it now."

But Archer only shook his head. "I brought this to your doorstep. You and your sisters. The rest of this town."

"You didn't—"

He stepped back towards the door, interrupting her. "I'll go now. I needed to bring her back. But I won't be a burden on you. Or your family. You don't deserve that."

Tatianna didn't move. She was rooted where she stood. The ache in her chest twisted tighter, too many feelings knotting at once—grief, anger, confusion, and something deeper, more painful than all the rest: heartbreak.

He turned. Paused. "For what it's worth, I wish I could take it all back and do it all over again. I should have told you everything as soon as I remembered. It was wrong of me not to. I was wrong not to. I should have trusted you the same way you trusted me. Instead, I let my pride get in the way, and I will regret it for as long as I live."

Then he was gone.

The door closed softly behind him.

Tatianna looked down at Celestine, tears falling from her eyes. The fight wasn't over. Not yet. But the cost was growing steeper by the minute.

Chapter 27

Tatianna sat beside Celestine's bed, her hand curled protectively around her sister's limp one. Morning sunlight filtered in through the pale pink curtains, casting a soft light over Celestine's pale face. Her breathing was shallow, but steady. Whatever Malric had done to her, the bracelets she'd once worn to suppress her magic were gone—so was the aura that always surrounded her, and the vitality that had always vibrated through her. Tatianna just knew the spark in her sister's eyes would be dimmed if she was ever to open them. She blinked back tears, there was no time to cry, not if she was going to save her sisters.

A quiet rustle at the doorway broke through the emotion-filled silence. Leondria stood there, her hair loose around her shoulders, robe cinched tight. Rhiannon hovered behind her, eyes wide with worry. Both of them were exhausted, eyelids heavy even though they'd just woke up from their magic-induced slumber. They'd slept through both Lady Cordelia's and Archer's visit.

The thought of Archer caused a sharp pain in her chest. She was still so angry. Every time she looked at her sisters, her anger bubbled to the surface until it almost overflowed. But there was something about what he'd done, what he'd risked, even what he'd said, that made her want to run to him, throw herself into his arms and let him shoulder some of the weight pressing down on her constantly. Return to when they were working on saving the town together, like he had promised her so many times before.

"She's really back then, and asleep?" Rhiannon asked softly, moving into the room and taking the chair across from Tatianna.

Tatianna nodded. "Unconscious. Archer found her like this and she's been like this since he brought her here."

Leondria walked slowly to the end of the bed and sat on the edge, careful not to disturb Celestine. Tatianna waited for her sister to settle before she told them all about her morning, beginning with Lady Cordelia's visit and revelations. Ending with Archer's arrival with Celestine after rescuing her from Wrenne.

"So, it's true. She really ran off with Malric Wrenne." Leondria's voice was strained with both relief and guilt. "And Archer—he risked himself to get her back, even knowing what that man could do to him."

Tatianna looked up sharply, her exhaustion worn thin. "He never should have let it get this far."

"Of course not," Leondria agreed. "But he brought her home. And from what you've told us . . . that was not an easy task for him. He's been manipulated too. Used by Malric. Maybe even cursed. You said it yourself—he didn't remember what Malric had done to him until *after* you figured out the spell."

"That doesn't excuse him for hiding it from me once he remembered," Tatianna said bitterly. "If I had known, I could have stopped Celestine from running off."

"I'm not excusing his actions, but I'm not sure knowing sooner would have changed anything. We weren't even sure warning Celestine of the little we did know was the correct thing to do. She's stubborn," Leondria said gently. "All this to say, Archer is not our enemy. And perhaps you're so hurt by his actions because you've fallen in love with him."

Tatianna stared, but remained silent. Her sister's words hit too close to the truth for her to say anything.

Rhiannon's voice chimed in, quiet, barely above a whisper. "And he's the only one besides us who knows Malric for the reprobate he is, and his experience with Malric could help you."

Tatianna stared down at Celestine's pale hand. "I just don't know if I can trust him again."

Leondria crouched beside her. "You don't have to trust him with your heart, at least not yet. Just . . . with this." She wiped away a lone tear trickling down Tatianna's cheek. "With saving us, saving the others, before Malric drains everyone like he drained our sister."

Tatianna closed her eyes, took a deep breath, and stood.

"I'll go to him," she said. "But he doesn't get to lead this. We do."

The scent of strong tea and burnt toast clung to the corners of the room like remnants of a forgotten spell. Archer stood at the center of the study, surrounded by stacks of books, loose pages, and half-drawn sigils. Aisling lounged on the sofa, her arms crossed and her expression wary. Lilith leaned against the hearth, flipping through a leather-bound volume with increasing irritation. Both women looked exhausted, having only recently woken up after another night spent dancing away their magic at the cursed ball. Lysander was the only one who looked ready to throw himself into battle—his sleeves rolled up, a wicked grin in place.

"This spell is too big for Malric to be managing alone," Lilith said, snapping the book shut. "He's got to be tethering it to something."

"Or someone," Aisling added, glancing at Archer meaningfully.

He knew she was worried about him, concerned Malric would find a way to use him once again. But he was wiser now. He knew the man was not his friend. He knew he needed to take steps to protect himself.

"I know," Archer muttered, rubbing at his temples. "That's why I need to find what, or who, this is tethered to—with the right spell we can end this madness, stop him from doing any more damage. But if we rush, go in unprepared, he could—"

"Hurt someone," Lilith finished.

"Or finish what he's started and drain the entire town of its magic," Aisling said, not looking away from her brother.

Archer met her gaze and slowly sat down. "This isn't your fight," he said quietly.

"Oh, not this again," Lysander groaned, flopping dramatically into a chair. "Don't start the noble sacrifice routine, Archer. It's become boring."

"I'm serious," Archer said, voice hardening. "You've all helped me more than I deserve. But Malric is dangerous in ways none of you fully understand. I've seen what he can do—what he's already done. I won't let any of you be his next victim."

"We're already his *victims*," Lilith snapped. "More importantly, we aren't children. This is our decision to make, not yours."

"While all that's true, you're only a victim because of my silence," he said, his tone laced with steel. "I've already let too many people get hurt. I can't live with more blood on my hands."

There was a beat of silence, then Aisling rose, her expression inscrutable.

"If you're going to be a martyr about it," she said, "at least don't die like a fool."

She walked out without another word. Lilith sighed, offered Archer a look that was equal parts anger and pity, then followed her. Lysander lingered in the doorway.

"She might never forgive you," he said softly. "But if you do this all on your own and die, she won't ever get the chance to. You aren't meant to fight alone. And you have people who will stand by your side, who *want* to stand by your side, but if you keep pushing us away, one day we might actually listen to you and leave."

He left.

Archer sat in the quiet that followed, the weight of everything that had already occurred pressing down on him. He turned back to the pages on his desk—sketch after sketch, trying to create the runes from the ballroom floor, fragments of spell work, failed translations. His magic prickled under his skin, restless like waves in a storm continually crashing on the shore with little to no respite.

Maybe he could use his magic to remove power from a spell, just like he could amplify it. It wasn't something he'd ever tried to do, but if he could find the anchor point, maybe he could actually do something to fix what he had failed to stop. He reached for the chalk, drawing a half-formed spell circle on the floor.

"If the spell is rooted in a typical siphoning construct, like taking water from a stream," he muttered to himself, "then there has to be a vessel. Would Malric risk making himself the vessel, knowing the spell could overcome him at any moment? Is he arrogant enough to do that? Or is there an intermediary somewhere? Maybe that's the key: redirecting where the magic goes after it fills the intermediary vessel."

He stopped. While his logic was all well and good, it didn't mean he was correct. In fact, he wasn't sure of anything. The exact shape of the original runes was lost to him, the pages from the spell book weren't here, and if anything was off, it would have disastrous consequences. He needed Tatianna.

But Tatianna hated him.

And she had every right too.

The soft creak of the front door interrupted his spiraling thoughts. He froze, head lifting, not daring to hope. It was probably Lysander checking in on him, hoping he had changed his mind.

Footsteps in the hall. Then a knock on the study door.

He stood, frowning. It was too soon for anyone to be back.

He opened the door—and froze.

Tatianna stood there, windblown and flushed from the walk, eyes sharp and unflinching.

"I hear you've been trying to plan a takedown," she said coolly. "But if you think you're doing this alone, think again."

Archer stared at her, stunned—and then the smallest flicker of hope broke through the fog in his chest.

"What . . . Why . . ." He had so many questions, but none of them fully formed, so he stood there, sputtering.

"It's true then, you've sent everyone away," she said, stepping past him without waiting for an invitation.

"I did," Archer said, still stunned.

"Well, you're not getting rid of me that easily." She turned to face him. "This is my fight, too. And if you think I'm going to let you stand here and unravel the spell alone while Malric tightens his grip, you really haven't been paying attention."

Archer stared at her, speechless.

"Who was going to cast the spell for you? Did you even take a moment to think about that?" She looked over at his desk filled with scattered notes. "Apparently not."

Still, he said nothing, afraid if he spoke, he would say the wrong thing and she would leave him.

Tatianna met his silence with steel. "Now move. We've got a curse to break."

Chapter 28

"*Should one find herself repeatedly unsuccessful in casting a protection charm upon loved ones (particularly siblings under a nefarious enchantment), it is proper to maintain a composed demeanor, revise one's spell work, and refrain from weeping directly onto the spell diagrams. A lady may falter—but she must never unravel where others can see it. Note: Should a ward rebound and strike one's own chest, a polite cough and immediate repositioning of the corsetry are strongly advised.*" Miss Maplethorpe's Modest Manual of Magical Manners by Mistress Augusta Maplethorpe

The candles burned low. Runes shimmered faintly on the table between them—scrawled in ink and chalk, pages layered with notes, diagrams, and failed attempts. They'd been at it for hours, hunched over spell books, sketches, and other sundry slips of paper that should have carried the answers with them, but didn't.

Tatianna rubbed her temples. "It isn't enough. None of this is right."

Her shoulders slumped as she let her head rest in her hands, elbows on the table, supporting her dejected posture.

Archer watched her and pushed a book aside. Frustration crackled around the edges of his carefully measured calm. "It's a framework. If we can isolate the thread Malric anchored the spell to—"

"We still don't know how he *bound* it," she cut in. "Or where. We don't know if the siphoning is centralized or distributed, if there's a trigger or a failsafe, or—" She stopped herself, chest tight. "We're grasping in the dark. One wrong move, and instead of saving everyone, we'll be hurrying them along to their demise."

He didn't argue. That alone said how dire things were.

Tatianna stood and made her way to a window. His eyes followed her as she stared out it and watched the moon begin to rise over Bramblewick. "I thought we'd be ready by now. That we could break it tonight. Before . . ." She trailed off.

"Before he takes more from them," Archer said quietly.

She didn't nod in agreement. She turned back to him, eyes glistening, on the verge of overflowing. Her silence was enough of an answer.

"I tried to amplify a reversal ward using my magic, to see if I could use my ability to strengthen a spell to somehow weaken it, but it collapsed within seconds," he admitted, voice rough with wear. "Whatever Malric did, it's not just siphoning. It's anchored in blood, or bone, or—" He shook his head. "He bound it to something we haven't identified."

Tatianna paced, then stopped, hands curled around the edge of the table. "Then we're missing a piece."

"Maybe more than one."

They stood there for a long moment, surrounded by the soft scent of melted wax and burned-out spells.

"I don't know how to fix this," she whispered. "I can't keep watching my sisters fade."

"You're not alone anymore," he said. "Whatever we're missing, we'll find it. Together."

She looked at him, expression unreadable. "You're sure you still want to work with me after . . . everything?"

"I never stopped," he said, the words simple, yet heavy.

A moment passed— fragile, unfinished— and then she stepped back. She wasn't ready to see where these feelings would lead, not now, maybe not ever.

"I can't stay tonight," she said. "Not with them still under the ball's influence. Another night dancing might take something from them I can't give back. I'm going to try another protection spell, maybe this time it will work."

He nodded. "I understand. I hope it does."

Tatianna hesitated at the door. "Keep working. If you figure out what the missing piece is—send word."

"I will."

She lingered, one hand on the doorknob, as if debating whether she should say something else. In the end, she just nodded and stepped into the night.

Alone again, Archer looked down at the notes, the broken runes, the unanswered questions.

They were close. But not close enough.

The night air was cool against Tatianna's skin as she slipped through the quiet streets of Bramblewick, following the road that led to the cottage. Lantern light flickered in the windows of shuttered homes, and every now and then laughter could be heard from behind the illuminated glass, but her own thoughts occupied her mind, blocking out every other sound.

Combining magic.

The idea had been circling around in her mind all evening. Every time she pushed it away, it came back stronger, until it was the only thing she could think about.

What if breaking the spell required more than one source of power? It took two sources to create: Lady Cordelia and Malric Wrenne. Did that mean it needed two sources to stop it? Hers and Archer's together—maybe more? But if she opened herself to his magic, would she be able to stop taking from him? Could she trust herself *not* to pull too hard, too fast, too much?

She'd seen what greed and desperation could do. What it *had* done.

She shivered and wrapped her cloak tighter as the old iron gate creaked open beneath her hand. The cottage was dark except for the amber glow of a single lamp in the front window. Inside, everything was still. Too still.

Celestine was exactly as she'd left her—lying pale and quiet in her frilly bedroom, wrapped in a quilt. Rhiannon had charmed a faint protective aura into the corners of the room, but the magic was weak, wavering. Tatianna wasn't sure it would be enough to keep anyone away. Leondria and Rhiannon were asleep in their rooms, spent.

Tatianna crouched beside the bed and gently brushed a strand of hair from Celestine's damp forehead.

"You better come back to us," she whispered. "We're not done yelling at you yet."

On the side table, a folded note caught her attention. She opened it with fingers that already recognized the elegant hand.

Miss Wylde,

I'm in town. I believe I've uncovered something that cannot wait. The Hall's archives opened more doors than I expected. Meet me at the library in Bramblewick first thing.

We may be running out of time.

– N. Willoughby

Tatianna sank into the nearby armchair and stared at the paper.

Nigel rarely used that tone—curt, urgent, clipped of his usual politeness and general affability. He'd found something. Something that scared him.

She looked again at her sister, then down the hall where the other two slept in uneasy dreams, then down at her own shaking hands.

They were all running out of time.

* * *

The floor creaked beneath her feet as Tatianna made her way down the hall, every step heavier than the last. Her head ached with questions, with magic spells half-formed and breaking apart in her thoughts before it ever reached her hands. The door to Leondria's bedroom stood slightly ajar, and beyond it, the faint sound of breathing filled the dim room.

Tatianna slipped through the door, not wanting to wake them. This wasn't spell-induced sleep, it was natural; they were actually resting. More importantly, they were still here.

It seemed while she was out, they had decided to share a room, something they did when they stayed up too late talking, or like now, when it felt like everything around them was falling apart. Rhiannon curled towards the wall, one hand fisted under her chin. Leondria lay on her back, brow furrowed as though even in sleep she remained vaguely disapproving. Neither stirred as Tatianna closed the door behind her and crept farther into the room.

She stood at the foot of Leondria's bed for a moment, fingers clutched around the edge of her sleeve.

Please let it work this time.

She drew in a breath and thought about how much she wanted her sisters to be protected from Malric's spell—just like she'd done every night for the past week. She flicked her fingers to release the magic. It shimmered against her skin, reluctant and flickering. She shaped what she wanted in her mind, weaving detailed thoughts with quiet desperation and a prayer she no longer knew how to voice.

The spell lifted into the air like mist . . . then met the same resistance as always.

With a sharp *crack*, it struck Rhiannon's aura and ricocheted to Leondria's. From there, it rebounded twice, bouncing around the room, scattering sparks that danced over the room's rafters. Tatianna threw up a hand, but too late. The spell found her and smacked into her chest with a flash of light.

She stumbled backwards, catching herself on the edge of the window seat. Her breath left her in a short, frustrated gasp.

Why? Why wouldn't it work? Was Malric's spell that powerful, that once infected, there was nothing she could do to keep them from going back? Why were they still pulled into that cursed place night after night, losing pieces of themselves while she stood helpless to stop it?

Tatianna sank onto the cushions, burying her face in her hands. Her magic felt fractured, she felt fractured, like she was a million broken pieces just waiting to fall apart. She was unraveling.

And she was so—*so*—tired.

"I'm sorry," she whispered to the sleeping room. "I don't know how to fix this."

Curling onto her side, her arms wrapped around her, she pressed her forehead against the cold glass of the window. The spell crackled faintly underneath her skin—clinging to her, a ward against nothing, useless in the face of what truly mattered.

Exhaustion pulled at her limbs, and despite the tension wound tight in her muscles, her eyes drifted shut. Sleep overtook her so subtly she didn't even know it was happening. She slept curled up in the window seat, unaware that her sisters stirred and dressed for a ball. She didn't feel the caress of disturbed air from the door swinging open, or hear the rustle of their skirts as they were lured from their beds drawn out into the night towards a ball that only meant them harm.

Wrapped in a spell that protected only herself, Tatianna slept through the soft sound of slippers on the stairs—and the haunting silence that followed.

"Charm may be elegant, but timing is everything—there is no shame in letting determination outpace decorum when the world insists on collapsing before breakfast. Bewitching Tip: If he meets you halfway down the stairs, hair tousled and shirt half-buttoned, and still asks "What do you need?" —for heaven's sake, marry him later. Prioritize saving your sisters first." The Etiquette Enchantress: The Art of Charm and Beguilement by Anonymous, attributed to "The Lady in Lavender" Margin Note (flickering faintly): "Also: never underestimate the power of a dramatic entrance. Especially in boots."

Tatianna startled awake to the sound of the front door creaking open, followed by the soft hush of footsteps. For a moment, she was disoriented—the cool glass of the window against her cheek, the ache in her limbs from sleeping curled in the window seat, the faint static hum of a spell still clinging to her skin.

She bolted upright. Last night, the spell—she'd been so tired, but her sisters had still been here.

The room was dim with early light, but the atmosphere had shifted. Something was wrong. Something was always wrong. Her eyes darted around the room. It had happened again. She wasn't surprised, just disappointed that she hadn't been able to do anything about it . . . again.

The footsteps came closer. She heard a soft sigh. Then another.

Leondria and Rhiannon appeared in the doorway, both in their ballgowns, both pale and listless. Their eyes held that same unfocused sheen as before, their expressions dazed, as though their minds had danced far away and only their bodies had returned.

"Not again," Tatianna whispered, the words catching in her throat.

She crossed the room and reached for Rhiannon's hand—it was ice cold. She helped Rhiannon change into her nightgown. Then did the same with Leondria. Neither sister spoke. They were like dolls for her to dress however she wanted, silent, cold. They were in far worse condition this morning than any of the other mornings.

Tatianna stepped back, heart pounding. *This is going to kill them.*

The fury that rose in her chest came so fast it nearly choked her. All her carefully tempered restraint snapped. She would not wait another day. She *could* not wait.

Without bothering to change out of her wrinkled clothes, she flew down the stairs, grabbed her satchel, and flung open the front door.

The sun was rising over Bramblewick. Pale gold spilled over the rooftops and mist curled along the cobblestones. The air smelled of dew and desperation. Or maybe she was the only one who smelled the desperation.

She didn't care if the town looked like it belonged in a fairy tale. Right now, she was living in a nightmare. One she couldn't wake up from, because it was her life, not a dream.

She took off down the road, skirts hiked and boots skidding on the damp stones until she reached the Covington Estate.

She stood before the door and took a deep breath, trying to calm the pounding of her heart before she knocked on the door loud enough to wake the entire town, that is if it hadn't been sleeping the magical sleep of the cursed ball.

"Archer!" she shouted at the closed door, her foot tapping as if all her impatience had found its way there. "We have to go. Now."

The door opened while she was still shouting. A startled housekeeper blinked at her, and then, as if sensing the urgency, simply nodded and stepped aside.

Tatianna took the housekeeper's actions as an invitation and strode inside.

Archer met her halfway down the stairs, boots on, shirt half buttoned and jacket in hand. His expression shifted from confusion to alarm the moment he saw her face.

"What happened?"

"My sisters went to the ball again," she said, voice tight with restrained panic. "I tried to put a protection spell on them, Archer. I tried everything. But it doesn't work, it never works. And they're breaking. You should have seen them this morning. I can't—I won't let this go on."

"Aisling and Lilith went again last night. There's no stopping them until we break Malric's spell." He was already slipping his coat on. "What do you need?"

"We're meeting Nigel. At the library. Now."

Archer nodded, grabbing his satchel. "Then let's go."

Together, they stepped out into the waking morning, side by side, moving towards whatever answers the day might yield.

The Bramblewick library stood on the corner, everything about it quaint and cozy, especially in the pale morning light, its great doors yawning open as Tatianna and Archer approached. Tatianna's steps were quick, clipped—determined—but Archer could feel the tremor beneath her purpose. She was holding herself together by the sheer force of her will.

Inside, the library was quiet, the magic in its walls thrummed with a subdued tension, as if it too sensed the strain in the air.

Rhiannon was waiting in the small vestibule, perched on the edge of a reading bench, pale and anxious. The moment she saw them, she stood.

"Tati," she said breathlessly, "Leondria—she's worse. I didn't want to leave her, but she begged me to go. Said we had to stop this before it destroys us all."

Tatianna's jaw clenched, her eyes filled with tears. She dashed them away with a swipe of her hand. "We will. We must."

They moved through the stacks together until they found Nigel waiting in the eastern wing, a collection of books stacked high around him, scrolls unfurled and marked with ribbons and runes, tomes he must have brought with him from the Hall of Arcane Histories: their local library didn't have this extensive of a collection. He looked up at the sound of their approach, eyes bright with sleepless intensity.

"You came," he said, straightening. Then, to Rhiannon, "And you too—good. I'm glad."

Rhiannon's brows rose just slightly at the subtle change in his tone, her expression a little less guarded than usual. Tatianna noticed it, even now in the middle of everything: the flicker of something that one day could be more, buried beneath the exhaustion and grief. Tatianna hoped they could end this curse so Rhiannon would have the chance to explore whatever the moment between them was.

Nigel wasted no time. "Your trip to the Hall left me intrigued. I've been researching the runes and what purpose they serve ever since. I believe you determined it was a spell to take another person's magic. You were right—it's a siphoning spell, but you never mentioned anything else. With more research, I determined it has to be tethered. Fixed to a specific place. That's why it is so difficult to stop."

Archer folded his arms. "Where is it anchored?"

"I don't know." Nigel tapped one of the texts. "I believe it's bound to a physical location—most likely wherever the original runes were carved. If those runes are appearing at the ball, it means they're being replicated through glamour magic. They're not the source. They're reflections."

"So, we need to find the real ones," Tatianna said. "The ones I saw on the ballroom floor weren't the ones anchoring the spell.

They have to be carved somewhere close, probably somewhere connected to the ruins."

"And then what?" Rhiannon asked, voice tight with worry.

Tatianna turned towards her sister. "Then we break the spell, and we hand Malric what he deserves."

"I don't think it's going to be as easy as that. This is a spell that takes multiple people to cast."

"Yes, Lady Cordelia and Malric were working together, but she's lost control of it." Tatianna crossed her arms.

"So, it did take two people to cast this spell," Nigel said, voice grave. "Lady Cordelia didn't want it to become what Malric did. She had a specific purpose and didn't mean for it to become this … monstrous. But that means it will take just as many to unbind it. Maybe more."

Archer glanced at Tatianna. "Then we'll break it together."

Tatianna looked down at her hands, trembling with fatigue—ignoring Archer. She wasn't sure if she could do this with him. She shifted her gaze over to Rhiannon, who looked as though she hadn't truly slept in days, then to Nigel, still unshaven and ink-stained, fighting alongside them because he *believed*.

"We'll need help," she said quietly. So many lives were at stake, which meant there were very few people left in town that could help.

Nigel nodded. "That's why I'm here. Let's find those runes."

"I'll meet you at the Covington Estate. All the notes about where the runes could be are there." Tatianna grabbed her bag. "But I want to see Leondria first."

Chapter 30

The quiet of the Wylde home was heavier than usual, like the walls were holding their breath. Tatianna slipped through the front door without a word, the creak sounding too loud in the stillness.

Upstairs, the scent of dried lavender and bitter herbs clung to the air—evidence of the protective charms and desperate remedies Effie had tried, all of it in vain. Tatianna pushed open the door to Celestine's room.

Celestine remained unconscious, her breathing shallow, but steady. She was so pale, her magic a faint flicker Tatianna could barely sense anymore.

Leondria was in the room, reading to Celestine. Her voice was quiet, raspy. She sat propped up by pillows, eyes sunken with exhaustion and . . . something worse, her once-glowing aura barely a shimmer now. Yet, she smiled when she saw Tatianna.

"You came," Leondria whispered, voice hoarse.

Tatianna crossed the room in seconds and sank to the floor next to where Leondria sat. "Of course I did."

Leondria's hand found hers. "Celestine? Can you see her magic?"

"Still no change, but I'm sure she appreciates you being in here with her." Tatianna's voice cracked. "Nigel found something. We're going to end it. Tonight, if we can."

Leondria's brow furrowed. "Tati, you can't rush into this. This spell . . . it's dangerous. You don't need to prove anything to anyone, not even to us. I hope you know none of this is your fault."

Tatianna shook her head fiercely. "I guess I know, but I felt the spell being cast and protected myself, leaving the three of you exposed. You're all fading and I don't know if I can—" She broke off, pressing a fist against her mouth, willing herself to stay composed. If she started crying now, tears would turn into uncontrollable sobs. "I promise you, Leondria, I'm going to end this curse. I *will*. Whatever it takes."

Leondria squeezed her hand weakly. "I'd rather lose my magic forever than lose you."

Tatianna's breath caught. She stood, anything to stop her emotions from breaking through the wall she'd erected to keep them at bay.

"I mean it," Leondria whispered. "You think the only way to fix this is to throw yourself, your magic, at it until there's nothing left. But sometimes . . . sometimes love is *not* sacrifice.

Sometimes it's staying, letting people in. Letting someone else carry part of your burden."

Tatianna's gaze fell to their clasped hands. Leondria still gripped her fingers even as Tatianna wanted to run from her sister's words.

"I'm not saying forget what he did," Leondria continued gently. "But Archer brought Celestine back. He faced Malric not for her, but for you. Maybe . . . just maybe your heart isn't as broken as you think. Maybe it's just been waiting for you to open it again and let him back in."

Silence settled between them, soft but full.

Tatianna leaned in and kissed her sister's forehead, brushing away a few strands of sweat-dampened hair.

"I'll be careful," she whispered. "But I won't stop. Not until this is over."

Archer slammed the door to the library's study room behind him, shoulders tight with frustration. Nigel, Rhiannon, and Tatianna looked up from the cluttered desk of half-translated rune copies and spell diagrams.

"You're back," Tatianna said, scanning his face. "Where have you been?"

"I went to see Malric, to see if I could get something, any-thing, out of him." Archer shook his head. "He's too smug, too arrogant. I tried to prod him, steer the conversation towards the source of the spell—but he danced around it. Mocked me. Although, I wasn't surprised. He mocks me every chance he gets."

Nigel frowned. "Do you think he suspects you're trying to find the anchor?"

"He suspects everything," Archer muttered.

Tatianna stared down at the papers in front of her. "Was it a mistake to confront him? Does he know too much now?"

Archer pondered her question. "I don't think so. At least, I hope it wasn't a mistake. He did say something strange though."

Rhiannon coughed lightly, nodding. "Strange how?"

Archer hesitated before pacing to the window. He stared out the window, looking but not seeing what was in front of him. "He said—'You're always too sentimental, Archer. Still chasing ghosts down the garden path. But don't worry, you won't find what you're looking for. It was never real to begin with.'"

He turned, his brow furrowed, rubbing the back of his neck. "I thought it was just one of his usual taunts. But it's stuck with me. I keep repeating it over and over again, trying to make sense of it."

"'Chasing ghosts down the garden path'?" Nigel echoed thoughtfully. "Is that a riddle of sorts, or a metaphor?"

Tatianna stilled.

Her breath caught, her eyes wide, but unfocused—searching through her memories. "'It was never real to begin with' . . ."

Rhiannon blinked. "Tati?"

Silence filled the room as everyone waited for Tatianna to respond. She sat behind the table, not moving except for her eyes, unfocused but jumping back and forth as if they were scanning, looking for something. Suddenly, she stood and the room came into focus.

"I know where the original runes are," she whispered. "The glamour at the ball—the ruins. There's a garden path behind the ruins. I walked it once. It looped back on itself, over and over. I thought it was just illusion magic, meant to keep people at the ball."

Archer straightened, his eyes alight with something that looked like hope. "But it might be more. The glamour making the garden path loop back to the ball could also be the true anchor."

Nigel nodded, already reaching for his bag. "Which means if we break through the illusion, the real runes might be underneath. Hidden by the spell itself."

Tatianna looked between them, a spark of determination returning to her eyes. "Finally, we might be on the right track to stop this curse, and Malric."

The afternoon air was cool and damp with the promise of rain, the kind that somehow hung in the air and soaked through a person's cloak before they realized it. Tatianna adjusted the strap of her satchel as they stepped through the outer edge of the ruins, the familiar shimmer of glamour magic tickling her senses like an itchy wool sweater.

"Ready?" Archer asked softly beside her, his fingers flexing in the air, already blocking the threads of magic that tried to attach themselves to his magic.

They walked through the stone arch together, the others following behind them. She couldn't see the glamour of the ball, but she could feel it hidden beneath the surface of reality.

Tatianna nodded, voice quiet but resolute. "I'll go first. I think I remember the way."

Nigel murmured something and cast a minor warding spell to keep them veiled—just in case Malric had watchers hidden in the ruins.

The garden path was almost impossible to see. The only reason they were able to find it was because Tatianna had once before traversed the path. She led the group through what seemed like thick undergrowth, but at her touch, the plants shifted and shimmered, revealing a narrow trail paved in uneven, time-worn stones.

"Here," she whispered. "This is where I got turned around last time."

The air thickened with magic the farther they went. It didn't hum—it *whined,* like a penned animal straining against its own boundaries. Tatianna glanced over at her sister. Rhiannon leaned against Nigel for balance, her magic barely a flicker in her aura, her resolve unwavering. If the Wylde sisters had anything in common, it was their stubborn nature.

As they reached another twisted arch, this one made of iron and swallowed by ivy, Tatianna stopped. "This is it."

Archer stepped forward, brow furrowed. "It looks like the glamour repeats here, like an infinity knot. But there's a resistance—like there's something underneath that wants to be seen."

"I think the anchor is here. That's what's trying to push through," Nigel said, crouching to press his palm against the stone at their feet. "It's not just an infinity knot. It's a seal."

Tatianna knelt and searched through her satchel. Once she found the pages she was looking for, she pulled them out. Her hand shaking slightly as she unrolled them, laying them out in front of her. The runes still glowed faintly behind the black ink. "We need to break through the glamour without destroying the protective layers, all while being aware of any alarms Malric might have set to stop us. If we disrupt the wrong part . . ."

"It could collapse the spell in on itself," Archer finished grimly. "Which could hurt everyone still trapped in it."

"We'll work together," she said. She looked at Archer before turning to the others. "We're going to have to, all of us."

His eyes searched hers for a moment. Then he nodded and knelt beside her. She didn't know what he was looking for, but he must have found whatever it was.

Nigel joined them, murmuring the incantation to strengthen their circle. Rhiannon stood as watch, her spellbook open and a flickering light of protection drawn at her feet.

Tatianna reached out with her magic and Archer met her halfway. The joining of their magic crackled through the stones, a tug-of-war of currents learning each other's rhythm. For a breathless second, the glamour *fought* back—and then, it yielded.

The ivy at the archway shriveled away. Iron and stones shifted.

Beneath them, carved deep into the grey stones of the remnants of the castle floor and glowing with an eerie pale light, was a string of runes far older than any in the books Nigel had shown them.

Tatianna inhaled sharply. "This is it. The anchor."

"And it's active," Archer said, his voice low. "Very active."

The magic in the clearing pulsed around them. They had found the spell's heart.

Tatianna knelt by the glowing runes, her hand hovering just above the surface. The spell radiated from the rocks. Magic crackled at her fingertips, a shimmering echo of Archer's power flowing with hers heightened all of her senses. It was like her body was feeling the things around her for the first time. Nigel was murmuring calculations under his breath, translating the ancient symbols in real-time as their combined magic hummed through the clearing.

"This is it," Archer said. "We can redirect the siphon here. Break the connection at its source."

Tatianna's brow furrowed as she studied the symbols. "We redirect the active current of magic to reverse where the power is siphoning to, then close the new circle. If we time it right—"

"Stop!" Nigel's voice burst through her concentration. His voice was sharp, urgent, and entirely out of character.

Everyone turned towards him with questions in their eyes.

"We can't break it now," he said, stepping forward, his face pale. "The spell is interlocked with the glamour . . . but its true power comes from the event itself. The cursed ball."

Rhiannon frowned, swaying slightly, steadying herself with one hand on a tree trunk. "You mean it only activates fully—"

"—when the glamour is in full swing," Nigel finished, nodding. "During the ball, the spell renews itself. That's when the energy is at its peak. If we break it now, we won't destroy it—we'll *awaken* it. Strengthen it. It will start taking magic from everyone at all times of the day."

Tatianna stared at the glowing symbols. "So, what you're saying is, we have to wait, again." Her shoulders slumped. They were so close to ending this, she didn't know if she couldn't handle another delay.

Nigel's expression was grim. "Yes. And not just wait. You'll have to go to the ball. During the glamour. You'll have to break the spell while it's *active*."

Archer's jaw clenched. "That's when Malric will be at his strongest. Magic from everyone dancing siphoning into him."

Nigel gave a heavy sigh. "Which means . . . it will be the most dangerous moment possible."

A long silence followed, broken only by the eerie hum of the runes pulsing below them. Tatianna sat back on her heels, the weight of the choice anchoring her in place. Leondria's words rang in her head, quickly replaced by her worn-down appearance.

"But it's also the only chance we have to break the spell for good," she said at last, voice steady. "This gives us the time we need to ensure we're prepared."

Archer's gaze slid to hers. "We'll face it together."

She nodded, even though in the back of her mind, she questioned whether it was wise to accept help from anyone, especially him. She was still worried that she would take too much when the time came.

Rhiannon looked between them, then at her trembling hands. "I doubt I'll be able to help tonight, but if I could, I would be with you, all of you. Please stay safe, Tatianna. Even if it costs us the last of our magic."

Nigel nodded. "I hope it won't come to that: we have time to plan. Not much—but enough."

The runes at their feet flickered once, as if aware they'd been seen. As if daring them to try.

And Tatianna, standing there with the burden of her sisters, her magic, and the fate of Bramblewick on her shoulders, squared them and whispered to her friends. Or maybe to the runes.

"Then we wait."

Chapter 31

"Magic is not embroidery—precision is lovely, but passion is power. Magic responds to intent more than incantation. So, if your spell wavers, don't reach for a rulebook—reach for what sets your blood alight. Rage, love, defiance, hope—use that. (And if the duchesses clutch their pearls over your lack of form, tell them I said you may borrow mine.)" The Charmed School: A Guide of Magical Etiquette for the Modern Witch by Elspeth Rosemoor

T he sun was low by the time they returned to the Wylde family cottage. It burned a gold thin line under the weight of heavy grey clouds that looked about to burst at any moment. It was as if the sky itself knew what was coming.

Inside, the sisters gathered. Rhiannon sat curled in an armchair, pale but alert. Leondria, though too weak to stand on her own, offered soft-spoken strategy from the settee where she rested in her dressing gown. Nigel laid out notes and diagrams of spell patterns across the kitchen table. Archer stood on the perimeter near the door, a sentry watching it all. The air buzzed with tension and urgency.

Tatianna paced, having too much fear and too much excitement to sit while they finished planning. "We know where the anchor is. We know when it must be broken. Tonight is our chance. Before Malric has taken so much that no one can heal from this curse."

"And we help Emelie too," Rhiannon said, firm despite the shakiness in her voice. "She's an innocent in this."

Tatianna nodded. "The siphon is what's keeping her alive, her magic is poisoning her . . . Malric is letting her have just enough magic that it keeps her allergy at bay, but not enough to let her heal. If we can reverse the flow, we may be able to return what was taken—setting aside just enough to heal Emelie."

Leondria cleared her throat. "But only if Malric is stopped."

At the mention of his name, Tatianna went still. Her green eyes darkened until little of the mossy shade was visible.

"I want to end him," she admitted, voice low. "Not just stop him. Strip him of his power. Leave him as empty and broken as the people he's drained. I want him to feel what he's done."

A heavy silence fell. Then, quietly, Archer pushed himself away from the doorway, unable to stay silent any longer.

"No."

She turned towards him, eyes flashing. "You don't get to tell me what to feel—"

"I'm not," he said, taking her hands in his. "But I *am* asking you not to lose yourself in this. You're not like him, Tatianna."

She looked away. "But I could be."

Archer tilted her head until their eyes met. "You're afraid you could be like him. You don't want to use my magic because you're afraid you won't be able to stop taking it once you start. But that fear, that *awareness*—that's the proof you're not like him. Malric takes because he believes he deserves it. You hesitate because you care."

She swallowed hard, unable to speak past the knot in her throat.

"You won't use his magic to stop him," Archer said softly. "You'll use *mine*. It's the only way."

Her head snapped up. "Archer, no—I can't. Today it worked because it was a moment. There was no battle of wills, no contest of strength."

"I trust you," he said. "More than anyone. If my magic can help end this, if it can save your sisters, save Emelie—then I want you to use it. I'm giving it freely. No lies. No tricks. Just us, together."

She shook her head, struggling. "What if I can't stop? What if I take too much? What if I hurt you?"

"Then I'll wake up with a terrible headache and a deficiency of magic," he teased, a flicker of the warmth he rarely showed others coming through. "But I'll still be here. Because I believe in you. I trust you."

Tatianna's breath hitched. Slowly, she nodded.

"Alright," she whispered. "Tonight . . . we end this. For my sisters. For Emelie. For all of us."

Nigel looked up from the table, holding a list. "Then let's gather what we need."

Archer stood there for a moment, like he wanted to say something more, doubting whether he should speak, or stay silent.

"I can see there's something else on your mind. Now's not the time to hold back," Tatianna said.

"I think we should include Lysander. He can help, if we . . . if I let him." Archer shrugged, not sure what he wanted her to decide.

She nodded. "Then get him here, and quickly. Now's not the time to turn away those willing to stand with us."

Archer bowed his head before striding out the door.

As night crept closer, they lit the lanterns one by one. Runic circles were sketched onto parchment, and vials of powdered crystal and enchanted herbs packed carefully into pouches. Cloaks and gloves and charms layered on. All of it meant to protect them from Malric's magic long enough for them to break the spell. Tatianna slid her grandmother's ring onto her finger, feeling the pulse of the inherited strength it carried. She hoped it would help remind her of what her family was capable of.

The clock ticked louder than usual as it moved closer to the time for them to act.

And outside, the curse shimmered faintly across the sky—it was a summoning disguised as an invitation to the nightly ball that waited, like a snare hidden beneath ballgowns and quartets.

The last light of day melted into indigo as the Wylde cottage filled with the soft rustle of cloaks, the scent of protective herbs and oils, and the crackle of low-burning candlelight. Shadows stretched long across the floorboards. The glamour had already begun to shimmer faintly in the distance, a haunting call none of them could hear without enchantment, but all could feel in their bones.

Archer had returned, not only with Lysander, but with Aisling and Lilith. While they couldn't help when the time came, they were there, offering what support they could until the curse entrapped them in its talons.

Tatianna adjusted the laces of her boots with trembling fingers. She couldn't tell if it was nerves or excitement. Whatever it was, a large part of her wanted this night to be over.

Across the room, Rhiannon sat beside Leondria, her hands twisted in her lap.

"I hate this," Rhiannon whispered, looking up at them. "I hate knowing I'll be there tonight—but not *really* there. That I'll be dancing while you're fighting for our lives. I wish I could actually *help*."

"You *are* helping. Believing me when I told you what was happening was the biggest help of all," Tatianna said softly, kneeling before her. "You've stood by us when it would've been easier to give in. You've helped figure out how to tear this curse apart, even as it pulled you under."

"Every moment you fought, it bought us time. That matters," Archer added, stepping beside them.

Rhiannon blinked the tears welling in her eyes away, then rose and pulled Tatianna into a tight hug. "Then promise me you'll come back. Both of you."

"We will," Tatianna murmured, her throat tight.

Next came Leondria, sitting upright with visible effort, her blonde hair braided back, a shawl wrapped around her thin shoulders. Her usual commanding presence was softened by exhaustion, but the fire in her eyes still glowed.

"You are my wildest, most reckless sister—next to Celestine, of course," she said with a tired smile. "So, I'm trusting you to go against your nature and be cautious while saving the day. Remember what I said earlier about needing you to come home."

Tatianna laughed, her cheeks wet with tears she hadn't realized had escaped and crossed the room to hug her. "You'd better be here when we come back."

"I'm not going anywhere. Well, I might be going to a ball, but if I could stay home, I would." Leondria then whispered into her ear, "You've always had the strength in you, Tatianna. Just because it's different, doesn't make it wrong, despite all of Mama's lectures."

The embrace lingered a second longer before Leondria pulled back, her voice firmer. "Go. Before I cry and make you all late."

They turned to the door, but Aisling stopped Archer with a firm grip on his arm.

"Hold up, hero." Her voice was quiet, but unyielding. "I've known you too long to let you slink off without saying anything."

Archer gave a sheepish half-smile. "I'm not really good at goodbyes."

"Good thing this isn't a goodbye." She looked him square in the eyes. "You're coming back. You're not just smart, you're good. And you're not alone anymore."

"I might be the weakest link."

"Don't be ridiculous," she snapped. "Your magic lifts people up. You don't need to take from others to be powerful—you give and they shine. That's rare. And it's worth more than you know."

He swallowed hard and nodded. "Thanks, Aisling."

"Now go," she said, softening. "And if Malric so much as breathes wrong, punch him in the face for me."

Archer laughed despite himself.

"If he doesn't, I will. Malric deserves that and so much more for what he's done to all of you." Lysander walked to the door. "Shall we get on with it? We have a town to save."

With a deep breath, Tatianna and Archer stepped into the night. Those that could help followed behind them. The sky over the ruins glowed, as if the ball had already started—the glamour awaited everyone's arrival. The music of the cursed ball played in the distance, but it was there, beckoning everyone towards it. Faint as a heartbeat, sharp as a dagger.

They walked into the snare by choice, for the last time.

Tatianna's fingers brushed Archer's. Everything that needed to happen etched into her brain.

"Ready?" she whispered.

He gave a single nod.

She raised her hands, thinking about her family's old protection spell, how it worked, what she wanted changed, and who she wanted protected. Power gathered like breath held in the air. She pushed it out with a sharp flick of both hands. A shimmering bubble of energy unfurled around them—soft gold and silver threads weaving into a dome that pulsed with her will. It engulfed her, Archer, Nigel, and Lysander, giving them a layer of protection on top of the spells they had cast earlier.

Only then did she reach forward and slip through the veil of glamour.

Crossing into the enchanted world was like stepping into a dream laced with hidden danger. The light was too perfect, the music just off enough to make her skin crawl. Twinkling chandeliers floated above their heads, suspended in the air like stars, and flower petals drifted from nowhere.

And there—among the revelers—were her sisters.

Leondria, pale and sluggish, turning slowly in time to the music, her gown wilting at the edges, her normal golden glow gone, tarnished, even in the magical light.

Rhiannon's eyes were wide and glossy, her smile fixed but wrong, her movements mechanical as she fought the curse, but didn't have the strength to win.

Even Celestine, supported by the spell, danced in slow, sweeping circles—her body betraying her even while unconscious in the waking world.

Tatianna's breath caught. "They're *all* here."

She turned to see Aisling and Lilith moving across the floor, just like her sisters.

Archer put a hand on her shoulder. "We can still stop it. Look."

Behind the glittering illusions of the ball, the garden entrance lay crumbled in silence. But beneath the illusion's skin, a pulse—runes, flickering like fireflies along the broken stones, revealing themselves only when you *didn't* look directly at them.

"There," she said. "The anchor."

They moved quickly now, navigating through the dancers—none of whom seemed to notice them—and knelt before the half-buried symbols. Archer began stabilizing the space with quiet murmurs. Tatianna traced the runes with her fingers and placed the sigils they'd prepared: a strip of ribbon from Celestine's hair, the salt of tears, a lock of Rhiannon's hair, a page from Nigel's translation.

When it was time, Tatianna stepped to the center. She raised her hands.

She spoke the spell as written. Clean. Precise. Perfect.

Power answered. The air thickened, shivered—like the glamour itself was beginning to unravel.

And then—nothing.

The shimmer snapped back like a taut wire. The runes dulled. The music surged louder, burying her spell under its enchantment. The dancers kept dancing.

"No," she breathed. "No, that should've worked—"

She'd done everything right. Just like she was supposed to. She turned to cast again, heart pounding, palms sweating. This had to work.

Archer stepped in front of her.

"Tatianna," he said gently, his voice cutting through the chaos. "Stop."

"I have to try again—"

"Not like this."

Her brow furrowed. "What are you talking about?"

"It's too formal. Too rigid. You're trying to force your magic to fit something it *isn't*. This—"—he gestured to the still-pulsing glamour, the cursed ballroom, the anchored runes—"—this isn't a spell that will respond to the traditional murmurings of precisely pronounced words: it's more than that."

Her hands trembled. She knew what he wanted her to do. "But it *has* to be perfect. I don't want to hurt anyone. I have to control it—"

He stepped closer. "No. You have to *trust* it. You have to trust *yourself.* Use your magic your way."

She blinked at him, chest rising and falling. The idea both terrified and freed her.

"I don't know if I can," she whispered.

"I do."

Their eyes locked.

Tatianna turned back to the runes. Slowly, she took a breath. She closed her eyes.

And instead of reciting the spell, she let herself *feel.*

Her sisters' laughter. Her mother's fierce pride. Her friend's gentleness. The sharpness of betrayal, the ache of love, the quiet hope Archer hadn't let die in her. Everything she wanted back, everything she wanted to continue to develop. She let it *all* in.

And then—she let it go.

Magic burst from her, raw and alive, shaped not by syllables, but by will. Her way.

Chapter 32

The runes glowed like coals, flickering brighter under the force of Tatianna's raw, untamed magic. The surrounding glamour rippled, the air humming with imminent collapse. Light fractured across the ballroom, catching on the sweat-damp brows of dancers mid-spin, eyes vacant and sparkling with false joy.

Then the music stopped, halting with such haste discordant notes tore through the air.

The dancers stilled, suspended like marionettes with no one there to pull their strings.

A shadow stepped forward through the fractured light, cutting through the dying illusion with casual arrogance.

Malric Wrenne.

He clapped slowly, a sardonic smirk tugging at the corner of his mouth. "Beautiful, Tatianna. Absolutely breathtaking. I knew there was more to you than spells and etiquette."

"That's not a revelation. My mother would have told you as much. You only had to ask." She shrugged calmly as if she wasn't destroying an ancient siphoning spell cast by the man in front of her.

Archer stepped in front of her, raising his fists, preparing for a fight.

Malric rolled his eyes. "Don't be tedious, Archer. You've already played your part."

Tatianna straightened, her jaw set. "Get out of my way, Malric."

Wind whipped around them, sending cherry blossoms spinning into the air. Her hair seemed to float as she stood there holding her spell together. She felt Lysander and Nigel draw on their power, ready to use it to protect them.

Malric stepped closer, the air bent around him like he was the eye of a storm. "You still don't see it, do you?" His voice dropped into something reverent. "The magic you just used—*that's* what I've been after all along."

Her stomach twisted. Had they fallen into a trap? Did she lead them all to their doom?

"I've tried to recreate it. Every wielder of wild magic I found, I took—Celestine, that boy at the academy, others. But it never worked. It always turned to ash in my hands." He bared his teeth. "Their magic refused me. It fought. It was *chaos*. It tried to turn my magic against me."

He took another step forward, rubbing his hands together. "But yours—yours is different. It *listens*. It doesn't just obey you—it *adores* you. It bends the natural world to your will."

Tatianna's hands curled into fists. "It's mine, no one else's."

"That's what makes it so powerful." He raised his hand and grabbed the air, and her power—her magic began to slip away from her.

It was slow at first. A quiet tug beneath her ribs. A whisper of loss almost like heartbreak. Then the drain intensified—tendrils of her power unraveling like thread, pulled from her spirit.

She gasped, her knees buckled, and she fell to the ground.

"No!" Archer shouted, lunging forward, but Malric slammed him back with a flick of his hand, using her power to send him skidding across the stones.

Tatianna gritted her teeth, struggling to hold on to the warmth that was the core of her power. The light flickering in the runes faltered, changing colors as they weakened and Malric gained strength. The glamour rippled, the dancers stirred again like puppets twitching to life now that their puppeteer was back in control.

"Don't you see?" Malric said, breathless, voice full of awe. "You're the final piece. With your magic, I can remake the world. *Without limits.* No more spells. No more rules. Magic—pure, unleashed. It would all be mine. Everything I've been searching for, everything I deserve."

Her limbs trembled. Her vision blurred. Searing pain ripped through her as he continued to take.

But even through the pain, Tatianna realized something, something he could never understand.

He thought the power came from freedom. Magic without constraints. Without rules.

But he was mistaken.

It came from love.

From connection to others.

From choice.

Her magic didn't obey her because she demanded it.

It came because she asked. Because it wanted to.

And now, with her knees to the ground, her heart breaking, she did the only thing she could.

She *asked* it to come back.

Not to win.

Not to punish.

But to protect the people she loved.

For a brief moment Tatianna felt the warmth of her power return, pulsating through her, answering her call. But before she could do anything, it slipped away from her like water through her fingers, siphoned by Malric's hunger. Her limbs shook with the effort to hold on. The edges of her vision dimmed. Darkness surrounded her.

And then—

A hand touched her shoulder.

Warm. Steady.

Archer.

He was bleeding at the temple, one arm pressed tight to his ribs, but his eyes held nothing but fierce, unwavering clarity.

"Take it," he whispered. "Do it. Now!"

She looked up at him, hollow with pain, her eyes pleading. "No—"

"Take my magic." His voice was hoarse, demanding. "Use *me*. I'm not afraid of you."

"But I am." Her voice broke on the words. "What if I can't stop? What if I drain *you*— What if I become—"

"You *won't*." His hand cupped her cheek, thumb brushing away a tear. "You are not him. You never were. You never could be. You ask your magic to help you—you *never* demand. And I'm not offering because you need me. I'm offering because I need you. Your sisters need you."

Tatianna stared into his eyes.

No fear. No hesitation.

Just love.

Slowly, painfully, she reached for the bond between them, just like before when they found the anchor together. His magic came to her not with a crash, but a gentle trickle that grew into something stronger. It was eager, steady, bright. It felt like the sun breaking through a storm.

Malric's grip on her power shattered.

He stumbled back, confusion giving way to rage. "*What did you do?*" His scream echoed off the stones.

Tatianna stood, Archer's magic strengthening her every thought, every move. She met Malric's gaze with fire in her eyes.

"I asked for my magic back. I guess it likes me better."

She lifted her hands and let her power flow.

Not with words. Not with runes. Not with any spell scrawled in a dusty tome.

But through her connection to her power.

Through trust of herself and those she loved.

Through love, freely given and received.

The runes pulsed in answer; the glamour flickered between reality and illusion, and for the first time—the dancers stopped mid-step, blinking like dreamers waking up from a dream, finally aware of their surroundings.

Malric screamed as her magic pushed back, tore itself away from him, not just resisting his control, but destroying his grip on it. Tatianna didn't take his power.

She broke it.

And behind her, Archer stood tall, his power steady in her hands, his breath slow and even, as he gave her everything she needed.

Thunder struck, and the sky opened up, dousing everyone in pouring rain. The surrounding stones became slick under the raindrops.

Malric dropped to one knee, panting, but not defeated.

Not yet.

"No," he rasped, voice like stone scraping against rough stone. "You don't get to win. I won't let you. Not after everything I've done—everything I've *sacrificed.*"

His fingers clawed at the wet earth beneath the glamour, digging towards the anchor—those ancient runes carved into the stone beneath the illusion he created. Cracks of dark light hissed from his palms as he gathered the last of the magic he stole.

"I built this spell from my blood and my power," he snarled, eyes glowing from his fraying magic. "You think love and sappy sentimentality will stop me? You're nothing but a silly girl with a romantic heart and a pretty face. That kind of magic breaks. *I don't.*"

The ground pulsed with dark energy. The runes flared to life, trying to surge with him.

Tatianna stumbled as the force of his desperation roared through the ruins. The storm raged around them.

But Archer's hand was in hers, and behind her, the spell she'd cast with his help still shimmered—imperfectly perfect, alive. Still waiting to be finished.

Malric raised his hands to strike—

Tatianna stepped forward. Ready for anything he could throw at her.

"You've never understood. It's impossible for you to," she said, quiet but clear. "You're so obsessed with control that you can't see what true magic is."

She opened her palm and let her magic—*their magic*—answer her. She asked it to stop him from taking what wasn't his. To stop doing the bidding of someone that didn't appreciate it. The spell was cast; she wasn't sure it would work, but she trusted her intuition and let her magic do what it wanted.

The runes rejected Malric.

With a sound like an ice lake cracking moments before some-one plunges into the deadly cold, the stone at the center of the anchor split down the middle, and threads of dark power emanated from the crack, unraveling in the air like smoke in the wind.

Malric screamed, not in pain—but in disbelief. "No. No, it's mine. *It was all mine—*"

The last of the stolen power snapped back, tearing through him. He staggered, eyes wide in horror, as the spell he'd fed with greed and arrogance turned on its creator.

And then the anchor broke into hundreds of pieces.

The glamour dissolved like mist in sunlight.

The chandeliers disappeared, leaving only the full moon to light the ruins.

The music stopped.

The dancers woke from their cursed state.

The storm stopped, and petals fell, covering the stone like a carpet.

And Malric collapsed, a shadow of his former self, crumbling beneath the weight of his own ambition.

Chapter 33

In the aftermath of magical mayhem, it is both polite and essential to reacquaint oneself with toast, tea, and one's sisters. Emotional equilibrium is best restored not with further enchantments, but with honey, scones, and the sort of quiet company that lets you cry, laugh, or sulk without explanation. To Spell or Not to Spell: Navigating Society When Your Temper is Enchanted by Lady Mirabel Northwick

Silence fell like snowfall. It was soft, light, so unlike the crushing silence that Tatianna had become used to. There was no music. No tinkling of bells. No laughter. No cursed rhythm compelling the dancers forward.

Just blissful silence.

The air sparkled around them, glittering fragments of the glamour dissolving mid-air and drifting to the ground like glittering ash. The ruined castle lay bare beneath their feet—crumbling stone, trampled silvery pink petals, and ancient roots covered the ground.

Tatianna stood frozen, her hand still outstretched. Her breath trembled as she gasped for air. She could feel her magic humming quietly under her skin—fragile, frayed at the edges, but hers. Still hers. There was something else there, mixed in with her magic. It wanted to stay, to fix the frayed edges, to make what was hers less frail. She shook her head and asked it to go back home. It pulsed under her skin, disagreeing with her. But she pushed back until it reluctantly agreed.

Archer lowered his arm slowly from where he'd shielded her. His hair was mussed, his coat torn at the shoulder, his forehead streaked with dried blood, but his eyes were steady. She had used every drop of his power to defeat Malric. Archer's magic had run dry, but he hadn't let go of her once. He had given her everything he could give and was still standing.

"Is it . . . over?" he asked, voice hoarse.

His body jolted as if shocked. She stared for a moment until the corner of his mouth twitched into a lopsided grin. Only then did she respond.

"I think so," she whispered.

Then she turned.

The dancers stood, dazed and blinking. Some sat down hard on the stone floor, stunned, incapable of comprehending where they were or how they got there. Others looked around in growing confusion and fear; they knew something terrible had occurred, but had no recollection of it. All across the crumbled ruins, people were coming out of the stupor—it was as if they were waking from a dream they couldn't quite remember.

Rhiannon stumbled through the crowd, her eyes searching, her body swaying. "Tati . . .?"

Tatianna ran to her, catching her before she fell. "You're okay," she murmured, brushing damp hair from her sister's face. "You're really okay."

"I couldn't stop dancing," Rhiannon said faintly. "I wanted to stop, but I couldn't."

"I know." Tatianna pulled her into a tight hug. "I've got you now."

A sharp cry came from behind her—Leondria, half-carried by Lilith, collapsing to her knees beside Celestine, who lay just outside the crumbled arch. Her eyes fluttered open, conscious for the first time in days.

"Leondria?" Celestine croaked, blinking up at her sisters. "Why do I feel like I've been hit by a cart?"

Laughter and sobs burst from Leondria as she clutched Celestine tightly. Lysander knelt down beside them, looking somewhat disheveled, and took Leondria's hand in his.

Tatianna's knees gave out. She sank into the grass, Rhiannon still in her arms, and pressed her face to her sister's hair. Archer was beside her, holding on to his sister as if his life depended on it.

Out of the corner of her eye, she saw Nigel, with the help of the town sheriff, gather Malric up and toss him into a wagon. Later, she would ask where they were taking him, find out what punishment he received.

But for now, she relished in the knowledge that it was over.

Not just the spell. Not just the curse.

But the fear. The doubt.

It would take time. Recovery. Rest.

But for the first time in days—maybe longer—Tatianna could see a future beyond this night.

She looked up to find Archer watching her.

He didn't speak. He didn't need to.

She reached out, laced her fingers with his, and felt the smallest hint of a smile form through the exhaustion.

They had survived.

The Wylde cottage was not quiet for the first time in days.

There were no weird shifts in the air. No one was discussing how they heard bells in their dreams. The faint sounds of morning birdsong filtered through the window, as did the whispering of wind through the trees—not to mention the whistling of teapots and the clinking of teacups as four young women recovered from the night's events.

The sisters sat gathered around the breakfast room table, the same table they'd grown up around, where they'd shared secrets, squabbled over tea and toast, and listened to their mother's lectures on what was and was not proper.

Celestine was propped up with a pillow behind her back, pale but awake. Her gaze was clear, more present than it had been since before the curse. She looked down at her hands, new bracelets on her wrists, flexing her fingers as if still uncertain her magic was truly back and not still in the hands of Malric Wrenne.

Rhiannon sipped from her favorite porcelain teacup, the one with the purple flowers on it, her hands trembling only slightly. She was back to reading books, spending her time keeping to herself, quiet, not talking to anyone all that much. She didn't need to, though. The bond between the sisters ran deeper than words.

Leondria was bundled in a thick shawl, her magic quiet now—a gentle golden glow, no longer fragile and flickering. She leaned into her seat with a tired grace, watching her younger sisters with soft, pensive eyes.

And Tatianna sat between them, languishing in the feeling of her family being normal—for them, at least.

Leaning back in the chair, she felt light for the first time in ages, the burden she'd been carrying gone with the ashes of the glamour. Her hair was still wet and windblown from the night's ordeal, there was a burn mark on the sleeve of her dress she'd yet to notice, and a bruise was developing on her leg that she couldn't remember what caused it. But there was peace in her eyes and in her soul.

"Tati," Celestine whispered. "I'm sorry."

Tatianna turned towards her. "You don't have to—"

"I do," Celestine insisted, her voice filled with emotion. "I knew I should have listened to you. I did. But I wanted so badly to feel . . . desired. Wanted. Important." Her lip quivered. "And he used that. Used *me*."

Tatianna reached out and clasped her hand. "He used all of us. But he didn't win."

Rhiannon set her cup down with a soft rattle. "You broke it, Tati. *You* did it."

"*We* did," Tatianna corrected, her voice thick. "I didn't do this without you believing me. I couldn't have. And I wasn't alone."

Leondria smiled faintly. "But you led everyone. Without your strength, we might all still be trapped."

A long, quiet moment stretched between them.

The fire crackled. The kettle on the stove whistled low. Somewhere outside, the town began to stir with the beginnings of a new day.

"Do you think it's really over?" Rhiannon asked softly.

"No," Tatianna said honestly. "Not entirely. The magic's broken, but the wounds . . . They're deep and will take time to fully heal."

Leondria nodded. "But we have time now."

Celestine sniffed and reached for the honey pot. "Do we also have toast? Because I feel like I was nearly turned into a decorative corpse, and I deserve toast at the very least, or scones. Can we get some lavender scones today? And maybe some croissants. You know Mrs. Merryweather's croissants can fix anything."

That earned a huff of laughter from all of them. Real, warm, weary laughter.

They sat like that for a long while—talking, not talking, holding hands when they needed to, and knowing when silence was enough.

Chapter 34

The bell above the door chimed as the Wylde sisters entered Brambles & Butter, the smell of honeyed buns and warm cinnamon rolls wrapping around them like their favorite quilt. The cheerful blue and yellow decor brought a smile to Tatianna's lips as she took a good whiff, enjoying the homey smell of baked goods, even if her stomach responded with a demanding growl that could almost be heard over the chattering patrons.

It was the first time they'd all walked into town together since the spell had shattered. And while Celestine still looked a little pale and Leondria leaned on Tatianna's arm a bit more than her sister liked to admit, there was something lighter about them all. More color in their cheeks. The return of mischief to their eyes.

Mrs. Merriweather looked up from the counter and beamed. "If it isn't my favorite gaggle of trouble. I thought the town had grown far too quiet."

"You'll be regretting this within the hour," Leondria warned as she swept towards the glass case. "Celestine's sweet tooth is back, and for once, I intend to let her ruin her appetite completely."

Celestine clapped. "It all looks so absolutely perfect. And I'm famished. I want everything with icing."

"I want that lavender honey biscuit," Rhiannon added. "And the lemon tarts. Two of those. Don't look at me like that, I earned this. I don't know if you know this, but I spent night after night out dancing. My dresses have become quite loose on me."

Tatianna smiled quietly as she watched her sisters. The room buzzed with carefree conversation and clinking china, but it was the sound of *them*—laughing, teasing, nudging shoulders and trading insults—that filled her heart.

The bell chimed again. A familiar voice called out from the entrance.

"Well, well. The Wylde witches return," Lysander said, strolling in with Lilith on his arm. "And no one's turned into a frog. I'm shocked."

Leondria laughed. "There's still time. Are you volunteering?"

Lilith rolled her eyes. "Ignore him. He's been absolutely insufferable since the spell broke. He thinks he helped."

"I did help," Lysander said. "Tatianna, I was helpful, wasn't I?"

She raised an eyebrow and tried to keep her face serious, but the twitch of her lips was bound to give her away.

Celestine perked up. "Buy me a strawberry tart and I'll agree with you."

He handed her a coin before she finished her sentence.

Celestine squealed. "It's quite clear that Lysander was instrumental in ending the curse, and sending Malric Wrenne to some penitentiary somewhere, abandoned by his magic, left to be imprisoned and ordinary."

Moments later, the chiming of the bell alerted them to the entrance of more patrons.

This time it was Archer and Aisling, both rather windblown as they stood in the doorway. Aisling made a beeline for Mrs. Merriweather, declaring loudly that she'd walked through "the very bowels of curse-ridden society" and deserved at least three ginger scones, before making her way to Lilith and dragging her to an open table where they could enjoy their baked treats.

Lysander escorted Leondria to the table to sit next to his sister. Rhiannon and Celestine followed behind them with trays filled with an assortment of goodies. Tatianna knew neither one intended to share.

Seeing her sisters happily settled with Lysander, she let her eyes drift across the room, to Archer. Their eyes met.

She nodded, the movement only noticeable if someone was looking for it, but it was just enough to convince him to walk over to her. He stood close enough that his arm brushed hers when he leaned on the counter. The distance between them wasn't enough to satisfy propriety's standards, but it was far enough that very few people would comment. And not near enough for her own liking.

"You look . . .," he began, voice low.

"Don't say 'better.' I'll slap you."

He smiled the lopsided grin that caused her heart to flutter. "I was going to say 'dangerous.' But also, yes. Better."

She rolled her eyes, but her smile gave her away. He paid for her order and they made their way to their friends and family just in time to enjoy her sister's propensity for dramatics.

Celestine took a bite of her scone, her eyes fluttering shut as she savored the bite. She then dropped it on her plate in front of her and announced to the room, "If anyone even thinks about starting another magical catastrophe, please do it *after* I finish this."

Leondria raised a brow. "You really want to go through that again?"

"No," Celestine said. "I just want it on the record that if it happens *again*, it's not our fault."

Rhiannon sipped her tea, eyeing them all. "Famous last words."

Laughter bubbled up, unabashed and easy.

Tatianna sighed, content in this very moment. Love and laughter surrounded her, making the world feel safe again.

Celestine popped a sugared blueberry into her mouth and grinned. "So . . . should we dare ask Mrs. Merriweather to let us behind the counter again?"

"No," all three sisters said in unison, expressions aghast as each of them remembered what happened the last time they were let behind the counter.

Rhiannon gave her a pointed look. "Last time you tried to 'help,' you cast a spell on the butter, causing it to sing sea shanties."

"It worked, didn't it?" Celestine said, fluttering her lashes. "People loved it."

"Until it made each and every person who ate a croissant dance a jig," Leondria reminded her. "And the croissants are what everyone in town comes into Brambles and Butter to get. Except you, there's not enough sugar in Mrs. Merryweather's specialty to tempt you."

Rhiannon put down her glass of lemonade. "There was an entire day where almost every person who lived in Bramblewick were stuck dancing jigs to the shanties the butter was singing."

Celestine shrugged. "Details."

Tatianna chuckled. "Save your chaos for later. For once, we deserve a day where nothing catches fire. Maybe we can avoid casting any spells, at least for today."

That's when the door opened—and all laughter died.

Lady Cordelia stood in the doorway, arms wrapped tightly around her daughter. Beside her, Emelie leaned against the frame, her skin nearly translucent, breaths ragged. Her magic sparked around her like shattered glass—every jagged edge pointed towards Emelie like it was prepared to attack her.

The Wylde sisters moved first. Tatianna stepped forward, steady and sure. "Bring her in. Sit her down."

"I don't know what to do. I know I don't deserve anyone's help, but we've been to three healers this morning," Lady Cordelia said, voice thin with desperation. "It's not getting better. It's worse. The only thing I know for sure is her magic is poisoning her. The spell—"

Tatianna stopped her. "You don't need to explain any more than you already have."

"She's fading away. Soon she'll be gone." Lady Cordelia didn't even try to stop her tears.

"No," Celestine said, tone suddenly sober. "We're not letting that happen."

Emelie whimpered as the magic around her tightened. The sharp points hurting her. Her body couldn't contain it anymore.

"I studied the spell, what it was meant to do. It should work." Rhiannon stepped forward.

Tatianna looked at her sisters. "So, we all agree it's worth trying."

They nodded. Rhiannon, the strongest at spell craft, chanted the spell that their grandmother had devised so long ago.

"I'll go first," Leondria said, raising her palm and letting a shimmer of golden magic flow towards Emelie.

The spell didn't take much, just a drop. Tatianna saw the change in Emelie's magic as soon as Leondria's power interacted with it, the drop of gold mingling in with the shattered pieces of Emelie's aura.

Rhiannon followed, then Celestine—each sister offering some of their power.

Emelie stirred. The jagged edges softened, but it wasn't enough.

"I've got more," Archer said, coming forward.

"You always do," Tatianna whispered, and together, their joined hands created a stream of soft, steady light, curling around Emelie's form and quieting the attack on her and her aura.

Lilith and Lysander came next. Then Aisling. Then Mrs. Merriweather, flour still dusting her sleeves.

"Poor girl doesn't deserve this," she said. "She should be out frolicking in fields of flowers, not barely able to stand."

One by one, more people entered. The tailor. The apothecary. A pair of farmers. Mrs. and Mr. Featherstone from the Gilded Kettle. Even the aloof Mr. Grimble from the bookshop.

Each stepped forward. Each gave a glimmer of power, a sliver of magic.

Everyone did it willingly, of their own free will.

The air in the bakery shimmered with something ancient and beautiful—not a spell, but a gift. Magic given, not taken. Everything that the broken curse was not.

Emelie gasped, her whole body trembling as the aura around her steadied, settled, and finally . . . quieted.

She opened her eyes. "It's . . . gone?"

"No," Tatianna said softly, kneeling beside her. "It's yours now. Just yours."

Lady Cordelia knelt beside her daughter, tears rolling down her cheeks. "Why? I never believed this could happen. Especially not after what I did. I thought they'd never help. I was so wrong about this place. About all of you."

"Your actions were motivated by a mother's love, something many of us understand." Effie Wylde stepped forward and placed a hand on the older woman's shoulder. "We all make mistakes. The important thing is how we fix them."

Lady Cordelia stood and faced the crowd. "I've taken too much from this town. I can't change what I've done, but I'll give back all that I have—my home, my land, my knowledge. Anything to make this right."

And not a single soul in the room doubted her sincerity.

Tatianna squeezed Emelie's hand and looked around the room.

This was Bramblewick at its best.

Broken, stubborn, wild-hearted—and whole again.

Chapter 35

B ramble and Butter sold out of baked goods. One by one, the patrons filtered into the town square. The people meandered about, shaking hands, relaying stories, until it turned into a celebration. Eventually, the day turned to dusk and the town square emptied. The murmurs of gratitude and disbelief still lingered in the air like fairies dancing on the wind. Emelie had been taken home, her color returned, her mother weeping softly at her side, offering Bramblewick everything she had to give and more.

Now, the cobbled paths were quiet.

Tatianna sat on the bench in the town's park, arms folded, the cool hush of dusk settling around her like a shawl. Her sleeves were still faintly dusted with magic, their golden shimmer catching the fading light.

She heard him before she saw him. Boots crunching softly on the gravel.

"I thought I might find you here," Archer said.

Tatianna didn't turn at first. "I needed some time alone."

He stopped. "I see. I'll leave you then."

"No, stay. I didn't mean you." She smiled up at him. "Come, sit with me."

He stepped forward and sat next to her on the same bench where they once plotted how to break the curse. "It feels like everything happened so long ago. Like everyone is ready to forget it ever happened."

She didn't respond. They sat in silence. A gentle breeze stirred the blossoms above them, sending petals cascading down around them. Somewhere in the distance, a dog barked and was hushed by a soft voice.

"I don't know how to feel now that it's over," she said quietly. "I'm so relieved that it's over and we won. But saving them . . . everyone, it consumed me to the point that there was nothing else. Now that it's over . . . What do I do?"

Archer's voice was low, steady. "You don't have to know. Not tonight."

She turned to look at him. He looked younger somehow, more carefree. Or maybe he was just more himself. Free from the careful restraints he had put on himself, stripped away from the pain of what had happened in his past. Finally capable of making the choice not to hide who he was and what he could do. The shadows under his eyes were still there, but his posture was different now—open, waiting.

"I was so angry," she whispered. "I didn't want to forgive you. I wanted to hate you for keeping your past from me."

Archer started to turn away, but didn't. Instead, he let her look into his eyes and see everything he felt. "I deserved that."

"You didn't and I couldn't." Her voice cracked. "Not really."

He exhaled. "After what happened, I feared my magic: how he'd used it without my permission, turned it against me, hurt someone else with it. I thought if I kept it locked away, it couldn't hurt anyone. I thought it made me strong, letting everyone believe I wasn't like them, not worthy of their esteem, allowing them to believe I didn't have magic. I had to be strong to be treated like that, right? Turns out, I was wrong. It only left me alone."

Tatianna reached for his hand. He stared at their joined fingers as if it were the first time.

"You trusted me with your magic," she said. "Not just to use it, but to *not* use it cruelly. That meant something."

He looked up, eyes meeting hers. "You're easy to trust, even easier to love."

"Are you sure?" She searched his face before turning away. "You know, I've heard I'm quite insufferable. Some might even pity the man that falls prey to my charms."

He spluttered, "I should— I apologize—" He took a deep breath and dropped to his knee in front of her.

She was smiling, biting her lip to hold back laughter.

He grinned up at her. "You are quite insufferable. Good at almost everything. Magic does what you want it to simply because you ask."

"Almost?" She tilted her head.

"You are terrible at casting spells from a spell book," he teased.

She laughed. "True, but who needs spell books when my magic adores me?"

"And yes, someone needs to pity me, so I might as well do it myself. How else am I going to tolerate your wild ways?" He arched an eyebrow.

Their teasing stopped. For a long moment, neither of them spoke.

Then, softly, she said, "I don't know what comes next."

"We can figure it out together."

"I need to know we get along when we're not trying to save the town. Can we spend time getting to know each other when life is normal?" she asked, her voice soft, almost tentative.

"We can try." He grinned. "It does seem like an impossible task, though. When is your life ever normal?"

He leaned in slowly, giving her time to pull away. She didn't.

The kiss was gentle. Not rushed. Not desperate. A promise of something built, not taken. Something earned.

When they pulled apart, Tatianna rested her head lightly on his shoulder.

The Wylde cottage hadn't felt so full in ages.

They had sat around the long dining room table for a sumptuous roast for dinner and had retired to the parlor for port and games—if they ever got around to playing. The buffet was covered with perfectly matched teacups, cordial glasses and serving plates filled with sweet buns and seed cakes. Someone—probably Rhiannon—had set out a pitcher of rose lemonade and a second pot of spiced tea in addition to the sherry and the port. It was a festive setup that Effie Wylde would approve.

Tatianna stood by the window, watching her family.

Leondria was seated, still pale from the curse's aftermath, but gaining back strength and color every day. Her hands rested in her lap, and one of them loosely clasped in Rhiannon's. Celestine sat curled up on the settee, her head on a pillow, listening while Lysander entertained her with exaggerated impressions of Malric's cape swishing in the wind. Tatianna wasn't sure she was ready to laugh at everything that had happened, but she was happy Celestine had bounced back to her normal self so quickly.

Aisling sat on the arm of the chair next to Archer, both of them looking less haunted now that the worst was behind them. Even Nigel was there, perched on a delicate chair on the other side of Rhiannon, engaging her in quiet conversation about books and spell theory.

Effie Wylde stood near the fireplace, silent, wringing her gloved hands as she stood on the outskirts of the gathering.

Tatianna met her gaze.

"Mama," she said, her voice clear.

The room quieted. The chatter and laughter quieted as everyone pretended not to pay attention to Tatianna or her mother. They instinctively recognized an important moment was here.

Effie stepped towards Tatianna. Her hair was up in its usual precise chignon, but there were loose strands tonight. Stray wisps. Her mother's mouth trembled slightly as she looked at her . . . and then at Archer.

"I have been so wrong in so many ways," Effie said simply, her voice wavering but honest. "I was wrong to judge. Wrong to dismiss what I didn't understand. I thought I was protecting you—both of you. But I see now . . . I was protecting—actually, I don't know what I was protecting. But I can say I was wrong to judge based on societal standards."

Tatianna's heart clenched. Her mother admitted she was wrong. Tatianna was too shocked to speak.

Effie turned fully to Archer. "You saved my daughter. More than once. You saved *all* my daughters. I don't have the words to thank you."

"You're giving me too much credit." Archer clasped his hands, leaning forward. "Tatianna is the one who deserves the accolades. Without her, the town would still be cursed."

"I know, but you should know that I know you were an integral part of her success," Effie stated, refusing to be contradicted even in her apologies. "I was a fool to ever believe you weren't worthy of her."

Archer stood slowly. "I wasn't," he said. "Not then. But I'm trying to be."

Effie gave a small, tight nod. "Good."

She turned back to Tatianna, eyes glistening. "And you . . . you've always been more powerful than I knew. I should have seen it. Tried to understand it. I'm sorry I didn't. More importantly, I should have listened to your concerns. Instead, I . . ."

Tatianna blinked away the sting behind her eyes. "It's okay. We're all fine, more than fine. And I think we all learned something."

Effie hesitated, then reached forward. Tatianna met her halfway.

They embraced.

The room exhaled.

Laughter and warmth trickled back in, like sunlight after a storm.

Someone passed another tray of pastries, then came the champagne. Aisling began recounting a childhood tale of when Archer saved her from one of her wild adventures. Leondria laughed at the incident before gesturing for Lysander to join her. Rhiannon pulled Nigel over to look at a book she'd hidden beneath the tea table.

And Archer found his way to Tatianna's side once more.

They stood together as the cottage buzzed around them. Family. Found and chosen. Changed by what they had survived.

Epilogue

The meadow was aglow.

Lanterns floated in the twilight like fireflies, bobbing gently over heads and between trees. Strings of tiny lights held together by gossamer strands looped from branch to branch, casting golden halos over dancers spinning across the dance floor the fairies had put in place so patrons could experience hours of revelry.

At the edge of the clearing, music lilted sweetly, this time a waltz. The notes floated through the air, enticing everyone to the dance floor even if they could barely keep time.

Lysander dipped Leondria in a sweeping arc, her laughter ringing out like chimes blowing in the wind. Celestine twirled past them, dancing by herself with a plate of something sticky and delicious in hand, powdered sugar clinging to her nose.

Under a shady elm, Nigel sat with Rhiannon, a shared book open between them. Their heads leaned close, fingers brushing now and again as they turned the pages slowly, more invested in each other than the words written on the page.

Aisling and Lilith were off to the side near the refreshment table, giggling like girls at their first party. Lilith said something that made Aisling blush crimson, and both dissolved into laughter.

Tatianna stood at the edge of it all, watching her sisters sparkle like the stars just beginning to prick the sky. Only one thing was missing tonight.

Archer appeared beside her, as if summoned by her thoughts. "They're happy."

She nodded. "They are."

"And you?" he asked, offering his hand.

Tatianna turned towards him, her smile full of mischief and something she'd yet to put into words. "I'm happier than I've ever been."

Taking her hand in his, he bowed his head. "Would you do me the honor of this dance?"

"I thought you would never ask."

He guided her through the meadow, weaving through dancers and laughter, until they reached the old willow at the edge of the clearing—the same one from the first night, where their story had quietly begun.

"I thought we were going to dance?" she asked.

Archer shrugged. "We have all night to dance." He pushed the swaying branches to the side.

There, beneath its gently swaying branches, sat a wooden swing strung with silver ribbon and soft velvet cushions.

Archer helped her onto it, then sat beside her, wrapping his arm around her. The swing rocked lightly, their knees brushing, fingers intertwining.

"You remember this place?" he asked, pulling her closer to him.

"How could I forget?"

The music drifted over them, muffled and dreamlike. Tatianna leaned her head against his shoulder, the scent of lavender and magic still clinging faintly to the air.

"The last time we sat here we were interrupted," Archer whispered, "before I had the chance to do this."

He took her chin, tilting it until their eyes met.

She smiled, waiting for him. "What are you waiting for? Kiss me already."

He cupped her cheek and kissed her, slow and certain, like a vow.

And all around them, the meadow danced on, full of laughter and light—and the quiet, steady kind of magic that lingers long after the glamour fades.

* * *

The Book of Etiquette for Acceptable Societal Decorum and the Proper Use of Magic

by Honoria Penhaven, Third Duchess of Cheltenham

The definitive book Effie swears by, full of stern lessons on decorum and proper magical posture during duels and dances.

- "A lady must never cast while fatigued, unless the matter concerns life, death, or the safeguarding of kin—at which point, decorum bows to duty."

- "Protecting family is the main duty of a well-bred witch. It is the one of the few acceptable reasons to bend any of the rules in this guide."

- "A gentleman offering his hand to assist a spellbound lady must do so with both reverence and restraint, lest the magic misunderstand his intent."

- "It is a well-bred gentleman's duty to restrain his magic lest he accidentally charm the lady to her detriment."

- "A young lady must never levitate a tea service higher than her chin in company, nor duel before dessert."

(Proper posture while casting is the mark of a well-bred witch. Wand arm straight, chin lifted, and enchantments always performed with a serene countenance—even in the face of insult or incantation.)

The Charmed School: A Guide of Magical Etiquette for the Modern Witch

by Elspeth Rosemoor

A more modern (and slightly controversial) volume focused on the intersection of flirtation, fashion, and magic.

- "One may sparkle, but never shimmer unsolicited."

(Fashionable witches may weave minor glamours into their gowns or lipstick, but such enhancements must be subtle, seasonal, and never outshine the hostess at a gathering. Charm your hem if you must, but never charm your chaperone.)

- "It is entirely acceptable to brush fingers with a gentleman while retrieving a wand, so long as one does not also steal his composure."

- "A lady may conjure light with the flick of her wrist, but it is her restraint in shadow that reveals her true brilliance."

The Etiquette Enchantress: The Art of Charm and Beguilement

by Anonymous, attributed to "The Lady in Lavender"

A scandalous, but beloved book, passed among sisters and whispered about at teas. Rumored to contain enchanted margins that reveal different advice to each reader.

- "To enchant with a glance is no crime—unless one

means it." Magic meant to allure must never cross into coercion. A flicker of firelight in the eyes is flirtation; casting an actual flame to draw a suitor's gaze is uncouth (and highly flammable). One must never beguile unless prepared to be beguiled in return.

- "Beware the man who casts no enchantment and yet leaves you thoroughly ensorcelled."

- "A man that charms without charms is a unique kind of dangerous, he captures the attention of the right lady with little to no effort, changing the course of her life forever."

- "When your heartbeat hitches in the presence of a spell-partner, it is best to pretend it is due to a draft—until such a time as pretending becomes unbearable."

- "It is unwise to show where your affections lie, at least until you are certain they are returned. This is especially true when your heart flutters for someone, it is unwise to become too familiar."

Magic, Manners, and Mishaps: A Collection of Essays compiled by Mrs. Peregrine of Bramblewick Ladies' Academy for the Magically-Inclined

A collection of letters and lessons from generations of magically-inclined debutantes.

- "A magical mishap is no excuse for poor manners—but it is an excellent test of character."

(If one accidentally animates the soup tureen, the correct response is to apologize, dispel, and offer to re-ladle. If one's hair turns green mid-courting, smile graciously and pretend it's the latest trend from the Continent.)

- "Every young witch will encounter a moment when her spell falters, her temper flares, or her heart betrays her—this is the moment to reach for grace, not glamour."

- "No matter the frustration, a lady must always be in control of her emotions. A glamour to convince others of such control only hides the tempest inside her. It does not quell it."

- "No enchantment cast in haste ever ends without regret, scandal, or an alarming amount of glitter."

- "Always take your time when casting spells, it is a careful process that must be done with precision to avoid any unwanted outcomes."

The Enchanted Social Gathering: Conversational Cantrips and Ballroom Boundaries

By Sir Thaddeus Quillfeather

A dry but indispensable text outlining how to charm a suitor, without literally charming them (a major faux pas).

- "One may twirl the air, but not the minds of one's dance partner."

(It is considered a grave faux pas to use subtle enchantments to ensure an invitation to dance. If you cannot charm with your wit, refrain from charming with your wand.)

- "If a gentleman wishes to show his admiration, let it be through quiet magic—a summoned rose, a warming charm, a shield at her back when she does not ask for it."

- "It is unseemly to cast a truth spell in the middle of a flirtation; should one desire honesty, one must earn it the mortal way."

Miss Maplethorpe's Modest Manual of Magical Manners

by Mistress Augusta Maplethorpe

A pocket-sized book often gifted to young ladies on their fifteenth birthday. Contains fold-out diagrams for wand etiquette and what color magic one should never cast during supper.

- "No respectable witch casts in coral or chartreuse after midday, and never before breakfast."

(Color-coded spells are a matter of propriety. Yellow for greetings, lavender for affection, pale blue for cooling tempers. And above all—never casting crimson unless engaged, enraged, or fully endorsed by your chaperone.)

- "It is poor form to levitate a teacup during a tête-à-tête unless one is also prepared to catch a dropped secret with equal elegance."

- "A well-bred witch keeps her wand holstered and

her opinions cloaked—unless, of course, the room is poorly warded."

To Spell or Not to Spell: Navigating Society When Your Temper is Enchanted

by Lady Mirabel Northwick

A tongue-in-cheek, but widely beloved book on controlling emotions during high-stress social events—especially useful for magically gifted young women of strong opinion.

- "When in doubt, breathe before you hex."

(A lady may express strong opinions, but setting the upholstery on fire because one's suitor danced twice with a blonde is unbecoming. Cooling charms are encouraged; ice daggers are not.)

- "If you must storm away from a suitor mid-quarrel, ensure your cloak does not dramatically billow unless you truly mean it."

- "Should a witch's heart begin to thunder louder than her wand, she is advised to speak slowly, breathe deeply, and avoid hexing anyone she might secretly wish to kiss."

Sample Spells

A Perfect Cuppa

The Sun is up

Please pour a cup

Take the handle to tip the spout

And let the steaming liquid out

Buttered Toast Spell

Mornings here

So be a dear

Take the butter

And spread to cover

Every nook and cranny

Of the bread I fancy

With each swipe of the knife

Apply the perfect heat to the slice

The Perfect Cup of Earl Grey

For the perfect cup of tea it is important to follow a few essential steps.

1. Heat water and pour into your teapot of choice, swish around to warm your teapot. Pour water out into the sink.

2. Heat water until boiling in your tea kettle. Pour boiling water into your warmed teapot with care.

3. Place teabag or tea infuser in cup.

4. Pour hot water directly into cup on top of the teabag or tea infuser.

5. Let tea steep for 2 minutes, 3 if you prefer stronger tea. Do not dunk teabag or infuser.

6. Remove teabag or infuser and set aside.

7. Add cream, milk, and/or sugar to taste.

Note: this is for an individual cup of tea. When making a pot of tea you can put the loose leaf tea directly in the teapot after warming it. I recommend one teaspoon of loose leaf tea for every 6 ounces of water. Let tea steep for 2 minutes. Place tea leaf strainer over the top of your cup before pouring. Pour tea. Set aside the tea leaf strainer and add cream, milk, and/or sugar to taste.

Boiling water is specific to making black tea. The temperature of the water is one of the most important steps in making a proper cup of tea. It is important to note that different types of tea require different water temperatures. As my specialty is Earl Grey, I am only discussing the temperature for black teas.

Cucumber Sandwiches

It wouldn't be tea time without tea sandwiches. A favorite at The Gilded Kettle is, without doubt, the cucumber sandwich.

Ingredients

English Cucumber

Cream Cheese

Sour Cream

Magic infused Herb mix (Simply Savory Dill Dip Mix or create your own mix of dill, parsley, onion powder, salt, and pepper.)

White bread

Directions

1. Mix cream cheese, sour cream, and magic-infused herbs.

2. Thinly slice cucumbers and pat them dry.

3. Spread cream cheese mixture on two slices of bread in

a thin layer.

4. Place cucumbers on one slice of bread in a thin layer.

5. Place remaining slice of bread on top of the cucumbers with the cream cheese mixture facing down.

6. Cut crust off the sandwich.

7. Cut sandwich into 4 triangle pieces.

8. Serve and enjoy!

Optional: you can salt the cucumbers to help remove excess liquid, to do this you would salt the cucumbers, let them sit for a few minutes, rinse the cucumbers off and pat them dry.

Acknowledgements

Writing a book is hard work, every time I finish one, I think of the viral sound clip, "I don't know how I did it, but I did it, and it was hard." Which, when it comes to writing, is one of the truest statements I have ever heard. Not only that, but writing actually takes a village. Everyone thinks of it as an isolated activity, and in many ways, it is, but I wouldn't be able to finish my books without having people to talk my way through my ideas. In fact, the ideas are the simple part, it's turning them into a fleshed-out story that is truly difficult.

This book started with my dear friend, and fellow author, Jamie Dalton, saying she wanted to do a cottage core themed set. I, of course, said yes. Then I had to look up what cottagecore was when it came to books and found Pride and Prejudice mentioned over and over again. If you've ever met me, you know Pride and Prejudice is my favorite book and while I will watch every movie and television version of it, none of them come close to the wit of Jane Austen's original publication. Did you know she was born 250 years ago? Anyway, my love of this story and the tensions between these characters became a glimmer of an idea. Then in my head I kept seeing this image of a beautiful meadow, surrounded by willow trees, completely decked out in gold and silver, and fairies floating by with trays of champagne and other *amuse-bouches* while couples danced the night away. This scene became my "aha moment" what if I combined Pride and Prejudice with Twelve Dancing Princesses and make them all witches? It was an idea; I even think it was a creative idea. But that's all it was. There was no story, no conflict, just this vague idea. It wouldn't have become more without my mom listening to me go on and on about it, and how to add mystery, or my dad helping me figure out how to fit in a Wickham character, or my editor Sarah (another Pride and Prejudice stan) leaving comments about the nuances she liked, or asking how this other part would fit in.

And I can't forget, the reader I met at WonderCon with the name that inspired my take on the Lizzie character.

I hope everyone can accept this heartfelt thank you. Really, I couldn't do it without you.

About the author

Stephanie K Clemens is known for many things: an author, photographer, dog mom, instagrammer, adventurer, teacher, lawyer, and more. When she's not sitting behind her laptop she can be found on some adventure. Most of the time it's a road trip with her two doggos, but recently it has been in the pages of a book.

Also by

Ladies of WACK Series

A Study in Steam

A Practicum in Perjury

A History in Horticulture – Coming Soon

Ladies of WACK Prequels

The Daring Adventures of Honoria Porter: Volume 1

Wynterfell Romances

For the Love of Hot Cocoa

Villain Rehab – Coming Soon

Fantasy Books

Stripped Away

Cursed by Bandits

Mundane Mornings & Enchanted Evenings

Children's Book by S.K. Clemens

Frankie Wants to be a Sled Dog